Phoenix Eyes

AND OTHER STORIES

Russell Charles Leong

UNIVERSITY OF WASHINGTON PRESS
Seattle and London

This book is published with the assistance of a grant from the Scott and Laurie Oki Endowed Fund for the publication of Asian American Studies

ISBN 0-295-97944-5 (cl.), 0-295-97945-3 (pbk.)

Note: This is a work of fiction. The names, characters, incidents, and dialogue are products of the author's imagination and are not to be construed as real. Any resemblances to actual persons, living or dead, are entirely coincidental.

The paper used in this publication is acid-free and recycled from 10 percent post-consumer and at least 50 percent pre-consumer waste. It meets the minimum requirements of American National Standard for Information Sciences—Permanence of Paper for Printed Library Materials, ANSI Z39.48-1984. ♾ ♻

The male phoenix sings by itself, as it dances alone.

—*Shanhaijing*, The Book of Mountains and Seas,
   third century BCE

Born in places East or West, between samsara and paradise, the people in my stories long to speak and struggle to love.

Some—sons and daughters, monks and mothers, refugees and runaways—leave their homelands and leave their pasts, and thus entangle themselves anew. Others attempt to liberate themselves from samsara— the world of attachment and the cycle of rebirth.
—Russell Charles Leong

Contents

1   Leaving

Bodhi Leaves

THE TREE, and the verdant flora and distant purple mountains that offset it, were part of an Indian landscape, not a Vietnamese one, said the monk. "You must imagine how a bodhi tree appears under the skies of another country."

But neither the youth nor the man could paint the trunk, branches, and leaves of the bodhi tree exactly as the monk had wanted. The problem might have been the canvas that the monk had bought from Builder's Emporium and stretched and nailed onto the crumbling drywall behind the main altar table of the temple. The canvas surface was uneven to the eye, and, given the dim lighting and the smoke of burning joss sticks in the room, awkward to prepare or paint.

Moreover, neither artist had painted larger-scale murals before. The monk had showed each artist the Thai prints of the Shakyamuni Buddha—sitting under the bodhi during his enlightenment, teaching his disciples, or meditating in the forest. The thin, gaudy paper prints themselves were torn and stained, because, as the monk explained, they had been damaged during his stay in the Thai refugee camp ten years ago. But that is where the monk had originally met the two painters: then, one was a child and the other a teenager who belonged to the families whose boats had been capsized or plundered off the Strait of Malaysia that summer. Everyone who survived the journey ended up, sooner or later, in Songfa camp.

The first artist, Vu, came from a family of lacquer craft workers. In Vietnam, the family specialized in pictures, trays, and commemorative objects of black lacquer inlaid with mother-of-pearl and abalone shell. The process was a delicate one: selecting and curing the light wood underframe, procuring and thinning the lac itself, incising the designs and laying in the fragments of shells and pearl. Once the family came to the States, however, they no longer made lacquer wares but instead imported them and sold the works of their relatives. Vu had not trained formally, but as a child he had observed his father carefully sorting the shell and pearl shards by color, sheen, and size.

The monk had wanted the mural behind the altar of the wooden statue of Shakyamuni Buddha completed before July 15—the Vu-Lan festival. Those three days following, hundreds of people would descend on Little Saigon, Orange County, to visit the Buddhist temples and pay their respects to those who had perished in Vietnam, in America, or at sea. They would pray for the liberation of all sentient beings, including animals, who suffered in this and nether worlds.

With ingenuity, and hired Mexican day laborers, the monk had over the past five years transformed the plain three-bedroom tract home into a colorful yellow and red temple and combination living quarters, surrounded by elaborate tropical gardens in the front and back yards. After the L.A. riots in spring, jobless laborers were even more plentiful than before. They helped install the granite stupa that stood as tall as a man in the front garden. The laborers didn't like the temple food consisting of cooked vegetables and soft tofu, however, so the monk had to drive them to a Taco Bell for meat burritos and Cokes at midday.

The outside windows facing the busy street were trimmed in an auspicious red paint, as was the front door. From the Korean nursery where the monk once worked, he managed to obtain some concrete statues of the Buddha and the Quan Am, along with a chipped birdbath, to grace the front. Two stone lions guarded the temple, along with a symmetrical arrangement of azalea hedges, sago palms, aloes, and two ten-foot bodhi trees on either side of the entrance. The house and its exotic gardens were an anomaly on the run-down suburban street with its tract homes and fading plots of grass.

After classes, Vu had rushed to the temple on his bicycle and gone to Builder's Emporium with the monk to buy acrylic paints for the mural: violet, forest green, burnt umber, azure, royal blue, black, and carmine.

In the temple, the monk had showed him the printed images of the Buddha rendered in saturated tones of pink, green, blue, and yellow. Vu did not care for the brilliance, but listened attentively to the monk and nodded politely. The older generation, Vu thought, merely copied what they could remember of Vietnam. But now that they were in America, maybe they should paint in a new way, not drawing upon their memories or nostalgia alone.

Vu opened the can of burnt umber, using it to first outline the trunk and branches of the bodhi tree, which would take up the middle portion of the wall. He mixed in some red and green, as brown tended to absorb the colors around it. Without filling in the trunk he studied the form of the tree, slowly dabbing in the red and green, toning the color down with gray. After three hours he was happy with the enormous trunk, like an elephant's. It would extend above and over the wooden Buddha figure, once the altar table was pushed back against the wall. Chi, the old woman who lived in the temple and prepared food for the Sifu, told him that it looked more like the trunk of a banyan than a bodhi tree. The monk, after his nap, surveyed the painting. He was silent.

"Sifu, what do you think of the bodhi tree? I didn't copy the picture exactly."

"A great effort. But the trunk looks like that of a eucalyptus tree to me, with all the gray bark. Better look at this print again!"

Vu pretended to study the print. "I see my mistake. Let me paint for half an hour, and then I'll return tomorrow?"

Vu pursed his lips: everyone had a different idea of how the trunk of the bodhi tree should appear. In reality, he thought, the trunk and branches of the bodhi did not differ much from other trees—it so happened that Buddha was sitting under one. He could have been sitting under a banyan for all anyone really knew.

Finishing the trunk took longer than Vu had anticipated. It was ten o'clock when he returned home. He ate the rice porridge, fish cake, and eggs garnished with onions that his mother had left out on the kitchen table for him, and lay on top of his bed. He popped a disk of Jay Z's "Hard Knock Life" into his compact disk player and moved into another space, just past the four corners of his room, through a familiar open field, and into the thicket of his memory. Nameless, fishlike creatures leapt through vines wrapped around dark branches. Pale monkeys splashed in the river beneath overgrown bamboo and ficus. The same large tree again. Its gray branches thickened into arms that ensnared his body—swarthy arms of the pirates who had once tossed him into the sea. The knock-down pulse of "Hard Knock Life" delivered him back to his room, as quickly as it had taken him out.

He got up and dragged himself to the kitchen to get a glass of water. Ice cubes and 7-Up would soothe his dry tongue and throat. Sweat covered his body, and the scar on his forearm from the shark attack turned livid, as it usually did when he felt anxious or angry. He didn't want to go back to the temple the next day. After his Chemistry 1-B, he called the Sifu and told him that he had to study for final exams and that he wouldn't be able to finish the painting before Vu-Lan day. The monk said that he would find someone else, and thanked him for his help.

The monk also had had dreams that night. Awakened by them, he had arisen several times and lit a yellow candle at the altar, studying Vu's rendition of the bodhi tree. A painted branch was more than flat brush strokes; each stroke should carry the round pulse of the hand.

Yet he conceded that living like squatters in the refugee camps could distort a person's sense of balance and proportion, and alter their perception. What they had seen and endured on sea and land could make anyone forget the true nature of things. Vu was probably too young to remember the makeshift bamboo and thatched roof temple in camp, which could hold forty or fifty people at a time. There were no gilt statues or bronze censers to furnish the altar. They had nothing but paper prints of Buddha strung across a rope inside the doorless, open-air structure. Sun, monsoon rain, and wind flung themselves in at will. Once, as they were praying, a sudden gust lifted and tore the flimsy roof off, and they could see white albino rats whirling in the air. Without the hand of Buddha, he thought, he himself would be dead, or have gone berserk long ago.

Understandably, young people, once they were in America, wanted to forget the past and move into the future as quickly as they could. Vu tried his best. But the elderly temple worshippers, the monk feared, would laugh behind his back at the stolid trunk and stiff branches of the tree. It was roughhewn, unlike the refined frescoes they would remember in temples back home. A fidelity to familiar images was a way of positioning his life in the new land.

He had to find someone else to finish it before Sunday, when families would come to pay their respects to temple monks and nuns.

The monk heeded his own blunt hands: they were good for striking the mallet on the wooden fish drum, for tending vegetables and pulling weeds, and even for teaching martial arts as he did, but not for painting. But he trusted his eyes, his vision, and his acute sense of people: by looking at a person's face or hands for five minutes or listening to their voice, even hidden behind a screen, he could ascertain their motive or character. The monk saw, but he did not discriminate. Whereas the world did. Between rich and poor, male and female, high and low, between Mahayana and Theravada sects. One time a portly scholar from a Buddhist university in Hue came to visit the temple. He gave the monk a copy of his book on Vietnamese Zen philosophy, signed with a flowery signature, a Ph.D. in bold black letters after his name, and with all the names of schools he'd studied at in Paris and Vietnam. This angered the monk. When they came to the U.S., intellectuals flashed their credentials even more, he thought. Knowledge of books led to discrimination by the book.

For he himself knew what it meant to face discrimination by words, or the lack of them, when he first arrived. At first he could barely understand English or make himself understood in that language by others. Each morning when he left the temple to work, he tried to remember a new word. He'd washed dishes in a fast-food restaurant. He'd moved office furniture for a van company on Figueroa Street, near downtown. He'd worked in a Hollywood nursery, for a Korean. He memorized the common names of flowers and trees, the ones most popular with customers: daisy, rose, camellia, orchid, maple, bamboo, pine, birch, cherry, peach. His new vocabulary was both small and large. It was provisional, yet easily understood. For six years, he'd stayed at the main temple at Ninth Street and Berendo, near Koreatown in Los Angeles, until he saved enough money to put a small down payment on a foreclosed tract home in Garden Grove. He'd planned to turn the house into a temple, miles away from L.A. A refuge—away from the blue and red graffiti on the walls, on the buildings, away even from the loud Mexican music that he somehow grew to like. Its melodies were endearing and sad at the same time.

In the inner courtyard of the downtown temple the monks who'd come before him had planted fruit trees: persimmon, kaffir lime, loquat, and kumquat. People from all over would find their way to this temple in the corner of a nondescript block with aging stucco apartment houses. Especially during the Tet holiday, young men would drive around in their shiny Toyota Celicas and rush in to make New Year's resolutions. They'd light three punk sticks, kneel, pray, then speed away with their long-haired girlfriends in tow. More often than not, they would cruise the temple, driving around the block to show off their cars to friends.

The next morning, the monk telephoned Thanh. Thanh had been laid off recently from the bank and had time to finish what Vu had started. He was ten years older than Vu. Though not trained as a painter, Thanh was well known in the community as a poet and watercolorist, albeit unable to hold down a job. Already his wife had left him, taking the two children with her to Las Vegas where she found work in a casino.

Thus his stanzas—published in the local Vietnamese paper or in the Bhiksu Buddhist Association journal—were ostensibly about Buddha, but also intertwined with feelings about his family. Startling images, line after line, were juxtaposed in his poems: a young Gautama washing himself in a muddy pond; a woman scrubbing her body raw with Mojave Desert sand . . .

Sometimes he would come to the temple, sobbing in front of the altar, seeking solace. The monk was at a loss. Even the Buddha's placid countenance could not allay his friend's pain—and it was three years since his family had left him. Painting might rescue him momentarily from his grief. Thanh hurried over to the temple. Again, the Sifu brought out his torn Thai lithographs, explaining that distant mountain peaks should be sharp, like mountains in Nepal or in India, not rounded like the hills found in the lowlands of their own country. Both of them laughed, because neither had ever seen snow on mountains in Vietnam. Last year, however, the monk had driven through the Sierra and seen snow-capped western mountains for the first time. Thanh would give it a try. He assured the monk that he could have the wall painted over if it wasn't right.

By late afternoon, the trunk of the bodhi tree had grown slimmer, and far-away peaks flushed with violet and pink began to appear on either side of the tree. The monk seemed happier, and Thanh came back the next two days to finish drawing the green heart-shaped leaves. The leaves, unfortunately, looked like solid clumps of philodendron, not like bodhi leaves at all. The monk thought it ironic that such clumsy rendering could come from Thanh's small-boned hands. Exasperated, Thanh shrugged his shoulders; he was not in the mood to paint the finely veined leaves required for the tree. "The tree lacks spirit," Thanh admitted. But the Sifu said the rest of the painting was fine, and reached into his pocket to pay him. Thanh refused the dollars, saying that the temple had helped him many times before and that the Sifu should keep the money.

That evening, the monk explained to the half-dozen worshippers why he was being so particular about the way the leaves and branches of the bodhi were painted.

"When you walk into this temple, the first thing your eyes see is Shakyamuni and the wall mural behind him. Everything on the altar, from the fresh color and scent of flowers to the smooth-skinned fruits, must move the heart in the right direction. Physical beauty is not just for the eyes alone."

The worshippers, mostly old women attired in gray cotton Buddhist robes, nodded in assent. One spoke up: "Master, you are right. Sooner or later my colored photograph will be hanging here with the other photos on the ancestors' wall, together with my ashes in a bronze urn on that table. I hope my nieces and nephews will come to pay their respects to their dead auntie. Of course the more beautiful the temple and the painting, the happier my soul will rest."

The other ladies guffawed at the stout black-haired woman who had just spoken. One whispered too loudly: "She'll probably outlive all of us, that's why she's agreeing!"

With a sharp glance at the women, the Sifu continued: "No matter who dies first, the tree will outlive all of us. You remember back home how large the bodhi tree grows, its roots can envelop the whole land below a house. I'm afraid this painting won't do."

Early the next morning, after dawn prayers, the monk drove his van to pick up one of his former martial arts students, Tinh, a nineteen-year-old who lived with his family in a beach town south of Little Saigon.

As the monk headed toward the coast, block after block of Vietnamese shopping malls disappeared in the van's rear view mirror. Then, a blue line of Pacific entered his vision.

Already the air glistened with heat. Cars and campers along the beach road were jammed bumper to bumper. Sweat ran down the back of the monk's thick cotton robe. He opened the window completely and let the heated salt air fill his nostrils.

He pulled his van up to the entrance of the beach parking lot. There were no guards here, as he remembered from the Thai camps. Because he was a monk, they had let him through the barbed wire gates to the beach beyond, facing the gulf. Under merciless sun or drenching monsoon rain the monk would meditate for hours on the white sand. But the exact meaning of his prayers, chanted in Pali or Vietnamese, had eluded the ears of the guards.

The American beach was different. No guards, only lifeguards in the wooden towers spaced evenly apart on the beach. He got out of the van and began walking toward the water. He tried not to notice the bikini-clad bodies lying on the sand, the pale breasts and thighs sprawled on bright beach towels. The coconut aroma of suntan lotion glazed the air. His bare foot almost caught on the jagged neck of a beer bottle buried in the sand.

Fastening his eyes on the horizon, he began humming part of a sutra to himself, the same one he had chanted a thousand times in camp. He touched the cloth pouch that dangled from a cord on his chest. Folded inside the pouch was a paper tablet with the "Heart Sutra" written in Chinese characters that his own teacher had given him.

Reaching the line where the tide wet the sand, he dug his feet into the water. He did not feel as liberated in America as he had hoped. The temple carried a fifteen-hundred-dollar monthly mortgage that had to be scrimped from weekly donations. The bank clerks, machinists, beauty shop manicurists, factory workers, and families who came to the temple helped out when they could. But the recession had reduced the amount people could give.

His breathing tightened. Maintaining the temple grounds and red altar candles and incense cost money. Then there was auto insurance, his frequent driving tickets, and remittances to his home temple in Saigon, now Ho Chi-Minh City. Everything had to be paid in dollars, and rich Chinese or generous Vietnamese donors who would buy a plot of land or donate a building for the temple, as they did in Vietnam, were not to be found in America. He turned abruptly around, made his way back to the van, and continued his journey.

The monk reached the dilapidated pink wood-frame cottage in back of the seaside motel that Tinh's family managed and cleaned. Tinh was already sitting on the steps waiting for him, in his striped surfer shirt, baggy shorts, and tennis shoes. As they drove back to the temple, Tinh explained to the monk that he was forgetting how to read Vietnamese, and feared losing more.

The monk was smiling at the gentle, dark-skinned youth sitting before him in the temple: "You spend your spare time surfing with Americans. Come to temple more often and help me out. And your hair, tied in a mane behind your head!"

"Sifu, I've been reading about the Buddha. In India, he had long hair, but it was coiled up into a topknot, like mine. So I'm following the Buddha's hairstyle."

The monk laughed. "You've a way with words, Tinh. But that was twenty-five hundred years ago. Only hippies wear their hair like that, or rock musicians."

"But master, does my hair matter? I believe in Buddha. I follow the five precepts. I don't drink, lie, steal, kill, or sleep with other men's girlfriends. If people judge me on my appearance, then they don't understand what you taught me." Gingerly, Tinh removed a small gold ring from his earlobe and offered it to the monk. "I don't need to wear this, can you keep it for me?"

The Sifu laughed and pointed to the unfinished mural. "You see the bodhi tree, it needs a hundred, maybe two hundred leaves. The leaves look like avocados or green fruits. Go out to the front yard and sit there for an hour. Look at the leaves, then come back and try to paint them."

Tinh went out to the front yard. Oblivious to the cars on the boulevard, he sat himself on the stone bench in a lotus position, right foot over left thigh, left foot over right thigh. Focusing on the leaves, Tinh narrowed his eyes and slowed down his breathing. He noticed how their colors changed with the flickering of sunlight. Brightness and shadow moved over the branches and leaves. He walked back into the temple without saying a word to the monk or to the wrinkled Chi, who held a glass of hot tea in her hands for him.

He had found a way to begin. Others, he felt, saw only one color. Tinh opened all the cans of paint at once: violet, black, green, azure, carmine. Leaves were not just green. He took a dab of each color, spreading it out on the tin tray that the Sifu had supplied. The first leaf he painted was not green, but violet, thinned down with white. He colored the second leaf azure, and the third, gray. Leaf by leaf, the bodhi tree took on character, its leaves reflecting myriad hues. For the next five hours, Tinh did not stop for tea or water, or glance at the altar behind him. He painted, not counting the number of leaves. He transferred the images that existed only in his mind—molecules of light and darkness—onto the canvas.

From the doorway, the Sifu observed the canopy of bodhi leaves growing above the Buddha and the lithe outstretched arm of the youth, his shirt sleeve speckled with paint. It had taken three persons—Vu, Thanh, Tinh—to fashion the limbs of one tree. He saw that the youngest among them would finish painting the leaves. On his own sleeves, he could smell the sea salt that clung faintly to the yellow cloth.

Geography One

SPRING RAINS appeared as the month ended, heightening the tropical humidity that enabled me to sleep at night with only a thin covering. Still waking up alone in the small hours before dawn, as I had been doing all month, I decided to leave Los Angeles for a day. The empty cans I left scattered about my backyard had filled with tepid rainwater. Mosquito larvae were already beginning to hatch. I bought twenty tins of tuna fish from the Thrifty's Drugstore because they were fifty cents each. It was the easiest way to eat. I had pared my living habits down. Even the *Times* was stacked haphazardly on the steps: I did not bother to unfold the soggy papers or read the news.

In advance, I checked my car's highway map of Orange County, the region south between Los Angeles and San Diego. Fifty miles one way meant a daily commute for some people; for me, it was a rare journey, a hundred miles round-trip. I had never driven that many miles out of Los Angeles and recalled only the cross streets—Brookhaven and Katella—in Little Saigon. No address or phone number. Though Lac Hai and I had been to the temple twice, at the time I did not pay attention to the route. Today I would go there alone.

On the way home from work the night before, I had stopped by the Thai market in Hollywood and bought two large boxes of dried Chinese noodles for the Sifu of the temple. The market had escaped the burning of the riots here two weeks ago, but the block still held the acrid smell of other charred buildings, intensified by the May rains. I had placed two ten-dollar bills in a white envelope, scribbling my name and Hai's on the flap. The twin bills symbolized a kind of symmetry that I had hoped to achieve in my life. I placed a small framed photo he'd given me of himself into the shopping bag and put everything in my car trunk.

I needed to return to the place where I had felt at home, a stranger among fellow strangers. If Vietnamese had been refugees to America when they first arrived, I was, ironically, in this position now, a refugee to that house that served as temple, shelter, and garden for the Buddhist monk.

The Interstate 5 funneled my car smoothly past working-class industrial towns—Montebello, Commerce, Downey, Norwalk—southeast of downtown Los Angeles. The morning was warm, smudged with brown haze at the horizon. Sweat soaked my shirt. Billboard mirages of Las Vegas casino shows in the desert and sleek Japanese automobiles glittered between real palm trees and poplars. I held my speed at seventy miles an hour as my eyes focused on the towns ahead. Sante Fe Springs. Anaheim. La Palma. I drove on. The freeway sign said "22, Garden Grove Connector," which would lead me west to Little Saigon.

Housing on these suburban streets—Magnolia, Euclid, Beach—was arranged without regard for pedestrian life: one side of the street had fifteen-foot concrete sound barriers which backed middle-class housing developments. Directly across from them, older, single-family dwellings from the 1950s and '60s—the kind built on concrete slabs—faced the blank walls. Newer developments, built cheaply of beige stucco, segregated themselves from the older houses.

Finally, Brookhaven. My eyes searched its length for the simple tract home which served as the temple. The lush oriental arrangement of rose bushes, aloes, bodhi trees, sago palms, and the plaster statue of Quan Am—goddess of mercy—fronted the house. I stopped the car, took the shopping bag from the trunk, and walked across the street. A single pair of men's black shoes, not the usual row of a dozen pairs. The door was shut. I knocked once, then again. The window curtains were drawn. A black umbrella leaned against a windowsill. Hung outside the door was a talisman made of old copper Chinese coins laced up with red cotton string in the shape of a sword and a ceramic incense holder filled with burnt punk sticks. No answer. Ten o'clock. Maybe the Sifu was still asleep or out for the morning.

I resigned myself to waiting. The Sifu had cut the flowering bodhi tree down to almost half its original size. He said that the roots could spread under and beyond the house; in Vietnam they grew to gigantic dimensions. The smell of the roses he tended permeated the air. I paced up and down the narrow entrance way.

I rapped on the door again. Silence. In my anxious walking back and forth, I counted forty-five steps across the width of the house lot. A dirty blue

Pontiac stopped beside me. An Asian man about my size got out, walked up to the door of the temple, and knocked. Turning toward me, he asked in Vietnamese if anyone was home. I answered in English. He smiled.

"I'm in trouble. I need three dollars for gas." I gave him three rumpled dollar bills.

"Thanks," he said, stuffing them into his shirt pocket. "I haven't been here in years. When I first came to this country ten years ago, I visited the temple. I had promised Buddha that if the boat made it to Thailand, and I ever got to America, that's what I would do. Sifu was kind, and rented me a room until I could settle down."

When I didn't respond, he continued.

"I'm a welder, but I got laid off yesterday. Maybe my wife will leave me— because I took her forty dollars last night to the Bicycle Club. I lost it all. I can't stop gambling."

He sat himself down on a rock under one of the two bodhi trees at the entry way. "Here, sit down," he motioned with his hand, "it's cooler in the shade." I sat next to him on the other flat rock, absorbed by the droning of bees and passing automobiles.

"These monks sleep late sometimes. They study old books at night," he said.

"Maybe he went shopping for food."

"If you see the monk, tell him I came by. I'll come back later." He stood up. We shook hands and he hurried off without telling me his name.

After waiting two hours I got into my car and drove around the block to the corner shopping mall. Lac Hai and I had walked through here, the last time we visited the temple together. He bought yellow mums and gladioli for the temple altar from the florist.

I returned to the temple but the door was still shut. I left the two boxes of noodles on the step. Should I leave the envelope with the money in the mailbox, in the plastic bag with the noodles, or slip it under the door? I decided that the door was safest, but retrieved the framed photo of Lac Hai from the bag. The sun's glare obscured the image of Hai pressed behind the glass, the small petulant mouth and dark eyes set obliquely into the pale face. On the surface of the finger-smudged glass, I could sense my own features reflected.

The rains had swollen the door tight and there was barely space underneath. I nudged the envelope in. Barking from behind the door—Phuc, the temple dog. He tugged at the envelope, and it disappeared under the door for good. I hoped he would give it to his master. "Phuc, Phuc," I shouted. Perhaps he would recognize my voice.

Once more, I drove off. I was hungry. At a Chinese-Vietnamese restaurant, I ate all of the squid-and-vegetable lunch plate. Returning to the temple, I saw that the package of noodles was still against the door. The man who had gambled away his luck and money had not come back. I would return to Los Angeles.

The night you left me you avoided my eyes. With my right index finger, I traced the printed image of the pink lotus framed in yellow: Tra Man Sen, Lotus Tea / 100 grams or 3.5 ounces. Red cardboard box, now emptied. Empty. I stirred the last of the green leaves into a cup of hot water. The monk, I recall, had served us such a tea at the temple. But that evening we did not drink anything.

Now my throat is dry, as are my eyes. I refuse to cry over this common affair between men. *Chuntzu chih chiao tan ju shui*—between gentlemen, friendship appears indifferent but is pure like water. That's about all I remember from studying Chinese, and that adage comes in handy now. More clarity: tacked on my kitchen wall, a torn newspaper clipping. On the paper, words by Aung San Suu Kyi, the Burmese leader under house arrest for her political speeches. She had written about coolness which lies beneath the shade of trees, of teachers, and of Buddha's teaching. I cut the article out of the paper and retyped it. I am not Buddhist, but I was moved because she had spoken her thoughts to thousands of people, whereas I have no one to speak to now.

I lock and unlock my hands, from fist to open palm, tracing the fate lines without caring whether they mean anything. Rub each fingertip. The tea is not strong enough, its bitterness turning to sweet aftertaste on the tongue. On the kitchen sideboard the bottle of Crown Royal that a friend gave me for Tet, the lunar New Year. I uncap it, sniffing up the fumes, but recap the bottle. I want to see you, Lac Hai, your face clearly in my eyes. For I am a Chinese man from America, left dry by a man of water who was born in the delta between the Red and Black rivers.

I spit on the tile floor. Why were you born? Where did you come from? I'm standing in the kitchen, I realize, staring at the fissured plaster walls. At you. Offspring of Lac Long Quan and Au Co, who, between them, produced one hundred eggs according to legend. Fifty of their children returned with their father to the seacoast; the others remained in the mountains with their mother. Those who went to the seas and the deltas became the Vietnamese.

So goes the tale. And thousands of years later you were born, Hai. How you came to America is your own story to tell. But how we met is mine. You thought you had the last word. No. My story is the last word, since you will never say "yes" to me.

Blue outdoor floodlights spot the palm trees and bougainvillea, linger on Spanish roof tiles and French doors that link the hillside deck to the garden. The literal truth comes out in clichés: Hollywood Hills, a circa 1920s neo-Italianate stucco mansion. A living room dressed for parties: gilded Indonesian wood carvings on Plexiglass bases; stuffed white couches. A hundred decorative Asian men—Thai, Chinese, Filipino, Japanese, Vietnamese—are dancing on the hardwood floor together with voracious Anglos who never look as young as the Asians, even if they really are younger. Double platters of fried chicken, lumpia, chow mein, lots of rice, and American pies: peach, apple, cherry. Two cut-glass punch bowls overflowed with sangria and citrus rinds. You are a Gypsy floating about the room, a red bandanna around your shining brow, one silver earring, and a vest of dark leather. You never throw me a glance, but I follow your cheekbones and lips with my eyes as desire catches at my throat. Three days later, I telephone you.

The black Toyota pickup hurtles through the smog-white afternoon, heading south on the Interstate 5 toward Little Saigon, Orange County. You drive fast, sunglasses framing the bridge of your nose, hands cleanly maneuvering the stick shift with long fingers. Following the curve of the freeway, you tell me how you've traveled the roads of the world and ended up here.

Ten years ago, at eighteen, you went from Buddhist temple to temple seeking the peace of mind that each monastery promised. You shaved your head. You meditated on your knees. You talked back and forth past midnight over tea with your monks, wore out pair after pair of sandals strolling the muddy fields of Taiwan, Thailand, Japan, France. Skinny chickens, heat and cold, and thick-walled buildings were the same in every country. Bare floors. Old books. A few compassionate monks. Most of them, who just followed rituals without risking heart or mind, disappointed you in the end.

You observed their teachings well enough, but could not quell other desires. That desire which still causes your body temperature to rise in fever.

But neither meditation nor lovemaking could contain or release this heat, for your pleasure walks the same path as your pain.

"Just friends for today," you tell me. "Tomorrow is less certain than the past."

Traveling a route you know by heart, you seek the pure sky of a childhood that was never your own. From dawn to dusk, your sky was fractured with rockets and fragments of fuselage. For your wartime hunger, Catholic-orphanage nuns beat you with bamboo canes that bruised your child's skin. A stranger to your history, I am neither father, teacher, brother, nor lover. In the truck I touch your thigh but you draw back, not trusting me or anyone who touches you. Exit Little Saigon: we swerve past the green enameled sign onto Bolsa, a boulevard crammed with two-story strip malls—Vietnamese bakeries, banks, beauty parlors, stationery stores, coffee shops, bookstores. Snack on sweet rice cakes and drink iced concoctions of brown sugar, red dates, and seaweed. You drink and look away. I would have talked with you in a new language for me: Vietnamese. Now silence runs deeper between us, a blade dividing memory.

You want to stop at the temple to visit your Sifu, with whom you had studied for several months. First we buy flowers for the altar, pink, yellow, and white mums. Inside the truck, I bring the large bouquet to my face. The petals darken into fingers that gesture with a sudden life of their own, settling upon my eyelids and lips.

The conversation between you and the monk is all yours. You sit across from each other in a corner of the room. The monk does not look directly at you, and not to me at all. But I steal a look at him—at his face tanned from gardening and at his clean-shaved head and nape. Then I bow by the altar and leave the room, exiting the side door to the backyard. It's a derelict space that backdrops the temple, painted yellow and trimmed at the roof, eaves, and windows with red. For Vietnamese, as for Chinese, these colors must be auspicious.

The yard is large for a tract home. The diving board on which I sit overhangs the edge of the swimming pool drained of its water. A concrete kidney-shaped grave is swollen with the legs of odd chairs, cracked tables, and a hundred aloe plants in black plastic tubs.

Somewhere inside the temple the monk is chanting. His sutras seemed to unlock doors, lift windows and solid walls, sweeping past wooden eaves and alighting upon the aloes in the yard. I sit in the midst of the debris, discarding another layer of my life. Last week a friend told me that seven of his buddies had died of AIDS. No one wanted to know. In Asian families, you just slowly disappear. Your family rents a small room for you. They feed you lunch. Dinner. Rice, fish, vegetables.

At my feet, aloes thrust green spikes upwards from black dirt, promise to heal wounds and burns, to restore the skin's luster. From this ground pure light would surely arise over suburban roofs and power lines, illuminating the path of green aloes by which I would return to the house.

Inside the temple the monk is already cutting cabbages for supper on the nicked Formica table. I find myself alone with him. You are gone to some other part of the house. Sound of sink water running down the drain.

From eastern deserts, Santa Ana winds blow inwards to Los Angeles. Sand submerges my feet, then rises and fills my eyes. The wind plays tricks. I am alone in bed, listening to it. Noises of branches and leaves rush against each other as arms and legs brush over mine. Burying me. My body is bloated with chrysanthemum leaves, like a Mexican birthday piñata, waiting for children to break it open with sticks. What will fall out? Flowers float on the Cuu Long—Mekong. Do white petals heed death or life? I do not know. Santa Ana winds blow through cheap condominium walls in the City of Angels, currents which sap the vines of my desire.

Dry throat, the night after you leave. Fifth gin and tonic. I am at The Bar, drowning in the shadows of Asian men half my age who gyrate on the dance floor. An Anglo man standing beside me named Doug or Eddie is talking. I listen, laugh, but do not turn my face to him. I wait for you to walk in with a new friend, for both of you to cast insinuating glances, like violets, at this roomful of men. Only after I have seen this with my own eyes will I leave. Dark petals unfurl, mocking me. Maybe it is the gin and tonic. I take black coffee, and after that, another gin.

I probably look younger than my thirty-seven years, in a white nylon windbreaker, snug Levis, black sneakers. Yet I detest the remnants of youth on myself. In the photograph, Hai, you are wearing a long-sleeved shirt that covers your arms, but it was not your concealed body or veiled spirit that most intrigued me. It was your journey that directed my imagination, as I have never ventured outside the country of my birth. China was a mental atlas of winding rivers and mountain ranges; Vietnam was still farther away in space and time. Beyond the black-and-white images of soldiers, helicopters, and villages captured on my television screen, that southern land was once the impassioned object of an antiwar demonstration that I had joined twenty years ago.

My stomach turns, entrails holding in rancid water, petals, leaves. The churning of Santa Ana air gathers momentum, drowning out the DJ. If I make it home tomorrow morning, the sky should clear from the wind. The bartender does not want to pour me another drink. I insist.

"I will give you a flower," I tell him. "Have you heard of *Flowers of Evil*? By a French poet. But I forget his name tonight."

The barman relents.

Around me, floors begin to crack and sway. Chrysanthemums fall apart, their ravaged petals plucking up stray insects. Even hands to my ears cannot shut out the wind. Stop.

The television blazes. We live in the heat of the desert, in jerry-built towns of plastic pipe and drywall. I long for waters past.

In the tenth century, Ngo Quyen defeated a Chinese armada in the Bach Dang river. He ordered huge timbers tipped with iron to be buried in the tidal shallows. At high tide these were hidden, and when Chinese troopships appeared, the lighter Vietnamese boats went out to meet them. The submerged timbers skewered the Chinese hulls. Then Vietnamese boats, their prows painted with lucky eyes, swiftly advanced and burned the Chinese ships.

Reaching the alluvial plains, between the brows of the Red and Black rivers, you can see the features of the land. Your face is flushed, sweating. Heat rises from your belly and chest. I press a cool white towel on you. More cold tea. You fall asleep in my arms. Maybe a fever, via these erratic winds, has seeped into your nostrils.

You get a haircut. It's almost like being home—mirrors and bicycles casually propped up below the banyan trees, and men, young and old, having a haircut and shave. Only in Little Saigon your haircut is indoors, under cool fluorescent lights. But the same extended conversations, the same jokes. Your black hair falls to the floor in dark wisps and you flirt with the Amerasian haircutter. You feel almost at home, but not quite. Even at my apartment, settled on the black leather-and-chrome couch with your Vietnamese martial-arts novels and cassette tapes, you're awkward with my domesticity— your long legs angled out in borrowed sweatpants.

When we go out to eat with friends you joke in Vietnamese. The most I can do is utter the dishes in Chinese syllables, but that is not enough. Your accent betrays a thousand uprisings: revolts against forebears and foreigners; against the Chinese, French, Japanese, Americans. When we get home one night you have not spoken with me at all: English has disappeared from your vocabulary. I ask what's wrong. You turn your head away from mine on the pillow, muttering: "If you want soap-opera dialogue then just turn on the TV, okay?"

"No soap opera—Chinese opera. How about *Taking Tiger Mountain by Strategy?*" I laugh, deflecting your sarcasm. "Don't forget I'm still Chinese."

"How would you know anything about taking? You never had your home taken away like I did. By Communists. In Saigon my stepfather had a three-story house, with a small ballroom on the top floor. A balcony, with blue tiles, that we danced or slept on during the summer . . ."

Not wanting to hear the same story again, yet still wanting you, I smother your face with the coverlet and crawl quickly underneath, bringing my face to your belly and pressing my lips farther down. I take you in my mouth until all I can hear is your breathing. Your body tosses and turns. Wordless. You come without touching me, your hands slackened against the pillow. So your silence is against me, a being who is both American and Chinese.

Ignorant, I do not share your dialect. I shave the shadow off my face in the morning. I learned that Vietnam lies in one time zone. That's all I remember from Geography One, junior high, about Vietnam.

But we lie awake in many zones. You speak to me across one time zone, and I speak to you in another. Your thoughts turn away earlier or my words tumble out later. Or, just the reverse. Zones which divide us.

Whenever you are alone you drive to Redondo Beach and watch the water. Hai: the name for "water," which is your real name. Water which takes you back, to the plains between the Red and Black rivers. One day you asked me the English name of the *mai* tree, with small yellow blossoms that open during Tet. I do not know the English name. On the kitchen table: the green plate from which you ate, the cup from which you drank. You may not return, but I leave them anyway, as I leave your sandals at the door.

I fall deeper into sleep under which everything becomes transparent. My hands search for mineral places we once crossed together—blue veins, black quartz. Your eyes travel farther back, to limestone hills above the river, dredging up timbers tipped with shining iron. Buried in river water. Hidden at high tide. Timber after timber, a forest of weapons. I stare at the deceptive calmness of the water.

I drop the teacup on the kitchen floor. It does not shatter, but remains whole. The cup holds departed kin, a spirit which wants to stay here. Neither libations nor liaisons could free me of it. Nonsense. Superstition. I, Miles Mak, am a college-educated Chinese American, after all, raised in Queens, New York, by way of Connecticut, Seattle, and, finally, Los Angeles.

Wash the night away. Rinse the plates and cups. Put them away, less the one in hand. Leaves, dark as sand or seeds, cleave to the bottom of my cup.

A truck lumbered past me, forcing me to steer my compact car against the next lane divider. Soon the glassy towers of downtown insurance and banking companies thrust their heads through the smog. The drive back up was faster than the ride down. When I reached Hollywood it was still the middle of the afternoon. I went to the Holiday Gym, a pink stucco exercise palace with pop music piped in from dawn to dusk. In the mid-afternoon it was almost deserted. Methodically, on the chrome and red vinyl–padded machines, I crossed from one to the other, flexing back and biceps, doing sit-ups and leg lifts to bury the time. Though I had not seen the Sifu I felt relieved even to have located the temple again. The steel-chromed bars rose up and down in front of my eyes. Sweat lined my face. I was imprisoned in my exertion of choice. I needed to sweat, whether it was under the sun or induced within this air-cooled environment. A few middle-aged Korean women with rubber head caps were swimming in the lap pool. Their pale heads and shoulders, bobbing up and down in the green water, took on the androgynous cast of fleshy sea creatures.

After showering, I went home, opened a can of tuna fish and a can of cream-of-mushroom soup, and poured all of it over leftover rice. The kitchen clock read 5:30 p.m. Dead heat of traffic. I could wait a while. Maybe I would drive back to the temple tonight. Rewrapping the picture of Hai in white paper, I put it beside the door, intending to bring it back with me.

Night on Interstate 5 released the day's torpor: automobile headlights turned upon each other, thousands of metallic bodies feeding heat and carbon exhaust to the hungry darkness. I drove slowly, without ambition, yielding to the cars already in front of me. I reached the Garden Grove freeway which connected to Little Saigon, but the sign said "West Connector Closed." Darkness. So I got off the East exit, opposite to where I wanted to go. The faceless buildings of a vast suburban shopping mall in the City of Orange surrounded me; it was fifteen minutes before I realized I was traveling in a circle, around the perimeter of the shopping center's department stores, now closed. I continued driving down the empty streets.

Irritated, I did not think to stop the car and check my map. Instead my eyes searched for Vietnamese shop signs, oriental mini-malls, and people. The pedestrians on the sidewalk had dark hair and were not tall. I squinted at them, hoping they were Asian. More auto body shops, Taco Bell signs, and liquor stores. This was not Little Saigon but a Latino barrio, part of Anaheim or Santa Ana.

I stopped at a red light and rolled down my window, catching the attention of the Asian driver in a gray Nissan sedan beside my car. "Bolsa," I yelled, the main street of Little Saigon. He pointed his finger in the opposite direction. I thanked him and made a U-turn at the next light. Residential blocks had the same concrete barriers which obscured my vision and direction. I found a gas station not yet closed. The Pakistani said, "Drive down for a couple of miles, you will pass Euclid, then Brookhaven, and make a right."

The temple might be shut for the night or the Sifu already asleep. Following the gas station attendant's directions, I found Brookhaven. I pulled my car up near the door next to the temple and got out. As I approached the door, the one light shining in a back window suddenly turned dark. I knocked softly. In an instant, the window lit up again. The door opened.

An unfamiliar face peered out at me. In the porch light I did not know whether the smooth face was a man's or a woman's. The person greeted me in Vietnamese. In the back room, I could see the Sifu adjusting his robe.

"Sifu," I called.

He asked me to come in and sit and introduced me to his assistant. Under the light, the young man looked all of fifteen, but he must have been at least ten years older. The monk explained that they had been separated twenty years by the war, but ran into each other in Los Angeles. As a child, the young man lived next door to the monk's house, south of Saigon. After the youth arrived in the U.S., he attended a year of junior college but had to drop out. He ended up here at the temple.

I hung my head, apologized for the late hour, and hoped that I had not disturbed them. I explained that I had come in the morning, but that the temple door was locked. The Sifu said, "Oh, I thought it was some traveling monks who had dropped by to visit and left us those boxes of noodles."

I unwrapped the photo and showed it to the monk. With a look of consternation, he handed it back to me. Glancing away from me, he focused his eyes past the carved brass candlesticks and fruit-laden platters, to a point beyond the image of the gold-leafed Buddha that occupied the center place on the altar table.

In English, he said: "You need not say more." Switching to Vietnamese, he paused between sentences to allow his assistant to translate. "A bird wants more than he can eat, so he flies into the trap. A fish wants more than he can eat, so he catches the hook. Know when you have enough." He pointed to the curtained windows.

"There, in the daytime, can you see the two trees at the entrance to this temple? When birds alight on the leaves, the trees do not show happiness. When the birds fly away, the trees do not reveal sadness. Be like these two trees."

The room enveloped the three of us, our knees and feet touching the felt carpet.

"Being born is unhappiness, as being sick is unhappiness. Old age or dying is also unhappiness. But still another form of unhappiness is happiness itself."

I could feel my hands go warm and pressed my palms onto the carpet beneath my legs. It was ten minutes, if that much. The Sifu's words resounded, as sound does, in the spaces within me.

"Go home and sleep."

I thrust the photograph of Lac Hai into his hands. "He does not belong to me," I said.

I stood up and thanked his assistant for helping. As I reached the door, the terrier, Phuc, barked at me, wagging his tail. I looked back at the monk, about to ask if the dog had retrieved the envelope with the money. Sifu nodded his head in the affirmative even before my asking.

"Next time you come," he said, "we'll cook some of the noodles for you."

I put my palms together, bowed, and backed out of the doorway. Someone switched off the porch light. My shoes were dampened with night dew and I put them on in the dark.

Runaways

I DON'T GET UP early in the morning. Before Ma goes to the grocery store she wakes Ba and me up. She puts his walking cane right near their bed. I can hear the soft thud of his feet and the click of the cane on the tile floor when he makes his way to the bathroom. She knocks on my door and calls me *lan doi* or lazy kid. I never see her smile, only her puffy eyes.

Sometimes she mutters in Spanish. No one can understand her except, perhaps, the wooden statue of the Virgin Mary next to the Buddha altar in the hallway. The statue was one of the two things she brought with her from Lima, Peru, where she was born, raised, and stolen away by my father. The other thing was her torn brown leather photograph album.

One time she showed my brother and me a photograph of her and her mother, posed in front of a broad, European-style avenue with trees framing white colonial buildings. She was smiling and holding onto her mother's Chinese-style dress. "Lima," in a careful child's handwriting, was penciled in under the sepia-toned image. Her grandfather, who had been sent to Peru as a coolie to work on sugar plantations, had harvested sugar cane, tapped wild rubber trees in the Amazon, and dug for gold. Saving his money, he imported a woman from China to be his wife. They had worked hard and left the Amazonian backwaters of Iquitos, where they had settled originally, to open a general supply store in the capital.

Before we finish our rice soup, Brother has revved up the green pickup parked outside our apartment. He's the only normal one around here. But as soon as he finishes junior college he's planning to join the navy. Out of here for good.

Some of us go to the clinic in the morning, the rest in the afternoon. If we don't check in, the social workers call our parents or guardians, or our aunts or uncles who sign the state disability forms.

I go around noon when the clinic gets leftover donuts free from the Hop

Luck Pastry Shoppe around the corner. The Pacific Mental Health Center is on the southeastern corner of Stockton Street, beneath the Ping Yuen Housing Projects, right through this wooden and glass door.

Through this door is another world. It's murky as water reflected on the scales of a fish, any of the gray-white ones piled high on the aluminum pans on Grant Avenue. Daylight barely reaches the inside of the clinic; here, we are just soft bones, stagnant blood, and slow fins serving out our time.

But they can't lock us up. For sure we would die in the state wards. I remember visiting my ex-girlfriend at Agnew's Asylum in Napa. It took me two hours to get there by bus. Before I even walked into the large corridor waiting room I could hear the screaming and moaning. It was how I imagined cattle or ducks or pigs sounded when they were being slaughtered for market. She was pale-looking, and we had nothing to say to each other because her eyes were washed out. Emptied. They didn't see me anymore. From the screaming noises, I expected to see blood on her white smock. But it was clean. I left her staring at me because I couldn't stand to look at her. As none of us have yet committed serious crimes—kidnapped or gunned down anyone important—prison's really not the place for us either. You must understand that in order for them to keep their jobs they keep on prescribing pills and make sure we go to the outpatient care clinic. No one looks up at me when I arrive, just the social workers who, after all, are paid to pay attention.

The main room is lined with brown metal folding chairs, with big tables in the middle. Seven-Up bottles with one or two cut-out paper flowers decorate the tables. The back wall has a long counter. Behind that is where a secretary and a couple of social workers and staff have their desks.

I almost bump into Diana. She's hunched over as usual, staring down at the table, at a donut crust and a Styrofoam cup of coffee.

"Diana!" I yell in her face, otherwise she would not hear me, or pretend not to. Her gentle face peeps up from the yellow knit sweater with the Chinese symbols for longevity embroidered on it. She will live a long time, her mother hopes, and I cross my fingers that she will.

"Do you know what this red thing here is?" I ask her, pointing to my heart. Every time I come here I ask her the same thing, to make sure that she and I still mean the same to each other.

"It's me," she says, smiling and pointing to my chest. "It's me, and you, one on the left and one on the right. I finished my donut. *Nei yiu donut ma?*"

"Mmmm, Di. I don't see any left."

Someone taps my shoulder. "Welcome back, Lee. Good to see you. You haven't been to the clinic in a week. We were worried."

"Yeah? Miss Woo, guess if I don't come around, you don't meet your quota."

Miss Woo drops her smile and walks away. Quickly, out of the corner of my good eye, I see her scribbling furiously on a yellow legal pad and putting the note in Dr. Lau's mail slot. Dr. Lau is my doctor. He is the one who prescribed the orange pills. He is the one who sees me every Friday. Just another Chinaman, from Hong Kong. This place is full of them; half the people who come here, and most of the docs and shrinks and workers, are from there.

I find a seat next to Diana. John winks at me from across the table. He's the one you always see walking around Chinatown, wearing a checkered sports jacket, his head in the air, not looking to the right or to the left. One time I followed him for a dozen blocks, and he only stopped twice: once to look at a Chinese movie billboard and the other to look at a window display of plastic toy ducks dipping their beaks into a bucket full of water. He looked at the ducks for a long time.

John always looks like he had somewhere to go, but he just walks in circles every day. People around here are used to seeing him, unchanged over the past five years. Every morning rain or shine you can see him leaving the Victory Hotel on Clay Street at exactly 7:30.

Some said that he escaped from a Vietnamese fishing boat in 1973; others said he was the son of a rich Chinese-Vietnamese banker from Cholon who had sent enough money to the clinic to take care of John for nine more lives. He never talked. The social workers treated him nice. A man like that didn't bother folks. I had a gut feeling that he knew more than he could ever say. I wanted to be there just in case he opened his mouth one day.

This Wednesday is quiet, except for Rowena's radio: Smokey Robinson and the Miracles. Rowena Gee, five-foot-five in thigh-high boots with five-inch stiletto heels, walks in with her six-foot-tall boyfriend, Herbie. Baby-faced. She must have been over thirty but no lines, no wrinkles at all.

"Hi-ya, and you, and you, and Di, and Johnny baby," she coos. Today her makeup is thicker. Green eye shadow and orange lips.

"Herbie," Miss Woo says, "please turn your radio down. This is not a public park."

Herbie worked in a North Beach Radio Shack about a mile or so from here. He and Rowena had been tight for almost as long as I could remember. As the social workers had said, speaking softly among themselves in

Chinese, not only was he Black, but five years younger than Rowena. "But at least he has a job."

I keep track of people, where they go and what they do, especially the doctors. Got to make sure they're doing an honest job. Because no one else here does.

About Rowena and Diana and John: I have to point out that most everyone in here has two things in common: they are baby-faced and they never wear hats, including me. Our faces stay smooth because we don't let the world bother us too much.

As for hats—none of us have been, or ever will be, accepted into the U.S. military. None of us are businessmen—with the black fedoras; none of us are old China women—with the tight knitted skullcaps. None of us work in poultry and fish shops and wear those white paper hats. No felt hats, knit or paper hats, or greasy hats. We bare our heads to the air and sky. How many times have we uncovered our heads to Chinatown social workers and doctors who don't know what to do with us?

Hatless, we're part of Chinatown. Yet we're not. Not working. The state pays us general disability and we're supposed to get taken care of by these greaseball social workers. The truth of the matter is: I'm the caretaker for all of us who wear no hats. The hatless family. They're my best friends. That's why I'm writing this in my own long-winded way, before they change the medications on us or ship some of us to the funny farm like they sent my ex-girl.

I don't know exactly what changes each capsule causes in me. I take them though—it's been two years now. Otherwise I get edgy and nervous. Don't know much about the different ones they give me, but they're supposed to calm me down. Don't get me wrong. I am a lot calmer now. That's why I'm still coming here. Until I get perfectly calm.

Maybe Doc is right. Sometimes I need those pills. Especially with Ma yelling at me at the grocery store. I hear her yelling all the time, even though no one else can hear her.

Brother says I'm crazy. "Ma's not yelling at you, all she said is will you go downstairs and turn the fire down beneath the pot of abalone on the stove." I thought she was yelling at me.

Ba gives me a drowsy look. I wish he would fall flat on his eighty-two-year-old face. That's not nice for a son to say, I know. But he might as well fall. He sits there, dreaming of when he was a middle-aged man. When he went to Hong Kong to marry my Ma. They sent my beautiful Ma—she was only twenty-one then—from Lima to Hong Kong to marry a fifty-year-old man she had never even seen before. She was one of five daughters, and there weren't enough eligible Chinese men in Peru at the time to marry all five off.

Through family connections, what she saw was a photograph of a much younger man, not the old one who finally met her at the Kowloon wharf in 1958. On the ship, she told me, she had made friends with a young Chinese man, from Caracas, who was coming to Hong Kong to meet the village girl arranged for him. An arrangement in reverse. Talking about her trip was the only time I saw her eyes soften, but she quickly brushed her eyes with the corner of her apron and told me to get back to work.

I think she remembered that man because of the Chinese customer from Venezuela who had come into the store one morning to buy Canadian beef jerky and dried Hawaiian pineapple for a trip he was planning to make to Latin America. From the back of the store where I was unloading crates of preserved duck eggs, I didn't see the customer clearly, just the shadow of his straw fedora. About an hour later, she began telling me about the voyage she had made over twenty-five years ago, but it was as if she was talking to herself. I didn't say a word.

She got a raw deal. Ba outlived his other two wives. I can see why. I think Ma cries alone in Spanish at home, after Ba, Brother, and I go to sleep.

She's yelling at me again. I duck behind the stack of boxes that read "Handle with Care, Soya Sauce" and stick my hands on top of my ears until the yelling stops. Then I walk down the damp wooden stairs to the basement kitchen.

The leathery odor fills the store. Dried abalone has been boiling for hours. I turn up the fire, then wipe the grease from my fingers on my pants. I go over to the sink and start washing the lunch dishes. The sink has no drainpipe so I dunk the cups, chopsticks, and bowls carefully into the plastic pan with cold suds and then slosh them through with hot water. After stacking the bowls and cups I carry the dirty water to the toilet and dump it all down. The water gets on my pants and sneakers. But I don't let it bother me. We live like fishes here. Fishes, swimming in clogged watery basements. Carp, eel, rock cod, salmon, flatfish, bass, floating clean or slimy, dead or alive, through the streets.

I don't wear hats, like the old folks. They're always protecting their heads, afraid maybe something is going to happen to them, that heaven is going to fall down on them. That somebody from a family association third-floor balcony will spit a wad or drop a cup of red Hawaiian Punch on their heads. I can't worry about such futuristic things. I'm swimming through my life, in the here and now. Fish don't wear hats, never seen any with.

I scramble up the stairs. Ba is still slumped on the wooden chair, the cold cigar on the ashtray next to him. He snores, right in front of the customers' faces. Longevity, what good is it? I hope Diana dies young, happy in her yellow sweater. She doesn't deserve to end up like Ma, in a fixed marriage, serving some guy old enough to be her father. He sits on that rattan chair snoring through the afternoon, then wakes up for dinner. After Brother drives them home in the pickup, he sleeps again, until his breakfast porridge. Sleep and eat. Day in and day out.

At least Diana still smiles when I yell her name. Ma just gives me a pained look when I call her name, and takes a five-dollar bill out of the cash register and hands it to me. "No gamble," she warns.

"Ma, I got to go to the clinic now."

"*Gei dim fan oak?*" she asks me.

"I'll be home around four," I answer.

Suddenly her eyes light up, with fire or something else. "Be sure you go. The doctors are good for you. Don't run away. *Chinos cimarrones*. If you don't go they stop the checks."

"Ma, I know they'd stop them—what did you say?"

"They used to call Chinese that when they ran away from the fields. Grandfather told me he ran away from the plantation once. Whipped because he still hadn't paid up his fare from China."

I turn out the door. I didn't tell her that sometimes I felt like tearing them up and dangling the torn checks in her face. Maybe she liked me to stay sick, as sick as she is for staying here with Ba. On the other hand, where would she go? She can't swim back to Peru because there is no one there for her anymore: her parents are dead and her four sisters are scattered throughout the world, from Canada to Hong Kong. So we hang together here, sinking in the basement water.

If I got well, clerks downtown would nod at each other and say to themselves. "Lester Kwok-Lee is finally well. Scratch him off the list. We only pay for sickos."

I sprint the three blocks up the hill to the clinic. Thursday is dance day.

The big room is empty. The mural on one wall shows Chinese laborers working on the railroads and digging for gold. Everyone's face is tinted yellow in the picture. Maybe they were eating the gold whole or had yellow fever or hepatitis. The corner of the scratched and dusty mural is signed, "James Leong, 1952." I wasn't even born yet. Strains of "The Hawaiian Wedding Song" drift into the clinic from the yard. I walk out the open back door.

Diana and John are hand in hand, marching under an arch of arms formed by Miss Woo and another social worker. They look like they are getting married, right here in the project yard, stepping delicately over gobs of weathered dark bubble gum pressed into the asphalt. Rowena is off to the side, by herself, fondling her Hawaiian lei made of pink toilet paper during craft day yesterday. I cup my hands, like I am blowing into a shell, and let out a big, fart-like sound with my lips.

I yell: "Hooray for John and Diane, hooray for the bridesmaids, happy Hawaii, happy Chinatown."

Rowena blows me a kiss and completes the ceremony by taking a dollar bill out of each of her black boots and giving it to the bride and groom. A half dozen people on the wooden benches look away, past the scrawny bushes below the project walls.

"Lee," Miss Woo interrupts. "Dr. Lau wants to see you. You go into the office in about five minutes."

She is afraid of me. She knew that I am running this place, making sure that all of them do their jobs, fill the forms, check the right names, pick up the pink box of stale donuts every afternoon. Behind her pointy Hong Kong face, under her polyester blouse and blue skirts she wears every day, she knows that I know. That's why I don't bother her much. As long as I come to the clinic two out of five days, they won't stop the SSI checks coming. She wouldn't dare.

Dr. Lau is waiting in his office, smiling. He strokes his receding chin with his left hand. He has one of those pickled smiles that look as if he has a sour Chinese plum stuck to both sides of his upper gums.

"Lee, have a seat. Haven't seen you for a while. Just thought I'd check up on you. We cut the Demerol, you know. You're getting much better."

"Doc. I get used to the pills. The color. Now that you've switched it to blue I feel lost. I liked those orange ones best."

"Lee, you know how you used to pick on Miss Woo, pick on Diana, and all the others in here. Since we've given you the new medication, Thorazine, you seem much more relaxed. Do you feel relaxed?"

"I don't trust you. Or Miss Woo. What did she write you in that note the other day?"

"You mean Wednesday? She just told me that you had showed up after a week's absence and she thought it was time for you to see me again. That's all."

"I don't care. Still don't trust her. Any of you from China."

"Lee, it is true that most of us were born in China. I myself am Chinese, but I was born in Burma. We can communicate better with Chinese—from everywhere. For instance, John is from Vietnam. He speaks *chiu chau,* another Cantonese dialect. But I'm able to speak with him."

"I don't think he talks to anybody. Does he say anything to you?"

"Not much, not much. But we want to find out about you."

"Doc, I want to tell you not to worry. The clinic is running fine. I've checked everything out. You don't have to worry about me, or Diana, or Rowena, or my mother or father or brother. They're just fine. But I don't want to talk to you anymore today."

"All of us feel antisocial at times. But that's perfectly normal. Just understand that I'm—we're here when you need us."

"That's it?"

"See you next week. I'm glad everything is working out. No more yelling in your ears?"

Doc's sneaky, like the oriental painting behind his desk of two birds on a branch. The birds probably just finished eating a hundred worms. But they just sit there looking all pretty and innocent. Doc's done his duty for the week, another mark on my chart. Seen Diana, seen John, seen me, and all the rest. He can go home and relax. He gets paid well. I should be the one paid. I take care of them.

Once you pass through the scales of the fish you never come out. Scales and bones and fins and gills get stuck in your throat. You don't see light in the same way again. No one understands what I'm trying to say. Maybe Diana, if she had five percent more brain cells. I'm not putting her down. It wasn't her fault how she was born or whatever happened to her, to Ma, or to me.

One Friday last year, we took a trip outside of Chinatown on the number 30 bus early in the morning. It was gray, not sunny, and I had my warm parka on. We had bag lunches. There were ten of us. We transferred to the 5 McAllister bus to Golden Gate Park. We were going to the aquarium and the Japanese Tea Garden.

I'll never forget that day. My orangeade dripped through the paper bag. It was a defective carton. That meant my roast pork bun tasted like orange drink later on. Then, as we were getting off the bus, Rowena almost got killed. She was standing on the street, on the pavement, adjusting her black nylon stockings. A motorcycle almost ran her down. That didn't seem to bother her. She blew a kiss to the motorcyclist, who was already half a block away. Miss Woo was panicky, I saw it in her eyes. I laughed and she threw me a dirty look.

In order to get to the aquarium section, we had to pass through the reptile section first. The glass cages were full of colored snakes that looked edible. That's what I heard—Chinese in China eat everything that can be skinned, fried, boiled, or steamed. That's logical, anything tastes good if it's prepared right.

I passed out copper pennies to everyone and we started to pelt the sleepy alligators in the algae-green pond below the steel railing. I could tell Miss Woo didn't like what we were doing, but she didn't say anything. I imagined we could, all ten of us, lift her up and toss her in.

The huge room was lined wall-to-wall with glass windows. Tiny fish as big as your little finger zipped this way and that. Some were like neon, with fluorescent coloring. These were live fish, arranged against backdrops of rock and ocean weeds. I would like to have one of those tanks one day. Diana stood tall and straight, her head at attention like a soldier, entranced by the little fish that were like electric blue sparks.

The fish room opened up suddenly to the dolphin chamber, with a wider and taller glass picture window. Rowena pressed the red button on the wall. We could hear dolphins yelping in their own language that none of us could understand. The dolphin pool was bare, no ferns, weeds, or rocks. They swam around and around in the blue water. My hands brushed the cool glass walls of the transparent tank.

We were watching them. Kids poked their greasy fingers, leaned their noses, and made funny faces at the dolphins. I stood with John and watched the dolphins and the people. I looked at John and he was smiling, not saying a word.

I turned away, without telling anyone where I was going. I ran out of the dolphin room and past the fish tanks. Making a left, I went through the dark hall of reptile cages, circled around the alligator pond, and cut out of the entrance.

The gray sky had turned to a light drizzle. My feet picked up speed, and I found myself between the green benches of the music concourse. I dodged an old woman with a white cane and ran through the wooden gates into the Japanese Tea Garden. We were supposed to visit here later, so my friends would eventually find me.

I rounded hills and bushes. Each tree was shaped by gardeners. I saw a Filipino man raking fallen leaves into piles of red, brown, and yellow. My eyes were wet, but not because of the rain.

Dolphins are beautiful smooth-skinned creatures. But their watery tanks that I thought were so big a while ago grew smaller and smaller until they shrank to a droplet inside my head.

I walked on the stone paths through the garden. No pathway was straight. Sometimes I found myself walking in small circles, back to where I started. Under a pine tree facing me, a greenish statue of Buddha sat peacefully with his hands folded on his lap. His expression looked like my kung-fu teacher's when he was doing his White Crane breathing exercises.

I wished I had a camera. I would stand behind Buddha and ask a friend to take a picture of me hidden behind. Nobody would be able to see me in the photograph. Only Buddha and I would know where I stood. Ma has her Virgin Mary, silent and wooden, which reflects the light of the votive candle Ma uses sometimes, on special holidays. But she bows to Ba's ancestral shrine and lights up incense at the same time. When I was a child, I waited to see which would go out first: the wick of the candle or the orange point of the lit punk stick. Who would win: virgins or buddhas.

I continued walking, past the wooden teahouse crammed with tourists drinking tea and eating fortune cookies. Glass wind chimes tinkled from the gift shop next door. I crossed a stream. Water was flowing freely. Over the pond a strange humped Japanese wooden bridge looked steep. There were no steps, just rungs. A few people were clambering up, taking photos. I watched until everyone had deserted the bridge. Then I started on the first wooden rung. Each rung was a piece of split bamboo that nicely caught your heel. Nineteen steps to the top, half of my life. Reaching the top rung, I stopped and looked at the green garden spread out below me.

It looked different from above. The people looked smaller. I could see some circular pathways that I had missed. About ten yards away, I saw my bare-headed friends straggling in, some eating from their lunch bags. Miss Woo, wearing a scarf to protect her permed hair from the drizzle, was leading them, holding onto Diana's hand.

Diana had the same kind of expression that my Ma had in the Peruvian photograph, holding onto her mother. Trust. I spit into the water. They sold you down the river, Ma. Now we are gone, and we can never swim back.

I decided to stay on top of the bridge, until they saw me. If they missed me, I knew how to get back to Chinatown by bus. I would tell them that they had gotten lost, not me.

Daughters

Today, as I drop my daughter off at the elementary school, I see her run to-
ward her friends, her knapsack bobbing on her back, her hair in pigtails that
my wife had braided. As I close my car window, make two rights, and enter
the freeway on-ramp, I think of another girl, who must be a woman by now,
if she survived. Where is she living today? Is she by herself, under the violet
skies of the humid Asian city where I was born? I leave that city—and
myself—unnamed for now.

It's curious how someone so inconsequential from my past should sud-
denly intrude upon my middle-class domesticity, pulling me back into a
world that I can hardly imagine now, and had almost entirely forgotten.

I am a man remembering a woman who did not speak a word to me thirty
years ago. Or she might have spoken, it was that long ago, but I have no
memory of what she said. She merely took the white towel from the basin and
washed between my belly and thighs with a mixture of vinegar and water,
then lifted up her blouse for me to touch her. She was beautiful and tender,
not yet even my age, sixteen, before I came to America. But I could not bear
to touch or kiss her like the others, and, red-faced, I just left the money on
the worn reed mat and descended the narrow wooden staircase through the
front room filled with other girls, to the alley.

The sound of memory. The voice of a woman I no longer recognize fills
the small spaces of my car, bouncing against the glass, vinyl, and metal fit-
tings. Does she live under the heated skies of this place where I work now,
traversing the freeways of the Valley? She is talking to another woman, and
their conversation forces me to pull off the shoulder of the road, leaving the
cars to hurtle past mine, toward other destinations.

"DO ME, won't you?" Mimosa teased. Haishan took the gold flacon of per-
fume and pulled out the stopper, unleashing the rich, heady smell of Opium.

She carefully rubbed Mimosa's back and shoulders with the expensive amber liquid. On Mimosa's twenty-fifth birthday, they decided to celebrate by going to Le Club Indochine, a fancy karaoke bar in Arcadia, an L.A. suburb where upper-class Asians lived in big houses behind tall cedars and iron gates. Mimosa could sing in Vietnamese and Spanish. April could sing popular Cantonese hits though she was Hokkien. And Haishan preferred to sing in English.

April had seen a fashion magazine spread, and decided on a black-and-white theme. Mimosa chose a short black linen dress that showed her legs, and pulled her hair back into a sleek chignon. April wore a one-piece pleated white dress, draping a chiffon scarf from her shoulders, tied at the waist, to accentuate her beautiful shoulders and back. Haishan decided to wear a man's tuxedo she had found and altered herself. She buttoned the black jacket over her bare breasts. Like Mimosa, she pulled her hair back and pinned a white gardenia to her satin lapel.

As they drove up Monterey Drive, they almost missed the club, discreetly hidden behind a grove of cedars. Le Club Indochine didn't need to advertise. The lot was filling up with pastel Acuras and Lexuses. The Latino valet took the keys to the white Acura that Mimosa had borrowed from one of her clients, a car dealer, just for the night. They walked past the fountain and shrubbery, down the stone steps to the entrance of the club. All eyes turned on them as the waiter showed the three to their reserved table, in the mid-level section. The pan-Asian menu that reflected the clientele didn't even have prices next to the items. "Seasonal" it read. They splurged—ordering just what they wanted—tiny plates of sauteed squid and shrimp marinated in basil, individual bowls of rice noodles with chili bean paste, soft-shell crab in Shaoshing sauce, Filipino egg rolls, and champagne. The three began to enjoy themselves and the room, which was divided into three descending levels, with a small platform in the front level. Black Sony monitors for karaoke images perched like bats at each corner of the ceiling.

At the next table, some young men talking in Korean gave them the eye. They wore identical dark Armani suits and kept touching their stiff, gelled hair. The three women were eating the soft-shell crabs when a tall man walked in and sat alone at a far table. He was dressed conservatively, in a pinstriped suit, with a white T-shirt underneath. His hair was pulled back in a short ponytail that revealed one silver ear stud. April said he was probably an Asian American, because of his build, and wanted to meet him.

Haishan said, "Let's wait, I'm sure he is waiting for some friends."

He kept looking at his watch, and glancing over at them. As he walked to the restroom, his brow revealed fine creases under the sunken ceiling lights. He was around forty, the perfect age. Then, through the door, a younger Asian man dressed entirely in white came in and walked toward his table. The man was slight and feminine.

Mimosa said, "They're gay, wouldn't you know it."

"Maybe they're just friends," April added.

When Haishan looked again, the older man's hand was lightly tapping the back of the younger man's wrist. She didn't quite understand men who were attracted to other men. But she understood how women could become close, when they wanted to feel more than just another man's desire or desperation.

Waitresses scurried among the tables collecting the pink slips with the names and the selections they had written down. The karaoke selections were in English and Spanish, as well as in Chinese, Korean, and Vietnamese. The video screens lit up. Stock images revealed flat-faced young lovers walking in parks under palm trees. After a few off-key attempts by the Koreans sitting across, Mimosa had had enough. She motioned to the maitre d', slipped him a five, and told him it was, after all, her birthday. Within minutes, the DJ called her name. "Now, Mimosa celebrates her twenty-fifth."

She rose, walked slowly down to the first level, and ascended the platform. Her dark eyes scanned the room, making every man and woman take in an extra breath, feeling they were her only partner, her secret lover. Then she began to lip-sync to the tango "La Cumparsita," sung by Jun-Jun, the Filipino pop star. Before the three women knew it, the far table with the older and younger men had ordered them a round of drinks.

Mimosa had the waitress invite them over. As the younger one introduced himself and began to speak, Haishan figured Mimosa was right, they were gay. But, for a change, these men weren't interested in their bodies. The older man remarked that they probably had good-looking boyfriends to match their striking beauty. "May I inquire why they aren't with you?" he asked, smiling at Mimosa.

She laughed. "Believe it or not, we're all still single. Because we can't find three men as pretty as you two." The younger man blushed. That gave them away, Haishan thought.

Ignoring her comment, the older man turned to Haishan and asked if she or April wanted a nightcap. "No more for me," Haishan said. But it was obvious that April still liked the ponytailed one. Sensing what was happening,

Mimosa told them that they were from out of town. She stood up, nudging April's arm. "Next time we're here, we'll give you boys a ring. So nice to meet you. Pardon us while we freshen up."

"Ciao," April said.

That was Haishan's cue. She rose and thanked them for the drinks. When she reached the powder room, Mimosa and April were already fussing and giggling like two schoolgirls. Haishan kissed Mimosa on both cheeks. "You're better than any boy, any day," she said. "Happy Birthday, Mimosa."

Mimosa opened the window. The freeway sound rushed into the room. She banged the window shut and lit another cigarette. Mimosa was in charge because she was smart and could smooth things out before trouble started between the women and the boss's wife, or between the women and the men.

"Who is pulling your hair tonight?" Mimosa asked Haishan. When she asked her that, it was almost like a secret code between them.

Haishan said, "You look outside. No cars. No men. No one yet, so how would I know?" Haishan had told Mimosa one time that, when she was young, her mother used to pull her hair before she'd fall asleep. Now, if only a good man could do that for her. Not just anyone. She would have to tell him exactly how to tug at her hairline. If he did it right, it would bring the blood up to her brain in five minutes. She would feel her blood rise and fall. Blood made her eyelids droop—better than a drink or a Valium. Only then could she sleep. But it wasn't her time yet—so she did it to herself until her eyes closed. She hadn't slept too well the past few nights. Nothing seemed to work, not even pulling hair.

"Don't leave the beef tongue boiling to stink up the whole house." Mimosa puffed on her Salem Lights.

Haishan laughed, putting on her eyeliner. "They come for me so if they smell cow who cares?" Haishan said. "We have to eat." She had been here six months, the newest one. She learned to make friends with everyone. Sometimes she cooked with whatever was left in the kitchen. She would mix fish paste and garlic and sweet oyster sauce and ginger and black beans and chili together. The "girls"—no matter if they were from Cholon, Bangkok, Manila, or Hong Kong—liked the mixed-up taste, as much as they liked her. So what, the stink, she'd tell them. Just put three Tic-Tacs into your mouth and crush them with your teeth before you kiss. No accidents to worry about either. The boss lady had insisted that they all have Norplant, the birth control capsule, inserted under the tender skin of their upper arms. Haishan could sometimes feel the capsule, like a fat insect caught under the skin of her arm, if she prodded her flesh with her thumb and forefinger.

You could end up worse, Mimosa thought. Like those Thai garment workers they found locked up in the house a couple of miles down, east of the boulevard. It was all over the American papers. At least she didn't have to slave away at sewing zippers on dresses or finishing hems for two dollars an hour behind barred windows and doors. She studied the photograph of them in the papers. Young, even pretty. But they looked scared. She didn't want to see anymore. But April read the paper carefully, the English and the Thai editions. She looked intently at each face. For a moment she thought she recognized a woman from her hometown. She tore the article out, crumpled the paper into a ball in her fist, and walked upstairs without saying a word to anybody.

But April, like the rest of them, felt pressure to make money for the bosses. The owners, a man and his wife, would come by every morning to collect the cash from Mimosa, who made sure everyone was getting their right cut, after deducting certain expenses.

On their days off, Haishan, Mimosa, and April would drive forty miles down to the Fashion Island Mall in Irvine to window-shop. They blended in with everyone else, with the tourists, guitar players, and people eating ice cream. Haishan studied the Asian students—Korean, Vietnamese, and Filipino—from UC Irvine or Costa Mesa College nearby. They were wearing tennis outfits and spoke perfect English, at least the ones who came here when they were four or five years old. Haishan would mimic their accentless English. Mimosa and April would listen and laugh in the cloudless, smogless air. Haishan thought that some of the students would be the same age as her brothers, whom she had not seen since she came to L.A. When the ocean breezes swept through the open-air mall, she could almost smell the sea kelp on the shores of her hometown, its tendrils trailing across the Pacific, pungent in her nostrils. Involuntarily, she clutched Mimosa's arm. "What's wrong, Haishan?"

Slowly, Haishan began to tell her about the smell of the ocean, and about where her family lived, near the shore littered with seaweed.

Mimosa nodded. "Home always comes back to you, even when you try to forget it." She patted Haishan's arm. "Let's get ice cream, okay?"

Haishan licked the gooey lime-colored cream. Mimosa continued.

"I can forget my home. Even my husband. But not my child."

"Boy or girl?"

"He took my son. To New Jersey, then across the border to Canada. No money to find them at the time. Later I did try. In Toronto. It was the dead of winter. I was cold as a rat. But I walked miles through the underground shopping malls and fogged every subway window that I looked out of. I must have been crazy!"

"That could drive you insane."

"I cried behind my dark glasses. Driving in the car alone, I wondered whether he missed me. He was only three."

"Did you get over it?"

"Either it would kill me or I would kill my feelings. I had to live. Maybe some ancestor had done something bad before. But I'll never know."

Haishan nodded.

"So, I light incense and say prayers anyway. I don't wish my lousy karma on anyone else. My bad luck will die with me."

As much as they enjoyed the American stores with blonde mannequins wearing coordinated sweaters and dresses, they would usually end up a few miles away, in the Bolsa Plaza shopping mall in Little Saigon. There, they could find everything in their sizes, have a bite to eat, and flirt with the Vietnamese hairdressers as they studied their own hair and complexions in the mirror.

Armand, their hairdresser, was French and Vietnamese, so he said. Mimosa laughed. Everyone said they had French blood, but probably their fathers were from Kentucky or North Dakota, not Paris or Marseilles. Mimosa herself was tall and olive-skinned, from her Mexican American father and Vietnamese mother; April had lustrous Chinese skin with an ivory undertone, small features, and delicate bones; and Haishan was somewhere between in size and shape, her thick hair usually falling in bangs over her brow.

"Mimosa, we have a new skin treatment."

"Do I really need it, Armand?"

"*Em dep lam!* You sexy lady! But women like you have to preserve their beauty. Otherwise you are spitting on what Nature gave you."

"If I were naturally ugly?" retorted Mimosa.

"Then my styling would improve Nature. Even you—too much Remy or no sleep could cause your eyes to puff up."

"I don't drink that much cognac!"

"But someone might want to get you drunk, honey. Now look here. This is made by a French-trained chemist—Vietnamese, of course—who analyzed the components in a Swiss formula. Now he has this manufactured here, in New Jersey."

"So what the hell is it, Armand?"

"These are small capsules. Le Pearle. Beauty pearls. You just break one in your hand, your fingertips, and smooth the gel under your eyes before you sleep. It has emollients, three amino acids, Vitamin E, essences of citron . . ."

"How much, Armand!"

"I'm going to *give* you this sample packet free, if you buy a one-month supply. Thirty capsules, for thirty dollars. That's only a dollar a day."

Mimosa turned to April and laughed. "Okay, Armand, we'll split a package between us. It better make us sexier, or you'll have to swallow those capsules in front of me!"

Haishan liked riding to Disneyland or Santa Monica beach and other places with her friends, but the smoggy San Gabriel Valley, named after the mountains east of Los Angeles, was the place she knew best. In the Valley one town began or ended by the road signs—Alhambra, Monterey Park, Rosemead, Downey, El Monte, Temple City, Arcadia, Altadena, Monrovia, Hacienda Heights. On and on. The stucco house the girls lived and worked in was two-storied, with one and a half palm trees in the front and dying grass mowed short. Avalon Heights. It was on the border between towns, east of where Highway 60 dovetails into the 605. Avalon Heights was not high-class at all, due to the landfill just to the other side of the freeway, the one where the new townhomes were already sinking. Their house faced the back of a grammar school yard. Parents picked up their children in the afternoon. At night no one came around except for the men. A few blocks down was a mini-mall with a couple of restaurants and a Vietnamese beauty salon, where Haishan sometimes would have her hair highlighted with henna. She would have a facial and a back massage when she could afford it. Warm soapy water on her hair would trickle down her neck.

For as long as Haishan could remember, on the eighth day of the lunar New Year, her mother would burn rice straw until it became charred and crumbled into ashes. Then she would rinse the ashes with water, creating a mild lye, and soak her daughter's hair. The ritual was not only to prepare for the midnight offering to the gods; it was also an act reserved for mother and daughter alone. That memory sustained her even after her mother had changed. Even after her father, having caught her mother saving an egg for her, thrashed his wife with the back of his hand. "The boys need to eat first, so they will be stronger," he admonished. Her mother hissed back. He just hobbled away.

When he began to check the kitchen pots for stray morsels she might not have set out on the table for their two sons, she gave up saving anything for Haishan. No longer did her mother save a fish tail or smooth pork innard for her. Still, she washed Haishan's hair every week and, during the New Year, with burnt straw water. Somehow it was not the same. Haishan asked her mother what was wrong and she snapped back. "Nothing is wrong. Everything is in Buddha's hands!"

Haishan's brothers wolfed down whatever tasty morsels were set before them, never questioning their right to eat the best parts after their father had eaten his fill. The head of a fish would go to him, the soft bellies to the boys, and the tailbones and leftover broth to Haishan and her mother.

Zhihai, the elder, was named wise sea. Yet, Haishan thought to herself, he never questioned tradition. Bohai, the younger, who was named wide sea, ate copiously, never stopping to give his mother or sister a second look. After all, Father always favored Zhihai and Bohai over Haishan, coral of the sea. The mouths and feet of children devoured or walked according to whatever their parents wished or demanded. So Haishan, with her mother, ate the leftovers, after her brothers and father. And she walked behind them. She only walked side by side with her mother, or even in front of her, when they were alone together, collecting the black kelp that covered the beach like glossy undulating eels at low tide.

One day Haishan's mother brought her a set of colorful plastic combs. Her father, noticing the bright ornament in her hair, yanked at it, causing Haishan to grimace. "What is this?" he asked.

"The combs are for Haishan. You have your sons. Don't you forget—they were mine when they were snuggled in my belly."

"Crazy woman." He spit on the floor.

Haishan cowered in the next room. Only a thin blue cloth separated the space into sleeping and eating partitions. Every word was distinct and clear. Her father laughed. "Don't forget, she is my daughter too! She'll be wearing gold soon! I'm sending her to the city to work. We have a debt to pay off."

"What debt? I owe nothing to anyone."

"Shut your mouth. We owe thousands."

Haishan heard her mother sobbing, then scuffling, slaps, and a muffled scream. Her brothers just stood still, afraid to intercede. This was not the first time. Suddenly, the curtain parted. Mother was on her knees, nose bloodied, crawling to the basin filled with water from the well. Haishan rushed to clean her up. She told Zhihai to boil some water and Bohai to rinse some towels. Then Father shouted for her brothers to go out into the yard to pull weeds. They were torn between mother and father; Haishan could see it in their eyes. But they were already afraid and scuttled out.

Haishan's brothers took after their father in appearance, by inheritance or by accident. Both were thin and angular, with dark eyes and bluish black hair. Each had a mole above his right eyebrow, like their father. But beyond that she could feel some expression unlike their father's in their eyes. Zhihai was quiet, he accepted whatever privileges and food came to him, but he didn't seem to enjoy it. The younger, Bohai, was oblivious and happy to acquiesce in his way. As for Haishan, she stuck close to Mother. She felt free when they were walking along the beach, even when humidity and sandflies and sun would tire them out. The beach was formed of coral sand, fine and white as ash.

They were grateful for low tide, when the kelp was plentiful for gathering. Sometimes mother and daughter would linger, watching a local trawler and occasionally a larger ship that would make its way through the archipelago, maybe north to Okinawa or south to Brunei. Haishan imagined it would take days or weeks. She asked her mother if they could travel one day, away from their hamlet. Mother nodded, neither a yes nor a no, but more of a nodding to appease a child's questioning. But Haishan insisted on an answer and asked the same question again.

"Yes, one day you will leave here. Maybe on a ship. On a bus. Or a plane. But I'll still be here with your father, waiting for you to return." Satisfied this time, Haishan put her arms around her mother's waist.

With the kelp that they gathered and dried from the shore, Mother would make soap to sell in the town. What Haishan remembered most was the smell of kapok seed husks burning until they turned to charcoal, and Mother stirring the ashes and water with a wooden spatula. While the lye in one pot was cooling, she would boil the palm oil and lard drippings in another pot over a low fire until the chunks melted. After two hours or so when the mixture was cool she would slowly drizzle the lye into oil, stirring briskly. Then she would pour the mixture into large wooden trays looking for lumps or watery or oily patches, spreading the mixture evenly to the corners with her trustworthy spatula. She would cover the wooden trays with a dampened muslin cloth for three or four days, until the soap was hard enough to cut. Sometimes Zhihai and Bohai would help cut the soap. Those times everyone, except Father, worked together as one family. At last, Mother would have at least three hundred bars to sell. She would go around the town to sell the soap, along with brushes she would make from palm fibers.

Father began to get more demanding, accusing her of secreting money she made from selling soap. The two argued and cursed more often. Mother finally gave up after Father broke the handle of her spatula in two and tossed it into the fire.

Mother, after washing and drying her fourteen-year-old daughter's hair, plaited it through with red ribbons for the last time and placed a thin gold bracelet around her wrist, telling her never to take it off. She stuffed Haishan's plaid satchel with an extra blanket and clothing, ten dollars, a green plastic statue of Kwan-yin—protector of women—oranges, and two bags of peanuts that she had roasted herself with salt and anise. "Auntie will take care of you for a while, because there's not enough to feed and send all of you to school," Mother said flatly, before tears rushed to her eyes. "Listen to her, and work hard."

"Ma Ma, don't cry. I'll be back soon, to help you gather the kelp and boil the soap." Father, with the limp acquired in the army, could neither hold a job nor walk far. The family barely subsisted on his wife's earnings from sewing and washing, making and selling kelp soap, and occasional midwifery. On his part, he hoarded his measly soldier's pension for his own cigarettes and beer and tended the three chickens and single pig in the rear yard. That morning, Mother, and Haishan and her two brothers, walked without Father down the narrow path that led inland from the seaside to the main road. There, the bus that would take her to the county capital would make a stop. Zhihai morosely kicked the pebbles in front of him. Bohai, his mouth quivering, thrust a red rubber ball into her hand: "Haishan, find a place to play! I'll come to see you!"

Soon the four were spilling tears onto the dirt beneath their feet. The bus lurched past them, kicking dust at their faces, and stopped. Idling his motor, the impatient bus driver almost drove off without the girl. After finding an empty seat, Haishan smiled and waved to her family through the dirty glass window. She promptly fell asleep until the bus reached the capital, five hours later.

A jolt, then a stop woke her up to confusion. It was not the city noise, or the buildings or billboards. That didn't surprise her, she had seen and heard city people and city accents on television. But the familiar smell of salt and kelp was no longer with her. She placed her fingers to her nose. The scent was almost gone from her fingers.

The bus sidled into the terminal. Hundreds of people were carrying satchels and hauling wooden and cardboard boxes, or chickens or ducks strung up by the neck. Disheveled children were running pell mell, mothers hoisting hot water bottles, and elderly men clutching their glass jars full of tea leaves, with the metal lids screwed on. She peered out, searching for a woman the age of her mother. Where would she begin?

Hawkers smelled that she was a bumpkin, and threw bundles of cheap colored scarves, belts, and jangling keychains and toys in her face as she descended from the bus. With her free hand, she pushed them aside. A departing bus blew black smoke in her face, obscuring, for a moment, the clamorous humanity around her.

After the smoke cleared, Haishan began to look for a middle-aged woman of her mother's generation. It was futile—because most of the women had characteristics of distant kin—be it their country speech, shuffling gait, or sagging dresses printed with small blue or brown patterns. A young woman decked out in a violet dress, red lipstick, and high heels approached Haishan.

"Ah, Haishan, you are exactly like the photograph Auntie showed me. Such pretty eyes and thick, dark hair!" She brushed the girl's cheek and hurried to a waiting taxi. "Auntie will take care of you and buy you nice clothes, like mine."

The girl said, "I don't like those colors and I don't wear lipstick."

"You will learn to like everything that I like."

"Who are you?" Haishan asked.

"Me!" the woman laughed. "I'm one of Auntie's daughters, silly girl! Now come with me!"

The woman called the taxi over, and Haishan sat stiffly on one side of the back seat, her eyes wide open but unable to follow where they were going. The taxi crossed a concrete bridge over a dirty green river, then maneuvered wide boulevards, ducking motorbikes and carts. Finally, the driver swerved sharply into a narrow, dim alley. The characters posted on the building read: Lane 15, building number 7, Hung Liu Street. A skinny dog on the stoop paid no attention to the two women who entered through the unlatched iron gate.

Auntie was a fat woman with the same kind of makeup as her several daughters, except that her face was pockmarked. She neither looked nor smelled sweet, Haishan thought. She smelled musty, like an overripe papaya. Haishan wondered how they could even be sisters. "My mother gave me two bags of peanuts. Here's one for you, Auntie."

Auntie nodded, exposing her gold teeth and dark gums. She didn't seem to care about the humble gift, and ordered one of her daughters to take the new girl to the outdoor bath in the old Japanese-style house. "Check for lice on her hair and between her legs," Auntie shouted.

Two of the girls, a bit older than Haishan, were already inside the large tiled bath, more like a small heated pool. "Join us, little sister!" they cried.

"I don't have any lice," Haishan said, as she scrubbed herself down with the soap and cold water. Then she walked toward them and dipped one foot into the hot water. They smiled at her, then began to pull at her ankles and calves until she practically fell in. They began to paw greedily over her naked body with their hands, pulling apart her braids and tugging the strands until it hurt. Haishan drew back in surprise and began to climb out, but another arm pulled her back in. As they dunked her head in and out, Haishan felt their firm arms on her body and a probing finger between her legs. She fought her way up, gasping and crying for breath.

That's when she began to spit water at them and scream for her own mother. They just laughed at her and pulled at her hair. Suddenly Haishan became very still, trembling from head to toe in the warm steam. She looked at them without crying or saying a word. Something inside told her she would need to follow them in order to live.

A few days later, the same girls forced her arms and legs down on a pallet, poured whiskey down her throat, and let a man enter her for the first time. She felt her body bristle with pain. A sticky wetness overflowed from between her legs until she was overtaken by darkness. Groggy and sweating, she awoke in a fever under the solicitous care of the same girls and the auntie who had almost drowned her and let her be raped. For three days they forced rice gruel and chrysanthemum tea between her lips to cool her skin and blood. For the first time, she began to feel detached from herself. It was as if she were living outside of her own body, watching it breathe and move like something foreign. Her limbs felt deadened, like sea coral broken off from its stem.

Dusk entered the city, its shadows locking down the tropical heat until dawn. The young women began to paint their faces and pluck their brows. Haishan never thought of herself as beautiful, only that they were like so many dolls painted the same way. Everyone copied each other's beauty marks and moles, if they were located in lucky places on the face. Most of the girls were darker, being from the countryside; they too would dust white powder down to their necks. City men, no matter how poor, preferred pale-skinned women with red lips. After work they would saunter down the alley in their short-sleeved shirts, laughing, spitting, and telling dirty jokes. Some would peer at the windows trying to catch a free glimpse. But the girls had no time to flirt until they were through with daily chores—cleaning the tub, sweeping, peeling vegetables, or just preparing themselves for the evening.

Along with two male guards, Auntie would station some girls at the door stoop to entreat the men to enter and see her "beautiful daughters." They'd sit by the windowsills, smiling or fanning themselves. When business was slow, Auntie would send a few directly onto the narrow street. Haishan learned to pull directly at men's sleeves, elbows, even at their pants pockets and wallets. She'd persist, even after a few hand slaps, until they relented. Then, like the others, she would bring them up to her windowless cubicle upstairs, fitted with traditional reed mats or an old mattress, depending on the season.

A metal basin filled with water and vinegar, a condom, and a small white towel were set on a side table or chair. Vinegar in water was a disinfectant, "old-fashioned, good, and cheap," Auntie said. "Wash their private parts first; men are always dirty." Condoms were expensive, she added, and the girls were to use them only for certain acts. Besides, Auntie said, as the government tested them monthly for syphilis and other diseases, they would be taken care of if they ever got sick. Neither Haishan nor the others believed that.

From the other girls, she learned to pick the out-of-towners from the locals. Tourists tended to tip more and were satisfied with their lot. The locals were stingy, plus they wanted the girls to serve them tea like expensive club hostesses, crack black watermelon seeds between their teeth and deliver them on the tips of their tongues. That Haishan would not do—mixing private juices from her mouth with a stranger's. Nor would she allow any man to pull her hair until she found the right one. But after a while she could quickly size up any man's desire, whether they were young or old, handsome or plain. She'd lift up her blouse or skirt to whatever part they wanted to touch first. "Small Plums" they would call her, because of the aureoles of her breasts that were plum-colored and shapely. Watching men fondle her body, she learned to speak, laugh, and embrace them without feeling. Even the two men whose smiles resembled those of her brothers, Zhihai and Bohai, did not disturb her much.

Haishan cursed her fate. At the same time she learned to numb her feelings, creating an impermeable zone between her outer body and her inner self. Later, as she got to know even the two who had cruelly dunked her in the water, she understood how she had ended up working for "Auntie." One of the girls who had pushed her in was the daughter of a widow whose husband, a seaman, had left her to raise five children. The other girl's father had beat up his two daughters, for lack of sons. The mother could save them only by sending them to the city, where they were no better than slaves to their well-off relatives. They ran away, and ended up working in the same place.

Haishan did not blame her mother, her brothers, or herself. But she did blame her father. Yet, Haishan wired money home whenever she could. Now and then she would get a letter from her mother, or small items such as soap and religious trinkets. Haishan lied and told her mother the work was paying even better. Mother would thank her for the money, report on her brothers' progress in school, and always ask her to come home soon. Sometimes, in a fit of depression, Haishan would tell the other girls she would be better off as a Buddhist nun and asked them to help shave off her hair, to see how she would feel. "Only virgins can be nuns, silly creature!" they chimed at her. Haishan could imagine herself bald, freed of the desires of men. But none of the girls would shave it for Haishan, even as an experiment, fearing Auntie's retribution.

Auntie took most of their money, for food, housing, and the "guards" she supplied for their safety, she said. They could go to the movies, but only in threes and fours, to matinees. One man, who spoke the same country dialect as one of the girls, always went with them. They would tease and bribe him until he'd let them go off to coffee shops or shopping, unbeknownst to Auntie. The guards, who could have been the brothers of any of them, would warn them of bad customers, drunkards, and sadists. On her part, Haishan would always share with them whatever food her mother sent her.

"In five years," Auntie told Haishan, "your parents' loans will be paid up." Then, like other girls, she would be free to go after settling any debts she had incurred. By then, Haishan knew the loan was going to pay for her two brothers' schooling and that she had to endure it until she was nineteen. Endurance was painful, she found, whenever her menstrual period coincided with the full moon. Something in the tug of the moon and tide pulled her home to the sea, back to herself. She would feel her skin chafe at the slightest touch of another person, be it a man or a woman. Her brain began to spin out delicate invisible filaments that would cause her feet to trip on the stairs, her fingers to spill cups of tea or dishes of food, and her nostrils to become acutely bound to the smells of everyone around her. Under a full moon she could feel blood flowing from her being to hidden chambers of the brain, seeking inner space. As soon as her menses stopped, her sensitivity would subside until the next eclipse of moon and blood.

In this life, as she was quickly learning, a person was imprisoned by the greed of men, or by the greed of women. What was the difference? The knowledge of people fomented within her. At the end of her sixth month, Auntie had promised Haishan a bonus, depending on how many customers she had brought to the house, and how many of them returned. Haishan kept a small diary in which she would write down the number of men she had seen each day; at the end of the month she totaled them up. If the same man returned, she would add a star to the neat row of vertical pencil marks. At the end of six months, Haishan reminded Auntie about the bonus.

"A bonus, eh? You should pay me for all the work I've put into grooming you, turning a country peasant into a fine specimen of a woman," she retorted, spitting into her brass spittoon.

"But you have already deducted those expenses every month, Madame," Haishan responded.

"True, and I have put small change, a few coins, into buying incense and fruits for the Buddha altar in the hallways, my dear. It's to save your souls from going to hell."

"Buddha doesn't need more incense fumes on his face or rotting fruit for his belly, Auntie."

"Haishan, get on your knees and stop cursing!" Ignoring Auntie's comment, Haishan approached her, trembling, and thrust the diary into her hands.

"What in the world is this? I don't want to read your diary!"

"These pages and these marks are my sweat and blood. Each star is a man who returned twice, or three times. If you deny me my own sweat and blood, you will be reborn as a beast in the lowest basement of hell, Madame." Without thinking, Haishan shook the pockmarked woman's fleshy shoulders, over and over again, so violently that Auntie felt her perspiring back against the wall. She screamed for the guards, but once they came they just stood there, mouths agape.

"Boys, save me from this bitch," she cried. Slowly, they walked toward the two women, with smiles on their faces. "Auntie," one said, "we heard both of you from the hall. Even if you fire us or get rid of her, our boss, who owns all these houses, will hear about it. You'll find yourself strangled or dumped in the river where you'll sink like a stone for stealing what isn't yours."

Alarmed, Auntie began to cry, taking a different tack. "How can you all abuse me, your second mother? What's this world coming to? Can a mother stop loving her children? Haishan, here you are." From her bosom, she extracted a small purse and pulled out 150 dollars, double the usual amount. Haishan took it, gave fifty dollars to the two guards, and without saying a word strode off. After that incident, Auntie never bothered her again. Instead she tried to lure her into reporting on the activities of the others, promising more money. Haishan refused, because she knew that one day she would leave the house forever.

Though she believed that the Buddha would ultimately save her, Haishan realized that Ma's plastic Kwan-yin statuette was no protection against people like Auntie; the gold bracelet Ma had given her for emergencies Haishan hid in a tea box underneath large white envelopes, in case she needed to pawn it. In those envelopes Haishan kept every tress of hair she had shorn in the city. It was the only part of her body that remained her own, that hadn't been taken forcefully from her. Twice a year the girls would get a vacation, on their birthdays and the week after the New Year when the house closed. Most who had arrived here on hot creaking buses could now afford to go back to their country towns—loaded with presents for the family—on air-conditioned express coaches. Haishan was the exception. For three years, on the day of her birth, she would go with the guard she had befriended to the Kwan-yin temple at the eastern part of the city, nearest the grimy river, and place fruits and pink and white flour buns on the altar. Then, extracting a white envelope, she would toss it into the large outdoor brick oven, seeing it blaze along with the gold and red paper money that others had burnt for dead souls.

Haishan took secret pleasure in imagining each hair hidden within the envelope burning, coming to life, each strand glowing like a sharp needle, finding its way back to a body that had abused her, mentally or physically. She could almost hear the snap of each black filament as it took on a belated energy. Blood rushed to her head. She felt strangely liberated by her act. It was the most intimate expression of herself that she had ever shared with a man, and yet it was with the one whose job was to guard her.

Another year passed before she could muster enough courage to go home and face her family. She washed the makeup off her face, changed to a white blouse, skirt, and sandals, and put on her gold bracelet, which still fit her slender wrist. She had sent her packages ahead—a microwave oven, shoes, and a china set—so she would not have to carry any of them home. Haishan got off the coach one stop before reaching the road that led to her house, so that she could retrace the path by which she had left. Off the main road, the path was still unpaved, as she had remembered it. The sharp smell of the sea and seaweed decaying in the heat opened her nostrils and memories of gathering kelp with her mother at low tide, bundling it in baskets to make soap later. She took a deep breath and continued to walk.

The Buddhist temple with a two-story cement statue of Kwan-yin—a red strobe light stuck in the middle of her forehead—still dominated the shoreline. Through the night fog it would flash, a familiar beacon to sailors, trawlers, and local fishing boats. Farther on, ugly new housing where there had been only dunes before had gone up, seaside cottages built for city folk. Now, rusting machinery and sheets of corrugated tin were abandoned by the side of the road, along with overturned bathtubs and broken toilets, their plastic skins already crackled from the salt and sun.

Before Haishan reached the low-pitched one-story cinderblock house that was her home, she wiped her face of sweat and brushed the damp hair out of her eyes. As she opened the door, her mother's back was turned. She was fanning the skin of a glazed chicken hanging from an iron hook in the kitchen. "Ma!" Haishan cried. Mother and daughter stumbled toward each other and embraced. Father got up from the new television, bought with his daughter's earnings, limped over to the two women, then went back to his program after muttering his welcome. Mother began to pat every part of her daughter's body—arms, waist, breasts, and legs—as if to reassure herself that her child, now a woman, hadn't changed. Haishan felt suddenly naked, like a small, wounded swallow. "Ma, stop touching me before I faint."

The only thing that went wrong during her three-day visit was when her handbag happened to drop and spill its contents onto the floor. Lipsticks, rouge, powders, and small satin bags that held her jewelry scattered in all directions. Haishan, with a nervous laugh, quickly thrust them back inside her handbag.

"Ma—they are surprise gifts, and one is for you!" Later Haishan chose a carved mother-of-pearl pendant for her. Her father did not speak much with her, but had words about the county government, the prices of ducks or chickens, or about her brothers, who had just joined the maritime academy. He did not dare look his daughter in the eye. On the last day of her visit, she found herself with her mother alone in the back room. Over and over, the older woman stroked her daughter's hair.

"I will go to hell for sending you to this life. I don't ask mercy for myself. But I light incense to Buddha and to Kwan-yin every day, to protect you."

Haishan laughed and took out a photograph of herself with makeup, permed hair, and bright clothing. The cheekbones of her oblong face were accentuated with rouge; her thin lips were fuller and carmine-colored.

"It looks like another person, a beautiful fairy," her mother remarked softly.

"Or a beautiful ghost," Haishan said. "Maybe the Buddha, by giving me this life, is saving other young women for much better ones." But even her mother did not believe these words.

Haishan finally told her the truth. "Here you are," she said, "in this town by the sea, cooking, washing, working—making yourself useful to Father, a part of one man's destiny. Up north, I do the same thing. Only I'm part of many men's destinies."

"Do you want a husband and a family?"

"Of course," Haishan retorted. "Maybe in Australia, or Canada, or America, where I will blend in. Here, everyone will know me, being your only daughter."

Two years later, after settling her accounts with Auntie, getting a health check, and obtaining her freedom, Haishan did not go back home. The first thing she did was return to the Kwan-yin temple, this time alone. She threw the remaining white envelope of hair she had saved into the brick oven, watching the flames fan the filaments of her past. She bowed three times in front of the large polychrome statue, and thrust a few dollars into the wooden slot under the feet that was reserved for donations. After a week, Haishan landed a job in a hostess club, rented a small studio with another woman, and attempted to live again. Though she felt free, she also felt alone, like a prisoner who has walked out an iron gate into a changed world. But she had always depended on herself to survive, and picked up knowledge from everyone around her, old or young, male or female. Even at Auntie's, the women had sought Haishan out when they didn't feel well, usually during their periods. Haishan, after putting her fingers on a woman's wrist, could tell instinctively if her body energy was basically "hot" or "cold." She had, after one woman had been bruised by a sadistic customer, devised herbal poultices, steamed in boiling water, that helped her to heal quickly. Ironically, the establishment in which Haishan found herself—Jinhua, the Golden Flower Lounge—was only some ten blocks away from the brothel she had just left. The entrance gate, however, was not iron, but bamboo in the old Japanese style, flanked by two red-berried nandina bushes. In the bar, her lips were constantly wet, drinking the sugared water or tea in the bottles reserved for the hostesses, while plying the customers with expensive food and drink. She would merely indicate with a flick of her little finger what she wanted; the customer who bought the drinks had to pay the price of liquor, regardless of what was in the glass. Wealthy regular customers usually reserved their own decanters of their favorite liquor to go with the tiny plates of spiced meat, seafood, or salty vegetables that stimulated their thirst. A spiced chicken dish soaked and steamed in Korean ginseng root and rice wine was popular among those men who measured themselves in terms of their sexual prowess.

Haishan would tell them, jokingly, "Whatever you put in your mouth will come out of your ears and nose, from your front and back . . . even out of your pores!" But she was serious. In the club, with men whom she analyzed as cold, Haishan would order dishes that were more spicy, that contained ginger and green onions to stimulate their glands. Watermelon, by the slice or juiced over ice, could quell the fire of men who were hot and sweaty. Or she would order foods prepared with wine, or more salty or sour, according to what she felt they needed beyond lovemaking. Thus, for some men, Haishan was almost "a part of their limbs," as close as their feelings toward themselves, as they would drunkenly confess to her. She let them believe all that about herself, that she understood their needs better than other women. That was what the chunky young businessman, the scion of a transpacific industrialist family, had said to her, after their fifth meeting at the club. At first, she had seen him as similar to all the others: urbane, smooth-talking, with money to drop for food, drink, and flesh. He liked Haishan to lie on top of him, so that he could wind her hair around his white fingers. He liked to feel his own thighs entangled in the thicket of her hair, and her mouth nibbling on his soft skin. Then he told her about his life, that he was divorced, lonely, and unhappy with the type of spoiled daughters of rich families that his family had arranged for him to meet, no different from his first wife. "They all pretended they were virgins. I hate that," he told her.

She began to tell him about her life, about saving her locks of hair to burn on her birthday.

"I want someone as pure as you in heart," he said. He listened to her stories, a small smile playing at the edge of his lips. What made him different, she thought, was that he listened.

One evening, as Haishan was about to leave work in the pouring rain, his chauffeured black Audi screeched to a halt in front of the club. He got out, opened his umbrella, and pulled her inside the cab.

"We want to see the ocean," he told the chauffeur. They drove through the downpour. Intersections were already flooded, bobbing with the debris of the city—floating orange peels, glass bottles, paper, odd chunks of wood, palm fronds, dead rats. She held onto him, enjoying the protection of his arms and the warmth of the smooth leather seats, as the car treaded the dark waters. Street lights blinked on and off randomly, yellow and green eyes of a city amuck in the monsoon. As they reached the harbor he pulled a small satin pouch from his jacket. "Haishan, this is for you."

She opened the pouch. A pale green carving of Kwan-yin, jade encircled in diamonds, was attached to a gold chain. Moved, she let tears fall from her eyes. She let him place the chain around her neck. She would even let him tug her hair, but he would fall asleep before she did. Haishan would gaze at him for hours, at the placid baby-faced man who had a reputation as a tough, manipulative businessman. After six months, he proposed to her and asked her to quit the club. He'd pay for her tuition at business school where, he said, she could learn English and go to America on a tourist visa. His office would arrange everything. English was hard to learn but Haishan listened to television and language tapes every morning until she could pronounce and understand conversational sounds well enough to get by. She spoke with foreigners—Europeans or Americans—whenever she got the chance.

Haishan took him to see an herbalist until his eyes and skin glowed, and other women began to notice him. With his encouragement, she changed her style. Whenever they went out, Haishan would wear pale fitted linen dresses, pearls, and low-heeled pumps. She pulled her hair back into a French twist and wore hardly any makeup. The jewelry he gave her she would wear sometimes; most she stashed away, except for the pendant. Though they hadn't discussed it, Haishan thought that, as his future wife, she needn't show off her status.

Mother's prayers for her had finally been answered, she thought, as she packed her shoes and clothes into her valises. She put a dictionary, language tapes, and a small tape recorder into her satchel and waited for his office to send the car to take her to the airport.

Not until three months after she arrived in Los Angeles did he tell her that he was already married, with a wife and two young sons. He was an "astronaut." While he shuttled back and forth across the Pacific on business, his real wife stayed in a Los Angeles suburb overlooking the Pacific, taking care of their expensive real estate and educating their sons. Haishan was dumbfounded, then angry. "I want to be your wife, not your mistress."

"It cost me a lot to bring you here."

"Then send me home."

He laughed in her face. "This Alhambra townhouse, furniture, and allowance every month. All yours! Besides, I still have your passport."

She pleaded with him. "I can work in your office to earn my fare back."

"You, what do you know! And my wife would find out."

For an entire year, he would come over three times a week, before returning to his family in Palos Verdes Estates. By the time he rang the bell, she would have snacks and drinks prepared, and his favorite CD music. Besides preparing herself and food for him, she would occupy her days with reading, television, or walking in the shopping mall a few blocks away. But his casual deceit gnawed away at her, and she grew thinner.

"Has he changed, or did my own instincts betray me this time?" she would ask herself. Food didn't stay in her stomach; after he left she would vomit in the toilet. Her lustrous hair was becoming dull, and noticeably thinner, even with the back-teasing she tried. She learned about Americans and the world from television soap operas, news, advertising, and public service announcements.

One day she told him, "I have no friends and no life here. I'm a prisoner."

"Prisoner? Who's stopping you? Here, take a taxi and go shopping!" he said, taking two one-hundred-dollar bills from his wallet. "Or join the health club down the street, you're getting flabby back there," he said, patting her thigh. "But before you leave, take my pants off." He grabbed her roughly by the arm.

They made love without feeling. Haishan thought of Auntie's house, with the two guards, the locks, and of her life in this place, slowly unraveling. As a last resort, she asked him for money to take driving lessons.

"I take care of you well, even better than my own sons," he smiled. "Why are you so unhappy? You wouldn't fly away from me, now would you?" He turned away, pouring himself another cognac, and turned on the television. As Haishan washed the dishes, watching him resentfully from the kitchen, she remembered her own father's thin profile, the day she left home.

Haishan was getting ready to go shopping when the doorbell rang. It was not his day to come. "Who is it?" she asked. She peeped through the hole. A woman she had never seen before, well-groomed, with dark glasses, was standing there. Haishan opened the door slightly, without unfastening the chain.

"You must open this door," the woman said.

The astronaut's wife, Haishan thought. She smiled as best she could. "Do come in and have tea. We know of each other, don't we?" Without replying, the woman strode in and surveyed the apartment. She took off her dark glasses. Her eyes glittered.

Making a sweeping motion with her hand, and looking directly at Haishan, she said, "All this is mine. And I'm taking it back."

"I think you're mistaken. These are gifts. Some of the paintings I bought myself."

"With his money. Whatever assets he has belong to our family. When he married me he had nothing but his brains, his pudgy body, and a good name."

"But he's smart enough to make his own decisions. He has me." So he was adopted into her family business, Haishan thought. He has no power, only over his mistress. She began to smile.

"What are you laughing at?" the wife shouted. "What are you? No better than a white worm that eats good rice. A whore."

Haishan felt her throat tighten and told her to get out. "Who's the whore?" she said. "If it's me, that's fine. Then you—and he—are the pimps. So much for your noble family!"

The wife pulled two thin silver objects from her Gucci bag—a pair of knitting needles.

Haishan kept her distance. "Put those down now. I will call the manager."

She lunged for Haishan, drawing blood from her arm. Haishan kicked her in the shin. The wife was screaming now. "I will destroy your fox face!"

She lifted her arm but Haishan dodged her blow. With her free hand, the wife began scratching Haishan's face with her red nails and tearing at her hair. As she raved she dropped one needle. Haishan snatched it up. The wife backed away toward the door, still cursing, flailing her fists and flashing the single needle. Haishan locked the dead bolt and ran to her dressing room mirror. Her face was bleeding; blood was running down her nylons. As best she could, she used a wet towel to cleanse herself. The scratches looked shallow. She wondered if they would leave scars. Haishan could feel her scalp burning, where the wife had torn off an inch of skin and hair. She quickly tossed some clothing, the jewelry box, and cash she had hidden under the bed into an airline duffel.

Haishan sat on the edge of the bed and closed her eyes, exhaling and listening to the voice that she had relied upon since birth. What should I do now? she thought. She dialed 911, as the Chinese TV program had said to do. "Hello, please. I need a battery women's shelter. Please."

"Ma'am? You mean a shelter for battered women?"

"Yes."

She had seen such an announcement on television a few days ago, the first time she had heard of such a thing. A recording gave her the choice of two numbers and Haishan called one of them.

"The Monterey Shelter, may I help you?" The voice on the other end of the line was steady and clear.

"I've just been attacked by . . . my husband," she said, in her best English. "No need for police. But I need a safe place to stay." The voice gave her an unlisted address and she wrote it down for the cabbie.

When Haishan entered the nondescript building the Black receptionist rose from her desk. "Miss, you're bleeding. We've got to get you to a doctor. Just have a seat."

"No, no doctor," she said. But within the hour, their staff doctor had seen and bandaged her, given her antibiotics and painkillers. Haishan never went back to her apartment again or tried to call her lover. In the back of her mind, she wondered if he'd purposely let his wife find out where she was staying, so he could get rid of both of them. She'd kill out of pent-up hate, then she'd be arrested and put behind bars for murder. Before they let Haishan leave the shelter she had to speak with their psychologist, and go for counseling. She lied and told them she had enough money and a place to stay. After four days of observation, they let her go.

Haishan had just enough cash to rent a motel room with a kitchenette. After her money ran out, she began to pawn her jewelry, a ring or a pin at a time, for less than they were worth, at the Chinese gold store in the mall. It was pure luck that she ran into a woman there trying to buy a pair of gold earrings. The olive-skinned woman turned to Haishan.

"Do you speak English?"

"Not that good, but I understand you."

"Where did you buy those beautiful emerald and gold earrings?"

"From my boyfriend," Haishan said, "but maybe I need to sell them soon."

"They're exactly what I've been looking for," the woman said.

"Well, maybe later I'll sell them to you, then." The woman left Haishan her phone number.

A month later Haishan called the woman, Mimosa. Over coffee, they discovered they had more in common than they had ever imagined. Haishan ended up selling Mimosa the earrings, and she, unlike the Chinese jeweler, offered to pay her even more than they were worth. Haishan protested, but Mimosa wouldn't have it any other way, and thrust six fifty-dollar bills into her hands. Mimosa suggested that Haishan work with her until she could get her life back together. The next day Mimosa picked her up at the motel and drove her to Avalon Heights.

Like men, women don't rush to tell the truth when they open their mouths. Haishan became "Coral," easier for men to remember. Most of the men wanted a fifty-dollar "regular"—her breasts and her lips because they were afraid of getting AIDS. When they were about to come Haishan would pull it out of her mouth and use her hands on them or put it between her breasts. None of the girls really knew where the men were originally from. Because they would say "Thai" when they were actually Filipino, or "Chinese" when they were really Japanese. If they wanted a "special"—with penetration—it cost them a hundred dollars and up. Half of everything went to the house, and then ten percent of what was left was deducted for their room, board, and "protection"—the Norplant implants and the security devices and hidden monitors in the rooms.

From the window the girls could spot the men's cars, everything from beat-up Mustangs to top-line imports. One day Haishan was looking out the window when she saw his black Benz with the gold license plates.

"I don't want him to know I'm here. But I want to see him anyway," she told Mimosa. Haishan could hear his voice downstairs, arranging what he wanted with April. Haishan stayed in the room next door with the see-through one-way mirror. April went in with him for a "special."

He took off his clothes. Haishan noticed he had gained back his paunch and was puffy around the eyes. Maybe he was drinking too much. She felt sorry for him. She wanted to see what he wanted from April. He hadn't changed; he had liked Haishan to sit on his belly, astride him, as he spread and entered her. April put a condom on him first, before she rode him. As he came sweat poured from his brow and he clutched at the bed. He still wore his wedding ring and gold link bracelet.

After Haishan saw his Mercedes back out of the lot, April came into her room. "So, what about him, Coral?"

"That was the man I used to call my lover. But he still isn't happy with his wife."

"Do you mind if I go with him?"

"No," Haishan said. "This is only temporary for me, I'll be gone in a month. He'll come back again if he likes you. Who knows what will happen?" Haishan felt her life was becoming entangled again, her body and soul twisted by filaments of desire and destruction. America was a country of dreams and dust.

The house had four bedrooms on the top floor. A windowless garage had been converted and divided into two cubicles for the "regular" jobs. The house had ten women who rotated days, evenings, and weekends. Three of the bedrooms were used just for clients. The other room was for sleeping. Some of the other "girls" stayed at another house that the owners had rented close by, but came here to work. Haishan usually shared a large queen-sized bed with one or the other. She didn't mind sharing the bed. It reminded her of childhood, when she and her mother slept together on a wooden pallet.

Nobody liked or trusted the bosses. The women were more afraid of the wife than of the husband. She was plain, with a large birthmark on her left cheek. She always wore matching red or blue silk ensembles and swung a black sharkskin bag over her matching shoes. They'd come every morning to collect the night's profits. Once a week she would walk up to the second floor to check the rooms. "Clean up this pig pen," she'd say, "Our customers are high-class." She'd pick up a can of Lysol from the bathroom and begin spraying it indiscriminately over the walls, chairs, and tables, then simply toss the empty can on top of a bed. The women had to clean up after her. Sometimes she even opened their purses, to check for drugs and pills, she said. She'd harangue whoever was nearest to her, while her husband would just bob his head up and down, like a useless, broken toy. "You beauties are helping to save the Asian family. Men can live peacefully at home because here they can take care of their needs," she said one time. The women glared back at her; Haishan just walked away.

The relentless routine drained Haishan. Her life seemed to be burning it-self at both ends and eating her up inside. Six months at Avalon Heights were like six years. Sunlight began to hurt her eyes. She took to wearing dark glasses, sometimes even inside the house. The cool-energy foods that she pre-scribed for men didn't work on her. Haishan even put herself on a diet of rice porridge, bananas, and melon for two weeks, lit incense to Kwan-yin—to no avail.

Her thick auburn hair was becoming brittle. When she showered, dark clumps began to fall out and clog the drain. She panicked. Mimosa insisted that her friend go to her Chinese herbalist, that she would pay for it. She even drove Haishan to his office in Temple City. He prescribed a natural kelp shampoo treatment that would restore the condition of her scalp and hair, similar to the one she had used as a child. After checking her tongue, he also prescribed some daily herbs—tiny black pills that she had to take three times a day. Eating one teaspoon of black sesame seed oil and honey daily would speed her recovery, he said, and told her to come back in a month.

Haishan was willing to try anything. But she couldn't tell him that if her hair wasn't strong enough to tug anymore, she wouldn't be able to rest. Now the moon was full and her blood was flowing freely. Unable to avert her eyes, she saw everyone whom she had known as if in a waking dream. For an instant, she even saw herself as a nun. She would shave her head as she had threatened to do long ago and toss the filaments into the burning temple oven.

Now she just wanted to close her eyes. Mimosa was the only one who could pull her through the night. But it was not only Mimosa who wove dark strands of Haishan's hair around her fingers.

It is I who caress her also. Her lips part. She is preparing to speak to me. Before she can utter a word, the sound of a siren takes her breath away. I glance in my rear view mirror at the black-and-white highway patrol car. A burly officer walks around toward my window. I roll it down.

"Driver's license, sir? Anything the matter with that car?" I pull out my billfold. The officer stares at my photograph. "Mr. Lampson Ko. You look like a different person in this photo."

"Officer, I've been in America a long time! I had short hair then." He nods.

"To the matter at hand. We got a report that a car was stranded on the shoulder, that a man was slumped over the wheel."

"No, Officer, I felt dizzy and had to rest a few minutes."

"Have you taken any alcoholic substances or drugs within the past twelve hours, sir?"

"No, in fact I just dropped my daughter off at school."

"According to my watch, it's two o'clock in the afternoon, sir. Next time, pull off the freeway. Otherwise, you'll get a citation."

I start up my car, pulling off the shoulder into the traffic lane. If I get off at the next exit, double around and take the side streets, I should end up at the place I left this morning. My only daughter should be there, waiting for me.

Sons

I

THERE IS NOTHING good about being a son. When you have to admit that you have a father, allowing people to think that you are a father and a son, as if any relation existed between those two terms.

And yet I usually find myself talking about my father, telling my friends and any strangers what he does and where he has been, trying to describe with exactness his activities, trying to grasp his life through what little information I have of him. Doing this, I feel like a small child pressing a string of hard beads to my chest, a rosary of sorts, chanting the same phrases and images a thousand times in order to derive an order, a strength out of them. But the polished beads do not yield a thing; it is a repetition of uselessness. Nothing comes out of them.

I know my father like this. I see him working in his white apron, flashing and sharpening his cleaver on the back rim of a white Chinese pottery bowl. Zhap. Zhap. Zhap. The gray steel cleaver on the sturdy bowl. After arranging different vegetables on the table, I see him grasping the handle of the cleaver firmly, then nudging the bitter melon under the blade, at a slant, so that the pieces come out in even green crescents, like perfect waves of a green sea, at the same angle; and then the carrots, in thin narrow ovals, cut and dropped to boil lightly in a pot awhile; and then the green bell peppers, the seeds and pale green mulch scooped out with a spoon, the flesh cut in quarters and sliced. Then all the vegetables arranged in neat piles on a large plate ready to be cooked, the hardest, fibrous vegetables to be cooked first in a dash of oil, and then the more delicately flavored ones, with purple and orange-tipped spears of heat, sizzling them in the heart, while all along the rice is boiling on another part of the stove, each white grain destined to be firm and separate from the others.

My father's hands were always busy preparing food and papers, writing and touching inanimate and ultimately useful things such as pencils and knives. Yet I do not know the real strength of his arm. I have never been lifted on his hand, brought up to see any life outside of my own. As a child I dreamed of my father.

Was this true, could I see my father dancing, away from the stiff and solemn pace of himself as father, provider, and businessman? Was it true, my father strong and bare, bravely dancing, using the wind as rope to catch all the worlds, flinging his arms and legs?

No, that is not him at all; his motions are never quick or free, but formal, stern, and placid for every emotion except rage.

At the door to my room, my father is glittering in anger, a knife poised in his hand. His face is pulsing pink, the once pale cauliflower flesh tinged with color and rage, and he is on one side of the room, about to throw the knife into me. I am just standing there, cringing; how can I defend myself against this violence, this dark pearl which I have struck?

So this is what is beneath my father's calmness, his layered dispassion, his view of my foolishness and ignorance and youth. It is this seething fury, not really his, but an inherited bitterness from some vague source, from a life not his, a frustration that has finally found its point in a knife, a silver gleaming tooth that will draw blood from my chest.

My father, I scream inside. But outside, I try to remain calm and rather disinterested in any personal aspect of the situation, as if his piercing my body is an event apart from the two of us, beyond any relation of father and son, as if any death or any son's death can happen like this, if the son does not observe and obey the rules—the correct way of doing things.

During these moments, I appear calm, waiting for the blade to fall, and I despise him even more when his arm suddenly drops down and the knife falls to the floor; he is not strong enough to go through with his convictions—he cannot even kill his own son.

I had heard the story about how Abraham would have killed his own son, Isaac, for God, because of his trust in God, but my father is not as good as that, because he does not believe in God in the first place. He will just kill me for no god at all.

When I am older, I begin to strike back against my father with a vengeance, with a force akin to hatred or love, with the urge to destroy all images of men or seek all images of them wherever and whenever possible.

Because I am a son myself I must realize my peculiar tendency to be manly, and so I search. I go out into the streets to look for this peculiar stuff of which men are made. Now I am in the middle of it, sunk into it. With love to the Father and to the Son.

II

Mantos. The loneliest man in the world. Also my friend. Stain of beer and cigarettes. Warm arm. I'm sweating. He eats, sleeps, sees. With arms, with all-seeing eyes. With a clarity that numbs. A blinding light. Blind clarity.

Mantos woke up from his mother's womb. He knew what he wanted from the start. He was an antibody to himself. Red corpuscle against the white world. Sun in the dark sea. A pulse in silence. That was the thing, he was not born to bliss. Ever. Before. In his past life. No paradise, no hope or hint of one. He was bound from the start always to travel, to see whatever had to be seen. But he was no genius though he saw how things and people worked in absolute fidelity, every part of the engine, of the features.

But he would not go as far as to say it was a consciousness of being. No. It was supremely frustrating. He wasn't ashamed of his flexibility, but then he wasn't any Christ either. He was just Mantos, all he could be to his friends and forever more. He was a Lord's Prayer. Amen was the beginning and the end. By the grace of God. By no one's grace, no one's vision but his own.

Sometimes he felt indelicate. No bliss for him. Not the happy innocence of ignorance. But not worn yet. Only twenty-six. Brought up on long, lean limbs. Limber. Stalking. Rigorous. Disciplined. Which he was of course. Mantos. Like Athena, Goddess of Wisdom, sprung full-grown from Zeus's head, wholly formed. Whole but not complete. The fate of never finding a person to talk with, to share his irreducible sight.

His desire was in the mind, to make the full use of it. In physical action he forgot, to some degree, the frustration. But not for very long. Afterward it was all there again, flooding back, filling his pores and his blood and the waters welling within him. There was no space for bliss.

I knew Mantos before. A few times, I have run across him. Beer and cigarette smoke will stay in my mind with him. Through night states. A gulf of mind. Mine is not so open yet, so strong. To have a strong mind. Strength is beautiful, is functional, is new. To keep it smooth, and from breaking.

To run my fingers over this clear, subtle mind, like a hard pebble found upon the beach, formed by heat and pressure, the most intense violence and fury. For the stone suddenly to explode and surround you in a forest, and I am lost. A tender violence. Violent tenderness. A mixture of his self impression, with regard, care. Violence to a point—tempered by love.

When I think about Mantos I cry, laugh. I am angry, frustrated, mistrustful, unsure. In transit. As I sit in the back of a streetcar at night going through San Francisco streets in the end seat that hugs both aisles, Mantos is gone. The streetcar is vintage 1948 and the lights in the ceiling are flat half-globed yellowish white disks in two rows on either side of the aisle. I smell someone's cigarette smoke, but not the sweet acrid scent of the night after, the odor of an ashtray full of soft gray stumps . . . this smoke is new. The streetcar is in front of me and I am behind all the moon-disked lights, somewhere back in the darkness.

Eight o'clock. Passing Duboce Park, its massive trees—clumped inert figures of silence. The streetcar goes on, rattling through the tunnel. Square niches on the walls with bare bulbs are like the entrances to catacombs or tombs. The night is like a heavy bottle pressed upon my lips.

Silence is round, like a sphere, a whole separate world curved between hands. I ask, what is chosen by silence? What is shaped within that is growing, brooding, going to be born out of it? May the word that is shining in the center of silence be yours. Cut to the core of silence, like the flash of knives or one green plant in a houseful of rooms. There is that sleeping flesh of yours, shaping a cool sheath around warm dreams. Silence has made a full circle around your life and mine. So I ask you again, what do you mean by that silence, behind your teeth, and all the past around your body like a thousand layers of cloth? My quiet friend, when word and skin and time can finally meet and sing, I will ask everyone I know to rejoice with me, with you.

Somewhere, there must be a tree, new growth pushing upon the bark, upwards now, forcing exultation. I must train my body to live a thousand miles away from you, to drink dry water, to inhabit a dry landscape like a desert rat, to harmonize into fate like a shifting dune. I ignite easily now; my face and arms and skin have become flaccid and layered with dust and I am growing old. Mantos, I wonder whether you are still alive.

This is my dry town, of dusty buildings that stem from dry rot, slaked on dust, with a dry ocean right beside lapping dunes through my arms, sweating dry sweat; even my blood is dry, a needle in my arm will draw a hole that will finally empty me, dry powder, like an old woman's rouge, the stuffing of a pillow or a doll, dry powder will come tumbling out in clouds and my eyes will fall out because there is no more dust to keep them. This is my dry town, a heedless neutral color between tan and gray, flickering below a gray sun. There is no landscape of green leaves, it is a brown abstract of points; even the animals, the rats and cockroaches that remain, have lost their oily sheen on fur and shell; we crawl dry.

Hot light that has blinded my eyes, that has gathered the darkness into black flames; face that I have seen a few nights; hands that I have fought and taken, and brown hair . . . Acrobat in the middle of the air, encircled by lights and canvas sky, floating on the clouds of a million human breaths, with sad eyes narrows into one single tear, as a drop falls imperceptibly through the net to the damp sawdust of the ring and the blind crowd storms the gates shouting cheated and money back; while I among them sit still, awed, feeling that one tear enter my mouth, drawn down my throat, heavy as mercury; and as it slips through my flesh it burns my belly, and my skeleton must be coated with poison so I do not stand but sit, alone on the bench, smiling, letting the mercury warm my own heat, nourishing the fumes of your tear, letting it course and burn and destroy my cells and though I cannot see my own face I believe that I am radiant, as I sit on the wood being devoured, benign as I am burnt; my bones are stiffening, I cannot move my wrist, my calcium has turned to hard silver, my flesh to nephrite, my blood to pure water, and my clothes are now gone to shreds.

If handwriting could have conveyed the touch of your body, the tenderness and breadth of your mind, I would have stuffed your pockets with pencils before you went.

So this note is written, from a son to his father, in the year nineteen hundred and sixty-nine.

2 Samsara

A Yin and Her Man

"WHERE DID YOU put that Buddha!" she quipped on my answering machine. She was three thousand miles away. That Sunday afternoon she had gone to the Isamu Noguchi Sculpture Garden, in Long Island City, with her new boyfriend. I told her that when I was there, a few weeks before, I had hidden a small bronze Buddha in the grass near the plaque carved with Noguchi's name.

After I returned to L.A., they went to visit that granite sculpture garden and searched for the inch-tall figurine I had left behind. The garden, I was told, was closed to the public from October through April. Whether it rained or snowed I would not be able to see the sculptures. So the bronze would be my surrogate there, taking my place.

But the two could not find it. The caretaker had discovered it, weeds had grown over it, or it had been swallowed by the ground below.

I remember the last meal she and I had together at the Chiu Chau Cafe off Mulberry Street. "Fortune Flavors." After each bite of meat or vegetable doused in shrimp paste, curry sauce, or garlic, she wiped her mouth, daintily, with the corner of the paper napkin. She devoured the fish head quickly. Ditto the slivers of green onion. There were no bones around her bowl or plate; mine was littered with them.

We went to her room, a fourth-floor studio just north of her haunt, the Strand Bookstore. The room was starker than the week before, except for her books, pens, albums of scrawled and blank paper, and a clear jelly glass with weedy-looking purple flowers on her desk. Her gamine smile and the way she lifted her feet out of her shoes and set those perfectly flat arches onto the rug provoked me.

Maybe it was her wide-set eyes that could take in a whole garden, stones, and me, at a glance. She let me unbutton the back of her summer dress and it slid quickly to the floor. Then she pulled down my zipper, fondling what was already straining under my black jockey shorts. She was not like a Noguchi sculpture at all, as dense as granite mass. She was lighter, a pale limestone that almost left powder on my flesh. Though she shared her body with me willingly, she always kept something hidden for herself.

When she lifted her elbow, the bend of her arm showed the untanned skin, pale until my tongue reached the pink aureole of her right breast.

"Tell me," I said, "how your new boyfriend enters this room."

"On raggedy wall-to-wall carpet. This is our last night," she said. "Why spoil things?"

"No, tell me, when I am gone, how you would make love to him."

"Why?"

"Because when I'm not around, I'd like to imagine you making love to his body. That's the most I can have now, isn't it?" I lay my head between the smooth lines of her back and held her closer to me, my teeth in her hair, which seemed to have grown an inch since last week.

"Okay," she said, flatly. "If it turns you on to hear about another Asian man fucking me, I'll tell you."

"I don't want to force you."

"Then I'll tell everything. But don't use it against me. Promise?"

"Promise."

"Well, he walks in the door, dragging his feet. Maybe he was used to doing this as a child. I look at his shoes, usually scuffed, and at his hands, his clean nails as he takes his shoes off. He doesn't usually wear socks."

I pressed her breasts against the palms of my hands, and she moved closer, almost whispering what she had to tell me about him.

"His lips are full, and beautiful for a man's. But he doesn't say much, you know."

"Not a word?" With my fingers, I silently traced the letters for W-O-R-D around her breasts, with the "O" encircling a nipple.

"He brings flowers instead. Those purple ones, there, on the table, he brought me."

"I brought them."

"No, yours died already. He brought those after you left, almost the same color, but deeper."

"I see."

"He likes to walk around in his white jockey shorts that he irons himself, I believe."

"Strange fellow. What do you think of my shorts?" I asked, tugging at my black waistband.

"I bet you paid retail for those."

"I don't do discounts. I don't even iron for that matter. Ironing's for immigrants."

"But ironing's old country, you know. He has nice short legs. Thick, muscular, with the calves and thighs all out of proportion to his long torso, chest, and arms."

"A native. Go on."

"And a nice behind, the kind I can run my hands over. Almost stick my favorite cards—an ace, a king of spades, and a queen of hearts between his crack."

I began to massage the small of her back. "So you and he play cards?"

"Yes, naked, and with a full deck. But never for money, only for love."

"And what about his . . . ?"

"There's always a bulge in his shorts when he sees me. In fact, men go crazy over that and his behind too. When we're in the Village or Soho I see them looking."

"Is he straight or bi?"

"I don't know. I don't care. We use condoms, Mister Interrogator."

"Does he take off his shirt when he makes love to you?"

"Eventually, after tea, or after I've read my latest poem to him."

"Read me a poem."

"Oh, I've memorized my last lines for you. They go like this:

> "'After the fruit of passion dries
> And the red worm shrivels around the pit
> Ploppy floppy it falls to the ground
> Floppy ploppy all good things must end . . .'"

My penis went limp for a second, because as she spoke she was smiling right through me. But I caught myself before she caught my chagrin.

"This person, do I know him?"

"You may have met him. Remember when we were marching in the rally downtown to City Hall? Protesting the visit of the Japanese Emperor?"

"Oh, you mean the rape of Nanjing, the Korean comfort women . . ."

"He had written 'Down with Japanese Militarism' on his cardboard sign, and he was waving his hands. It was drizzling and the words were running like blood. Like during my bloody period. Don't you remember—you hated my periods? But I guess his face is ordinary in the daylight. Unlike yours."

"And at night?"

"It absorbs darkness, takes on caves and angles. Each feature becomes fuller and darker. His lips, lashes, the blackness of his hair."

"He's a chameleon?"

"No, he's just more Asian than you."

I went down between her legs and worked my tongue in her until I could taste her juices budding. Our thrashing wrinkled the new pages of sonnets she had written, smearing them with my sweat and her scent. She was pulling my hair, and I thought I felt the strands snap in her hands.

"Easy, easy."

"Does my description of him turn you on?"

I pulled my tongue out, tasting her tartness on my tongue between my teeth. "I'm hard. But for you, not for him."

"I don't believe you. I get turned on by a pretty woman. Don't you get turned on by a good-looking man?"

"So, what does he do for you that I don't?"

"He likes to dip a small white towel in warm water, and bathe me first. Kind of like a dry-wet bath."

"You can't clean yourself off?"

"He says my skin is dry, and since I come from the tropics, a bit more humidity in my skin makes it glow."

"He is strange."

"Sensitive. Politically conscious. Knows how to make money and eat well. Then I pull down his shorts."

"What about you?"

"I usually wear one of his shirts and I'm already naked underneath. I slip right out."

"So, who's on top?"

"Usually me. I'm so pale against his tan. Against his muscles."

"I know I'm better."

"Who says? He can wrap his legs around me and I can feel his thighs and butt and toes against mine. Not all bony kneecaps."

I began to straddle her but something made me pull it out.

"Oh, dear! Full moon over the Hudson. And we have until morning, you know."

Maybe she had been faking it all along. How does she really like it, I asked myself. But I needed to hear it from her own mouth. "Does he enter you from the front door or through the back?"

"Does the kitchen have a back door? Silly. I do everything with him that I do with you."

"Why is this our last night then?"

"Because your mind is not with me when I am with you. Because you're a goddamned Shanghainese aesthete who puts more energy into lifting weights than lifting my spirits." She laughed.

I flexed my biceps and shrugged. "Feel this."

With her fingers she pinched her own left nipple. "Here, feel this."

As quickly as I touched her breast, she got up from the bed and walked away from me to the uncovered window. Her shoulders and back draped and wound about with a white bed sheet, she looked like a plaster studio model for the Tiananmen statue of democracy that I had seen in some magazine.

"So, you think you Wonder Bread yellow boys with your Reeboks, long legs, and Acuras are better?" she asked.

"So, that's how you like them? Is it give me your tired and huddled masses yearning to be free . . . with me?"

She turned, with a delicate ironic smile. "Them? I'm one of them, remember. Brandeis gave me a B.A. in East Asian history. But I'm still that country girl who uses wooden combs to comb out her hair. I remember the insects and lice that used to get into my hair when I was a child in Hainan."

"He likes that—affectation—I suppose?"

She stretched out a free hand to the seat of the chair and picked up a carved wooden comb.

"Ninety-eight cents, Canal Street. It's sandalwood, from the Pearl River China Emporium. Smell it."

"Well . . ."

Suddenly she started on my head, combing and parting it in the opposite way than I usually did. As she untangled the gel-stiffened strands and ran her fingers over my ears I felt flushed and strangely more excited. I could smell the sandalwood mingled with the scent of her body.

Next, she pressed her fingertips against my eyes, closing the lids. As my vision grew darker, I began to visualize what I had never seen before. Yet I wanted to know whether he loved her as I had. "Does he talk to you, tell you that he loves you?"

"He doesn't talk much really. He uses his lips and his tongue and his legs and butt. He uses up his body, all the rounds and squares of it on me. Sometimes I'm bathed in his saliva, from my toes to my brow."

I could almost see the two of them, their arching, twisted saliva-slimed bodies illuminated by streetlight through the window. I suddenly wanted this night with her to end soon. For good. "I think I need a drink, babe."

"Help yourself to the diet Coke in the fridge."

I got up from the bed, then changed my mind. "Later. I want to know, do you really like spit?"

"I really like spit. And he really drinks lots of tea, okay? I'll lay it out for you. He's the manager of a Sichuan restaurant on the Upper West Side. Shit-wan chop goey, he tells me. For tourists. He only eats Cantonese food."

"A diehard nationalist. You've met your match."

"Match? He's just a stocky Cantonese who drags his feet and presses his jockey shorts at midnight when he gets off work. An ordinary yang man who has made peace with his yin—and with me. So I tease him. I love him."

"What's his name?"

"I call him Mat."

"A doormat?"

"It's short for Maitreya. Buddha of the future. If he doesn't stop eating Chinese pastries and beer, he'll get fat. But his mind is as pure as geyser water. My Mister B."

"I'm the Buddhist, remember?"

"You do the rituals and chant the mantras—so you got the incense and knickknacks. But I'm not convinced."

"Exactly. Because you don't believe in anything."

"No Nirvana for me. But I do believe in hell. In our slow, inevitable descent." She smiled and continued. "No passion, no compassion."

I put my fingers over her lips to stop her driveling. Instantly, she set her feral teeth on my forefinger, drawing blood. Her eyes, crinkling to slender black arrows, mocked me as I pulled away stumbling to the bathroom.

She followed me and we made love on the floor without another word between us. The tile floor, hard as stone, grew slick with sweat and saliva. Both of us, separately and for different reasons, were imagining *his* brown arms and legs wrapped inextricably around our own.

Hemispheres

AT THE POINT in my life that I had decided to remain alone, I got three offers to become a father. The offers came within a week, via telephone, by e-mail, and through a chance meeting. This sounds hokey, like a bad script. But believe me, everything that's happened so far is true. Maybe it's because I'm in the film business. Not Hollywood—East Hollywood. I'm an independent. You could say I'm my own man.

I was clearing the glass coffee table of pad thai noodles and large plastic cups of Thai iced coffee.

"Thanks so much for dinner," he said.

"And to you, for bringing your handsome self to me," I replied.

"You're in great shape for your age, too."

He said he would have to leave, to go dancing with a friend. Since I didn't care to dance, I let him go. He hitched up his trousers over his slender hips and tied a rubber band over loose hair that reached past his shoulders. The photos he had showed me earlier fell out of his shirt pocket. He gathered them up.

"One for a souvenir," I insisted.

"Choose the one you like."

I shuffled through the dozen or so photographs: here he was at an AIDS benefit show in an Indonesian-style sarong; a series of fantasy drag get-ups showed him in shimmering blue silk stitched with white feathers. I chose the photo where he was most androgynous, his hair pulled back behind the ears. I wanted to remember him, as it was unlikely that we'd ever have sex again, though our paths would probably cross. That's how it was nowadays: I'd run into younger men at film screenings and charity benefits, in supermarket aisles, even at AM/PM gas station hamburger stands. A forty-seven-year-old man who'd been hitched up with a lover for fifteen years, then broke up, didn't have many options. There was a difference between thirty-two and forty-seven. At least my car impressed. I had traded in my late-model Celica for a lease on a teal green, two-door Lexus, loaded with options. Once inside the car, I'd surround my new friend with stereo and a natural sandalwood spray that I'd found at Pic 'n' Save. In the daytime, you could see the tops of palm trees through the sunroof; at night, the moon and the stars. I'd take him to my small condo at the top of Cedarhurst Avenue and continue the mood with the same music and fragrance.

The morning Francine called I was already on my stationary bike. I pedaled as we talked.

"Francine, *deem ma*? How're the Bloomington gals?"

"Bryan, the gallery is doing fine. Lynn got tenure after she got the book contract. And I have a great proposal for you."

"Let me guess. You want me to co-sign your mortgage for that bastardized Queen Anne Victorian you found—or you want my Maltese to cohabit with yours!"

"Exactly! How did you know?"

"Whoa, Fran. Which one?"

"Daddy."

"Then why don't you bring your dog out here to visit L.A.?"

"It's not about doggies, Bry. It's about you."

"Oh?"

"Well, you know, Lynn and I have been together for five years now. She says hi. Now I want an all-Chinese child—smart, with good genes. And I need a father."

"Hell, there's plenty of good-looking men out there. Go to Chicago. They've got hardworking young Vietnamese, Taiwanese, Filipinos. Better sperm count."

"I'm interested in genes. Creativity. Sensibility."

"Genes jump generations, dear. My bad ones may be ready to spring out on you!"

"I'm serious, Bryan. I want a man who isn't too fem, but gay. No Mandarins from the North. A rice-eater. A Southern Chinese. Someone I can trust."

"Well, you know I'm Chiu Chau. A bit north of Canton City proper. Famous for bitter tea!"

"No matter, same province."

"But since Lynn is Jewish, wouldn't it be nicer to have an Amerasian child? Maybe adopt one?"

"It's my body and my decision. My only tie to Hong Kong now—with the Communists taking over and all—might be you. I'm willing to carry the child."

"Have you considered the requirements—we'd have to make passionate love, you know?"

"As long as I'm on top. No missionary positions, please."

"Well, Fran. Give me a few days."

"You must have questions. Like do I want you to visit or support the child."

"Certainly, I'd take a paternal interest."

"I've checked a few lawyers. Everything's legit. Joint visits. Support or no support. But I can handle raising a child. I've saved up for educating one."

"I've often wondered about my son. He would be around twenty-three now. When I left New York I left him with his mother. She never wanted to see or hear from me again. I've completely lost track of them."

"Then, here's another chance. With me. We'd understand each other so well, Bryan."

"Fran. I've got to get outta here and run to LAFI for a few hours. We're screening the independent film documentaries for the grants. Final selections. Let me call you back Sunday, okay?"

"A big hug to you."

As I drove to the Los Angeles Film Institute a few miles down in East Hollywood, where Western Avenue meets Los Feliz Boulevard, I recalled my son's mother. "Vinny" was what she called herself in those days. She thought it befitted a Hong Kong gal transplanted to Greenwich Village. As fast as possible, she wanted to get rid of her Catholic school upbringing, including the name the St. Veronica's sisters had given her, "Ruth." Slightly bowlegged, she had a rakish smile, full lips, pale skin, and dark eyes that expressed all she felt. A year at the London Academy of Dramatic Art when she was eighteen gave her a British accent that had to be unlearned in America. A few good roles at the Pan-American Theater garnered her a nomination for an off-Broadway Obie in 1973. She got pregnant with our child, even with birth control pills. At that time I was making small independent films. I had discovered I was bisexual and made the mistake of telling her. She told me to leave. It was her seventh month but she would ask her mother to come to New York to take care of the child.

I continued to send 250 dollars a month to her, though we'd never tied the knot. When I heard she'd married well, to a Chinese businessman from Trinidad, I stopped. Through night classes at NYU I wangled an M.F.A. and took enough courses to get an M.A. in critical studies. Teaching part time, I began writing articles and ironically got into the administrative end of things rather than the creative. It paid the rent and kept me in touch with film-makers, writers, and actors, people I'd always felt akin to.

I pulled into my reserved LAFI parking spot and dashed into the building to the second-floor screening room. The final selection panel was milling about the anteroom, eating bagels and slurping down coffee. We had four hours to break down the selections into final rankings. My assistant had pulled to-gether the veteran multi-cult folks this year: the Raza Art for Action Con-sortium; the curator of contemporary film series at the Museum of Modern Art; the Feminist Film Forum folks; and the African Institute for Diasporic Studies. Without ceremony, we began shuffling through the final applica-tions as the assistant turned on the monitor. I reminded folks that since this was the finals, we would see at least ten minutes of each film, regardless of whether people liked it or not.

I don't know how the first film made it this far. It was a badly shot docu-mentary on twentieth-century anarchist movements utilizing stills from the Library of Congress and the St. Petersburg Institute of Social Sciences. The subject was great but the editing poor. The second film was a local produc-tion on Latino and Asian hotel workers in Los Angeles. It traced their strug-gle to unionize at the New Otani Hotel in Little Tokyo, which was owned by the Kajima corporation. According to the film, Kajima was behind the forced slave labor of Chinese prisoners in Manchuria during World War Two. It, too, was shot in black and white, with good profiles of some of the workers and organizers. The filmmakers needed the money to go to Japan to film the trials of three Chinese who were filing a class action suit against Kajima. I'd have to see the rest before I could rank this one. We went through the dozen films left—one that impressed all of us was on pediatric AIDS, a collabora-tion between a woman doctor and a filmmaker that didn't portray the chil-dren as innocent and the rest of us as "guilty." They needed money to interview more people. Documentary was one of the few avenues left for raising social awareness. Even black and white was coming back into vogue; younger filmmakers wanted that gritty photojournalism look of the thirties and forties. They'd rediscovered Leo Hurwitz, Gordon Parks, and Walker Evans. Seeing all that talent and commitment elated me, though sometimes I wondered if I'd left my own social conscience in the screening rooms.

After the screenings and rankings—the hotel workers and AIDS documentaries had tied for first—I went back to my office. Fifty e-mail messages popped onto the screen, the usual stuff about grants, festival arrangements, independent screenings, fiscal closings, and so forth. Ah, one from Tina Lau. Her message was typed all caps on the screen: "I WANT YOUR SPERM FOR MY EGG FOR MY LOVE CHILD, ALL LOVE TINA." I saved my response to her for last. I wasn't quite sure if she was joking. so I simply e-mailed her what I had told Francine on the phone earlier: "Warning: This might involve passionate lovemaking. Love, B."

Tina had made her reputation with an installation she had done at the New Museum in which she had smeared secretions from her vagina and blood from her menstrual period onto black and white photographs that showed her and her lover in various positions—masturbating with a dildo, in leather, eating each other out in male drag. This had caused quite a bit of controversy even among lesbians. She said even gays and lesbians needed to come to terms with what she termed the "psycho-biological essence of being postmodern performing lesbian bodies." Despite her edgy art, she and I had always gotten along. Whenever she came to L.A. from Washington D.C., where she ran a sex-boutique for middle-class women, we'd hit the clubs and go on eating sprees in Vietnamese and Salvadoran cafes.

That night I was going to a poetry reading downtown, in the warehouse/loft district. The event was "Breaking Silences"—that seemed to be the latest buzzword for the Asian American literary crowd. I didn't entirely understand the concept that Asians had been silent. Maybe for the younger middle-class Asian Americans raised here it meant being silenced in suburbia in their White grammar schools or high schools—that is, until they went to UCLA or Pepperdine or USC and found their voices through ethnic studies classes.

Born and raised in Hong Kong until the age of fourteen, I never found the Chinese, at least, to be quiet or voiceless. I remember our small flat in the

Central District. Noises made their way up from the streets—from stalls, eating stands, people. Voices of Amah, or of my mother on the phone, or the droning of BBC newscasters. The television, radio, and phonograph often were on in different rooms at the same time people were talking, playing mah jong, or bickering. You had to speak your mind if you wanted anything done above the din. Or you cursed until you won, at home or at school.

Before the reading I had gone home and changed to a black cotton shirt and Levis. I dabbed bronzer on my cheekbones and neck and slipped on a silver earring and Navajo bracelet. I resented the "old queens" of the overseas Chinese type—fingers loaded with gold and jade rings, in their tight silk shirts and expensive Italian loafers that pinched the toes. They overate on dim sum and drank too much beer—served them right. To maintain my physique I ate mostly brown rice, tofu grilled, steamed, or stir-fried, and chrysanthemum herbal tea. And did lots of sit-ups.

Homeless men lined the street next to their makeshift shelters built of cardboard cartons that said "Made in China," ". . . Taiwan," or ". . . Korea." Downtown was filled with wholesale businesses and warehouses selling toys, silk flowers, plastic goods, and shoes from Asia. I scooted my Lexus into the secured parking lot and found a place under the brightest light.

All the chairs in the ground-floor loft had already been taken, so I found a place to stand in back. Someone began to read: "On behalf of 'Breaking Silences,' the Pacific Writers Workshop would like to present three New York poets." Two of the women were Vietnamese, with the same surname of Tran—one was Pham and the other Mai. The single male was South Asian, Arjun. Both women wrote about their childhoods; one lived in Saigon, the other near Ha Long Bay, a fishing spot since the seventh century. Pham's last lines caught my ear.

> "Beyond these southern beaches
> Etched with my own child's footsteps
> Wherever I had walked, never to return—
> Ha Long. Song Fa. Vung Tau."

At the break, Melissana Angeles walked straight up to me. A striking woman, she was an inch or so taller than I in the black boots she was wearing tonight. This was actually her studio loft. She was hosting the reading, since one of her nieces going to Hampshire College was involved with the workshop. We hugged.

"Generation gap, isn't it?" she said.

"Yes, but it's good to hear these young folks holding their own, don't you think?"

"You might say that. Any of them could be my daughter, you know."

"Melissana—I thought you were married."

"That Swede left me with only the dogs and my clogs."

"Sorry. Let me buy you a drink?"

She continued as we walked. "Guess I'm not marriage material."

"I know a lot of men—straight and gay—who find you beautiful, Mel."

"They're attracted to my exotic mestizo Filipina looks initially, then when they find out my age . . . Oh, let's drop it. What do you think of the writers?"

"Pham's great. I'm also placing bets on Arjun."

"Beautiful, but way too young for me. Besides, I saw him checking you out."

"Really?"

Some people had left, and we found two seats. Arjun began to read about growing up in Sri Lanka, a poem that juxtaposed lyricism and bloodshed. Then, a simple homage to his mother, a widow who'd raised six children during the civil war. He concluded with a biting critique of European sex-tourists prowling the beaches for Sri Lankan boys:

> "Their light eyes cut into my limbs like knives
> But they will never take my heart or my country."

Melissana tapped my elbow and smiled. "Let me introduce you. There ought to be a connection between like souls."

"Not necessary, Mel. I can just listen to some people, enjoy their poems, and appreciate them for what they are."

"I insist. You'd have a lot in common. In return, I have a tiny favor to ask."

"Sure."

"Would you have coffee with me, sometime very soon?"

"Of course."

"I wanted to discuss something that could mean a great deal to both of us—your possibly . . . fathering my child."

I almost dropped my wineglass. I laughed. "Mel. You're the third woman who asked me this week, believe it or not. What's happening to me?"

"I don't know what's happening to you. Check your horoscope."

"But Mel. I'm sure any number of men would love to father your child."

"It's like this. I'm forty-two It may be—is—my last chance. I'm not seeing anyone seriously. Married men are out. And none that I respect as much
as you."

"Mel. I'm past my prime."

"Precisely. A second chance. A fusion of me and you running around the
studio. Can't you see that?"

"Mel, let's have that coffee next week. I see Arjun is making his way to
the doorway."

"Come." Grasping my arm, she deftly wove her way through the crowd
until she reached him. "Arjun. Let me introduce my very good friend, Bryan
Chung. He's with the Los Angeles Film Institute."

Arjun shook my hand. "I've heard of it. Your documentary grants. One
of my friends got one, in fact."

"Who?"

"Do you know Thelma Jagannathan?"

"She was doing a film on organizing Pakistani taxi drivers in New York
last year, wasn't she?"

"She's in post-production now. I'm supplying some of the voice-over."

"You have a wonderful voice. And your poem about sexual coloniza-
tion—a cautionary tale for us all!"

"I meant that to apply to Europeans, not to Asian men."

"But Arjun—if I may call you that—does this really have to do with ethnicity? It's more about proclivity, it seems to me."

"I have a lot more poems—my first book is due out in the fall."

"Love to see it. Here's my card. Let me know how much and I'll write a
check later, why don't I?"

"Would you like to hear a few more?"

"Anytime. When are you returning to New York?"

"I have a few more days here. You must have a busy schedule, but I'd like
to have a drink with you before I leave. Then I can tell Thelma we met."

"No problem. Are you staying . . ."

Melissa took out a silver pen from her hemp clutch, smiling and handing
Arjun her cocktail napkin. "So Bryan. Don't forget your cup of coffee with
me." I nodded.

By Friday I had gotten a second e-mail from Tina, considerably longer. A fax
arrived on that same day at my home. She was serious. She had already had

a draft contract drawn up by her lawyer. Clauses about paternity. Injections and in vitro fertilization. On my part, I would need to abstain from sex for the next six months and go to the clinic of her choice once a month for checkups of my blood, my T-cells, HIV, the works. I couldn't have sex between those visits, otherwise it would invalidate the results of my sperm count. She would pay for everything and assured me that the complete physical would really give me a new outlook on life. In fact, she said, when she came to L.A. she would take me to her Chinese herb doctor, to check for things that western medicine could not discern. The contract was four pages long. She told me she would have to monitor her temperature and her fertile periods for the next few months, so that the responsibility was really mutual. She wanted it clean and scientific. I e-mailed back to her that it would really be easier if we just fucked. I hated the idea of spilling my seed into a test tube or a bottle. She e-mailed me back. Nothing personal, she said, but she couldn't stand the thought of any man inside of her. Dildos were fine. But not an organ attached to a male body.

But that's what I needed, I thought. Tina was serious. I decided to call Arjun. He said he was free tonight. I told him I would pick him up in front of the motel he was staying at in the Fairfax area. Less is more, I assured myself, as I blow-dried my hair, took off my jewelry, donned torn cords and sandals, and stepped out the door.

I had forgotten to ask the room number so I buzzed the manager's window. Room Five. I made my way toward the end of the pool, purplish under the outdoor porch lights. The door was partially open. I knocked. "Come in," he said. He was sitting cross-legged on the floor, in blue shorts and a snug white T-shirt. "I was meditating until you came."

"Shall we go out for a drink or coffee?" I asked.

"I found a coffee maker in the bathroom, so I took the liberty of putting it on already."

He stood and opened his knapsack, taking out a loose-bound manuscript. He walked over to me. "Here it is, the original. I'm checking it against the galleys. Cream or sugar?"

"Black."

I skimmed the pages as he went to the bathroom to fix the coffee. I sat on the single chair. He put my cup on the side table and perched on the edge of the bed.

"Would you mind reading something for me? Just choose your favorite."

"Bryan, it's really unfair to make me read my poems right in front of you."

"Unfair! All is fair in love and war."

"So here's one just for you."

Arjun flipped through the pages until he found the one he wanted, and began.

> "Across hemispheres
> I carry my body
> A brick of clay
> eight corners
> no match for the moon's curves . . .
> I follow my hands,
> seek a ledge, a clearing
> where I can find your face
> and face my own . . ."

"Arjun, it's very moving."

"It's about someone . . . and it still reminds me of him."

Without speaking, he kneeled and nestled his head in my lap. I did not say a word and began to stroke his hair.

"Could you spend the night here, Bryan?"

He caught me off guard. "You're kind, Arjun. I didn't really come here to . . ."

He laughed. "Phooey! I'm not such an innocent boy—not one of those on the beach! I'm twenty-four. Don't delude yourself. And don't you believe for a second that you're the subject of my poem. It was I who was attracted to you when I saw you talking with Melissana, at the reading."

"Me?"

"The way you carried yourself."

"Shall we take a rain check? Let's meet in New York. I go there often. Then we'd have something to look forward to—if you're not married off by then!"

"Bryan. You may lie by my side anytime, even if I'm married. But at least give me a kiss. Now."

I could not delude myself about Arjun's desires or my own attraction to him. As I caressed his body, the gnawing sensation that he was about my son's age kept me from fully responding to his kisses. But it would be deluding myself to say I had experienced fatherhood, since I had never seen my son and wouldn't recognize him on the street. Yet it disturbed me that bodies and beauty were so provisional—women reached a time in which they had to make a choice about birthing, just as men reached a time in which they had to commit to something other than themselves.

Mel's message was on the machine when I returned home. She was psychic, as usual. "I'm ready for my cup of coffee anytime you are." I called her back and arranged to meet her for lunch the following Wednesday. During the week, I had a chance to carefully reread Tina's contract. As much as I enjoyed being with her, and her antics, something bothered me about test tubes. The mechanics of it grated on me. I placed the contract gently in a bottom desk drawer.

Mel was already sitting at the table with a cup of coffee in her hand when I got to the Cafe Kiki. This Hong Kong–style cafe served American food like lamb chops, steaks, and seafood, but with an Asian touch—rice, rather than potatoes, and stir-fried vegetables with the entrées.

I ordered a coffee and a grilled vegetable sandwich on wheat.

She began. "We've heard all about you and Arjun."

"There's nothing to report. We just had coffee, you know."

"That's not what I heard. Older men can be so wicked—but I forgive you."

"The more I protest, the less you'll believe."

"So be it. To the matter at hand. After we talked, I realized it was so gauche of me to just ask you point blank if you'd consider fathering my child."

"You needn't apologize. It was just unexpected, there, in the middle of the reading."

"Well, the next few days I went through my Rolodex, making a mental list of every man I'd ever dated, was interested in, admired, hated, detested, respected, or was attracted to. The categories were full, except for 'respect.'"

"What do you mean?"

"There were only two on the list who were even close candidates. Did you know that both of these men were gay? And I'm not a fag hag!"

"Certainly not."

"Who's the other?"

"The son of a famous Manila senator. But he died last week. SIDA."

"Sorry about that."

"So you see, Bryan, you're a majority of one. I'm assuming you're HIV negative, but just in case, both of us would need to get tested two or three times again."

"Mel. Did you know that I had a son, who is now around twenty-three years old?

"I didn't know."

"I can't really call him a son, though, because I've never even seen him. His mother and I had split up before he was born."

"Do you ever wonder about him? How he looks, thinks, acts?"

"Yes and no. I have wondered, then I realize that I'm really not entitled to that. Blood does not equal bond. So why not just adopt a child?"

"I've looked into that too. Did you realize how expensive the adoption process is on this end? Eleven thousand dollars, plus transpacific flights. Social workers. Lawyers. Visas. Clearances. It took a friend of mine two years to adopt a baby girl from China."

"So it would be cheaper to ask a friend?"

"Don't get me wrong. I wanted a good genetic combination, Bryan. Take it as an objective observation, not flattery."

"Frankly, I don't believe in superior genes. Aryan races. Enlightened Asians. I've seen the kids of too many of my friends whom I thought had terrific genes. One kid did himself in on crack, others are pale ghosts of their mothers and fathers."

"But you can't generalize from those Hollywood types you hang around with. Please, Bryan, think it over."

"Are you proposing natural or scientific child making, Mel?"

"What do you mean?" she laughed. "I don't have any qualms about making love with you, Bryan. I'll do what it takes. One of my girlfriends is actually thinking of getting her eggs frozen, but I'm not into that!"

By this time I was sweating under my polo shirt. Melissana's directness left me no room to move. She suddenly put her hand on mine, smiling.

"Bryan, I see that cornered look in your eyes. I'm not pushing you. Perhaps this just reflects my inability to commit myself to a nice, straight man."

"It's nothing to do with inability or capability, Mel. Or with being gay or straight or whatever. It's more to do with our not knowing who we really are—beyond what society tells us we are."

"Run that by me again."

"It's ironic that in the age of virtual reality and virtual everything, we are virtually ignorant when it comes to unraveling questions that the ancients—Buddha, Socrates, or even Nietzsche in modern times—delved into."

"You're better than fortune cookies! I mean you're quite the philosopher—and I'm not being facetious."

"This is going to sound New Age. But because you're an artist I can say this to you. I remember reading what the Buddha once said about life—that 'Karma creates all, like an artist; Karma composes, like a dancer.'"

"Got it. So I've got to just keep moving, changing, like my dances, like my art."

"I'm not Sogyal Rinpoche or Thich Nhat Hanh. But I think you can create something beautiful if you just go with the flow . . ."

"So this is your tactful Asian way of saying no to me, right?"

"Yes. I'm afraid so, Mel."

She was miffed, I could see it in her eyes, so we quickly concluded lunch and parted.

Exhausted after the luncheon, I decided to go the spa to work up a good sweat. I didn't realize how difficult it would be to extricate myself from potential fatherhood. It was no joking matter, I thought, as I began to run around the rubberized indoor track, above the weight-training area. Sweat began coursing down my back but I felt good by lap five—free, vital, and alone. I counted the laps—ten around made up a mile.

In front of me, the well-cut Latino was wearing spandex shorts that revealed his muscular thighs and buttocks. I forced my eyes away and began to think of Francine, the person whom I trusted and had known the longest, for twenty years, in fact. If I was going to donate my organ for a worthy cause, it would probably be to her. She knew herself. She had a good sense of politics, community, and her own sexual identity. Her ties to Hong Kong and her sentiments toward me were understandable. For her, sexuality was part of communication, and with her, any procreative acts would be an extended part of our long friendship.

When I got home from the gym I decided to drop her a line, to touch base as I had promised. I wrote her that I would try to arrange to stop by Bloomington on the way back from Washington, D.C., next month for an arts panel. Despite Bloomington being my least favorite college town, I said I'd love to have dinner, and talk about what it would all entail.

The possibility of real gay fatherhood would certainly be documentary material, I wrote on the card. Black and white? Hi-eight video or super 16 film? Digital. Badly scripted scenarios. I knew myself well enough not to propagate babies out of test tubes or provide fast solutions for women or men like myself going through midlife. Even if I carried my hands—and body—across hemispheres, as Arjun had done so well in his poem, I wondered if I would come up empty-handed. As I reread my message to Francine, I caught my smugness, tore the card up, and began anew.

Camouflage

THE MUFFLER AROUND her neck almost hides her mouth. She clutches the bottle of wine and package of meat to her coat, grimacing at the supermarket checker.

"Lady, you can't open the bottle of Manischewitz. Same with the hot dogs."

"Sir, you know me from before. I have been here many times. Let me speak to Schmidt the manager."

The clerk nods. "Smitty's off today, Ma'am. It's against the law to open liquor in the store. You know that. It's not the first time you've done this!"

She goes on. "Young man, I am very upset with you. I'm waiting for my tests from the doctor. I can't even sleep. Cancer, you know. I'm sick. I might die."

"Well, Ma'am, if you're so sick you shouldn't be drinking anyway. We'll have to take the bottle back, sorry." He reaches over to the woman but she pulls the bottle and package of kosher meat away from him.

"I don't mean to cheat anyone. I'll pay for this damn bottle and the hot dogs. I ate only one, I was so hungry!" She laughs and turns to look at me. "You needn't worry, Sonny, I won't get sicker! They're precooked!" I don't want to hear this old woman rant about depression, death, and cold hot dogs.

I juggle my bottles of orange juice and vodka and a veggie and cheese sandwich in my hands. Nothing's at home except for three-month-old frozen lumpia. The 24 Hour Food for Less is down the corner from my Fairfax studio. The Fairfax area's convenient to Cantor's all-night deli (too expensive), synagogues, and thrift shops (where I shop for retro stuff). Most of the night I'd been up listening to my Tiana Tabios disc. A friend brought it from Manila when he came through L.A. I couldn't get enough of her, maybe for my next show. Last night was my third time. I was the second Asian they'd hired. "The first oriental boy didn't work out," according to Orlando, the night manager. "He could get it up. But he couldn't come!" Twenty minutes into the music the spa customers were upset. A few walked right up to him. They had paid their money, they said, for a good show. The customer was always right. That's why the spa stuck to Whites and Latinos usually, for the Tuesday night show. The show brought people in. If you were good enough you went to the other spa, in Long Beach, after a few weeks.

In the car I wolf down the sandwich and wash it down with orange juice and vodka. My breath fogs up the rear window of the '91 Toyota Celica—the security guard can't see me. I throw the empty juice bottle and the vodka in my black nylon duffel, the one with the night's changes, towel, and my stash. I am exhausted. The "X" was cut with something that made my head spin. The Hollywood Hills behind me glow; it's only a few minutes past six o'clock. Sometimes I miss the humidity and the red and silver jeepneys at 6 a.m. Thousands of them jammed the streets of metro Manila, honking and fuming into the room in which I slept. I'd hold onto whoever I was with that night, my eyelids quivering under the delicate bougainvillea twisted around the iron window bars. No one could break in—but I couldn't break out either. Even if there were a fire like the one that had killed the Muslim family in Quiapo last month.

It was the last time I would call Papa for money. "*Ano ba ang akala mo sa akin, bangko?*" he sputtered to me in Tagalog. What did I think he was, a bank? He had worked all his life to retire in Canada and I'd be welcome to move back to Toronto with the rest of the family. Or I could go back to the P.I. and live with my Uncle Apostol. I knew he was mad and gently hung up on him. *Puñeta!* What a bitch!

Take the Cahuenga Pass over Mulholland Drive to the Valley. Get off on the 134, Vineland exit. Make a right, a left, then another right until the Pioneer Chicken on the corner. The spa is in a forgettable business strip of the San Fernando Valley, twenty minutes from my place—a small warehouse building with painted-over olive-drab windows and a single door on the right side. A steel plate on the door reads: Camouflage: A Private Men's Spa. The show starts at 8:30 p.m., sharp. Usually I get there an hour before. Touch toes. Clench butt. Open butt. Lift the knees. Spread my legs. Flash white teeth and shut up. I have my own room, No. 7, where I, or whoever's on that night, can change for the show. They already had the tape I'd given them last week. I never eat before dancing. Oil my chest and shoulders with coconut oil. Grease my cock and butt to catch the light. Thirty minutes is a long time. You work your heart out for one hundred dollars. I'm hardly a dancer. But as Orlando told me when I started, the clients didn't care much about aerobics. "Only that you could come." They wanted to be able to touch all the hard, soft, and wet parts of me. Like Uncle Apostol did when I was small. I lived with him and his family. Instead of letting Dora, the servant girl, bathe and dress me, he would do it himself. "You are my brother's son. I want to make sure you are growing right," he said to me in Fukienese, his father's dialect.

We'd bathe together. He'd ask me to soap his scrotum and between his thighs. A few years later, he would push his penis into my mouth. The first time I bit on it. He knocked me against the green tiled wall, blasting cold water on me until I shivered and cried for him to stop. Smiling, he just tightened his grip around my throat and said that my father would kill me if I spoke one word. Then he made me eat the rest of the soap. This went on for years, until I was twelve and left for boarding school. There, I had my first wet dream. I dreamt that a man with dark arms walked out of a glistening wet wall and pressed me against his chest until I grew aroused, then suffocated. By then it was too late: the other boys sensed I was different. They could smell me out, I think, the layers of lye, sperm, and water that left a permanent film on my lips, eyes, and skin. When I mixed up my catechism one day Father Lem took out his bamboo rod. He pulled down my pants in front of the boys. As he began to whip me, tears welled in my eyes. As the thin bamboo danced on my flesh, a warm feeling slowly arose and took over the pain. Maybe it was blood. I had an erection. The Father was furious and the boys howled as I tried to cover my small penis with my hands. From then on I would not trust or predict anyone's responses, including my own.

Some of the dancers could move, but they couldn't come on cue. Or they just dribbled it out. They weren't asked back after their debut. What more can I say? First thing I tuck my balls into a white g-string. Over that, a hip-length red kimono-styled jacket, usually a smoking jacket I'd gotten second-hand on Fairfax. I tie the sash tightly, slick back my hair and tie it into a ponytail. I snap a leather armband around my right arm, and that's it. From the bottom of my duffel I extract the small silver pillbox that an ex-lover had given me and pop the yellow capsule into my mouth. Orlando says no drugs and safe sex. But who sticks to the rules here? Within ten minutes I'd feel nothing but my own muscles gliding over themselves. The customers would disappear into the walls—Egyptian friezes, their flesh flattened, their cries muffled. I'd be floating and they'd stiffen into hieroglyphs on stone.

Knock on the door.

"*Cómo?*" I say.

"Orlando. Ready, babe?"

"Almost," I say.

He pushes it open. The Salvadoran night manager is stocky and handsome, poured into white jeans and a T-shirt that says Club Camouflage. "You look great!" he says. "Now, baby, one thing—one of our best customers complained last week."

"Whatever for?" I ask.

"He said you didn't pay him much attention."

"What? Hey, I can't keep track of every old tit! Who is it?"

"That blonde—the one who brings his own green towel! No favorites here. The boss says. Everyone pays the same money . . ."

"Okay—Orlando." I spit on the floor and smile. Orlando plants a kiss on my lips and grabs at my crotch, kneeling. I push his head away. "Easy, Orlando. Got to save myself for the boys."

I walk slowly through the narrow aisles of the bathhouse, past the tiny cubicles and fleshy naked men lying there. In my nose, the smell of Lysol, freshly laundered towels, and sweat. "Let the show begin," chortles a voice from behind a half-opened door. As I reach the "Jungle Room" I pause for a second just outside the dimly lit entrance. They've painted the walls with dark green camouflage-style leaves, and thrown some rope nets and black metal bars over the ceiling. Orlando's still talking.

"Remember, boys, there is no unsafe sex on these premises. The dancer is dancing for your E Y E S only. Please, keep your H A N D S to—I mean on—yourself! Now, give a hand to Sakoi!"

I'm mestizo—mainly Chinese with a bit of Malay thrown in—but I use a Japanese name. More exotic than Bernard Amador Angelo Tan, my given one.

The music starts and I step right into it. I'd taped Bambi Palanca for tonight. My hips rotate to Bambi's "Head Full of Love." On the carpeted steps that surround the darkened fifteen-by-fifteen-foot room, about two dozen men sprawl or sit, white towels tied to their hips or spread across their laps. The spa caters to Whites and Latinos, mainly, with a few Blacks and

Asians. There could be from twenty to forty guys on any given night. Orlando stands by the exit door. I grin as I let my kimono slide down one shoulder to the floor. Then I pick it up, as I begin to walk toward the men, flourishing the red garment like a matador's cape. The mirror in front reflects all 137 pounds of me: a tan, lithe, twenty-five-year-old body, five-foot-seven, straight hair, moving toward oblivion. I move in my own space, enjoying myself as I finger the white pouch between my legs. Count to five. Pop out my oiled cockhead. An inch at a time. Fifteen minutes to go. I have good abs and arch my cock toward them. Now their arms and wrists are moving under the towels. Some let their towels fall to the ground and spread their legs. Others begin to fondle the men sitting beside them. A few lie prone for a better "see," anticipating my walk up the carpeted stairs on which they are sitting. Loosen my ponytail, twirl and bend over from the back, giving them a glimpse of my solid butt and legs. "Beat it," someone shouts.

I go by the rules as best I can. But my tips depend on hips and lips. Orlando walks away just as some guy begins to finger my ass. Orlando stands by the door, his back to us, keeping track of the minutes on his watch. What he doesn't see he doesn't know—and isn't responsible for. A hand touches my balls. One man thrusts a bill into my hands. "It's a twenty—sit on my face for twenty seconds, babe," he asks. So I spread my legs and crouch down as low as I can. Good thing I'd shaved everything—front and back. Like Orlando said: "No fur—men want it smooth."

I find a space on the steps and lay down my cape. As I stroke my cock, fingers begin to tuck dollar bills under my black leather armband. My body's sweating, I can feel two hands, then three—ten, twenty—I don't know how many are on me. Orlando comes into the room again. He holds up five fingers—five minutes to finish. I walk back to the middle of the room and embrace my own body, stroking myself harder. With a shudder, I let my spunk spill over the red cloth on the floor. Like a wave, my energy gathers force and moves over the passive, waiting men. Uncle Apostol is drowning in my river. He's flailing his arms and his mouth opens and closes without a word but I stop only when the lights go on. I pick up my pouch and cape, smile, and wait for the men to drop business cards or a few more bucks at my feet. Pick-up trade. I stagger back to my cubicle. But I'm still throbbing. Ecstasy doesn't let me off that easy. On the table next to the condoms is a small bud vase and a single red rose. It says: Orlando. I close the door and find a Valium to bring me down again. Then I lie on the narrow bunk, counting the bills. Mainly fives and tens, plus that one twenty. Business cards from all over L.A.—

Beverly Hills to Montebello. Sixty-three dollars, plus a hundred for the night. I chuck the bills in the duffel and with my foot wedge open the door. I need a man.

Every Thursday I put in my time for (P)AIDA, the Asian AIDS clinic downtown. Auntie Aida is Filipino slang for AIDS, so the acronym means "Preventing (AIDS)." I am twenty minutes late already. As I turn the corner of the corridor, Marianne Martinez primes me: "You're late! They've been waiting for your artistic input. Bernard, we're having a 'card and candle' ceremony today. You know that Li-Li died, don't you?"

"No, Marianne, I didn't." I suck in my breath, put on my best smile, and walk into the dayroom. The windowless beige space is enlivened by sketches, bookshelves of magazines, and potted plastic palms in each corner of the room. The clients are more somber than usual. They aren't playing mah-jong or cards. Neither are they waiting for me or anyone else, really.

Li-Li was a graphic designer from Malaysia who, after living with AIDS for five years, had reverted back to Buddhism, the religion of his maternal grandparents. A gentle, handsome man. Gradually his health declined. After his last bout with pneumonia no one except his family, his caseworker, and I had seen him. I was with his caseworker one day, and she asked me if I cared to go to the hospital, since Li-Li had mentioned he wanted to see me. When we got there we had to put on gloves and wear paper masks over our mouths. They didn't want us carrying any germs into the room that might weaken him further. He was hooked on tubes and a ventilator for his weakened lungs, as I'd expected, and the doctors had maxed the morphine. It was not the Li-Li I knew. I don't know whether he recognized me. But I knew it was the same person inside that shell. I could not say a word. After touching his hand and the sheet over his body, I just walked out of the room and cried.

He'd been a regular at the dayroom until two months ago. I say hello to the half-dozen guys: Nestor, a Filipino rapper with a shaved pate; Lee, a Taiwanese who lived with his rich White doctor lover in the Los Feliz Hills; Ricardo, a transsexual mixed-blood hairstylist; Hoang, a former jewelry designer from Saigon; Rahu, an economics teacher from Thailand; and Chino, an aspiring Japanese American actor. Candles, colored construction paper, and flowers are already heaped on the table. We would write good-bye notes to Li-Li, as we had done for the others. His photograph is propped up on one corner of the table.

"You need a custom trim, Bernard! Come to my salon for the holidays."

"I can't afford you, Ricardo! Besides, I'm already smooth! My holidays are quiet, and . . ."

"And who are you with now?" he asks.

"Me and my hand! And you?"

Ricardo flings back his dyed blue hair. Today he's wearing a faux emerald bauble around his neck and a matching ear stud. "I'm very popular, Bernard. But I really can't say *who* in public!"

"He gets fucked, then just forgets their names!" Hoang adds.

"Bitch!"

I select a lime green sheet. Rahu hands me scissors. "I just got a part-time job as a substitute at L.A. City College. I'm so happy to be working again."

Marianne, the day worker, chimes in. "Isn't that great, Rahu!" I nod, "What classes are you doing?"

"Oh, I'm not actually teaching. Just assisting. Looking at papers and exams." Rahu adjusts his gold spectacles; his eyes are getting bad and the AZT isn't doing him any good.

I would cut out a palm tree, I decide. Across from me, Chino winks. I smile back. He's good-looking, masculine, in a pale, squarish Japanese way, with startlingly red, full lips. He walks over to me and hugs me, whispering into my ear. "Your kimono was a turn-on, Sakoi!"

My face flushes. "Chino—you still go . . . ?"

"Why not!"

If Chino knows, then everyone else knows. I look around the table, but the rest of the clients just smile or turn away, as if they don't hear a thing. I hadn't noticed Chino at the bathhouse—but then, I'm so high there I don't pay attention to anyone. I resume cutting out a colored paper card for myself and writing a personal note to Li-Li. I mean, it's no big deal working for (P)AIDA and being a dancer. I am pretty careful about safe sex.

Everyone has finished their cards. Marianne says: "Do we all want to read them? Share our inner thoughts with each other? That would be nice!"

"No, this is personal. I'd just like to place mine on the altar," Rahu says, taking a votive candle.

"But I'd like to read mine," Hoang says.

"Go ahead," Marianne smiles her empathetic smile.

Hoang takes a breath, pauses, and starts.

"Li-Li, now you're a star
Now you're in Buddha's hand.
Bright in Heavenly land
Shining over the China Sea.
Please shine over the rest of us
Who live still here on earth.
Because, Li-Li, now you're a star."

Nestor, who's been silent most of the afternoon, speaks up. "Li-Li, man, I know you're up there dancing your little butt off. I'm gonna join you soon. But not too soon, I hope!" He grins, revealing sharp incisors, and we join him. Then we each take a white votive candle, and Lee takes out his gold lighter, lighting our wicks. I notice the thick twenty-four-karat gold chain he has on today as it catches the candles' flames.

We stand up, ambling toward the altar in the corner. The altar, in a makeshift bookshelf, holds an assortment of statues, dominated by a gilt Buddha that Li-Li had donated to the room. He said that it was the real thing, not one of those tourist ones. Photos of others who died before him are propped on the altar, alongside silk flowers, packages of fruit candies, a plastic Virgin Mary, a Thai ceramic elephant, a Bible, and a silver cup with the names "Manny and Ernie" engraved on it.

Rahu, counting his fingers, quietly says, "In my country, they say that the energy of seventy lotus flowers equals the heat of one body at rest. You rest in peace, Li-Li." Marianne turns on the Muzak louder—some synthesized New Age stuff—and I wince.

One by one we place our cards with messages and candles on the altar. Hoang kneels and chants. I don't know whether it's Buddhist or Catholic because his voice is so soft. I haven't been to Mass for a few months, but for Li-Li's sake I make the Sign of the Cross on my chest and mutter to the Father, to the Son, and to the Holy Spirit. Some move back to the table, others wander off with their own thoughts. I slump down on the couch and flip through the gay mags that are distributed free to the agencies. Airbrushed White men dominate the pages of ads for everything your body ever lacked: abs, nose, thighs, teeth, hair, and amino acids and enzymes coursing through your system.

Chino comes up to me. "Can you give me your phone?"

"You can always catch me here, just leave a message."

"Let's go out for a drink—sometime soon?"

"It's against the agency rules to go out with clients, you know that."

"Then—just for coffee?"

"I don't drink coffee, Chino. Just Evian."

His smile suddenly drops. He hisses, "Jesus, you are a hypocrite, man."

"Everyone to his own."

"*Puta*. You strut your cock and ass for men in a sex club."

"Hold it right there, Chino," I say.

"Why won't you go out with me! I'm not asking you to take off your pants!"

His voice is getting louder.

"Come on, Chino—let's talk outside. Now."

"NO," he screams.

"Ay, man, cool it," Nestor says.

Chino calms down. Marianne comes over. "Can I facilitate anything here?"

"No, no, it was just a little misunderstanding," I say.

"Can I help? Really, you should let me handle this, Bernard."

"No, excuse me, I got to go to the head."

I take the wooden key off the wall hook and run down the hall. I open the door and lean against the sink. My stomach is churning. My breakfast spills out of my mouth and splatters everywhere. Chino has a point. Technically, I don't have sex with any of the customers. No penetration. But I bring customers into the spa where they have sex with each other. So, what's the difference? Maybe I'm adding to the caseload of men who become infected in these places. I wipe the sink and my face and pants as best I can, regain what's left of my composure, and walk slowly out of the restroom back to the dayroom at the end of the hall. Chino is waiting outside. I look past him but he grabs my arm.

"Look, Bernard, I'm sorry. We all gotta do what we gotta do."

"Chino, I've already broken so many rules in my life, what's one more? Here's my number." I smile, take out a card, scribble my name on it, and give it to him.

"How's the protease treatments, Chino?"

"My viral load is way down. They can't even find it in my blood. I have a part-time job now. East-West Players. Assistant stage manager."

"Good for you. And call me anytime, Chino. Anytime. Maybe we can go out," I tell him.

Chino calls the following week and leaves three messages on my answering machine. But I don't call him back. I'll face him later; I've been anxious all week. Whether I'd continue to work at Camouflage. Whether I'd go back to Cal Arts. It's a concrete bunker in the middle of the goddamned desert. At the scrubby edge of the suburbs, at the end of the twentieth century. Bored White kids with jeeps, lots of money, and vague notions of tribal postmodern art for the new millennium. My notion of tribe didn't quite fit in. Instead I'd spent my tuition on "X." Plenty of X-rated films were already in my head, reeling themselves around my brain and body. So I took a leave of absence because I never finished Project B—the mandatory ten-minute 16-millimeter film. At twenty dollars a hit for the purer stuff I was always caught short. I'd have to hustle, if I had any passion left for cutting-edge film and video. Maybe porn, I told myself, if I was really broke.

Someone I knew got murdered a couple of weeks ago. He picked up two White guys on Santa Monica Boulevard and asked them to pose. They were hetero. Anyway, their photos ended up in a gay porn mag a couple of months later. Pissed, they tracked my friend down to his studio and bludgeoned him to death, thrusting an icepick up his ass and a vibrator down his throat. It was still buzzing when they found him. They took the cameras and video equipment. After I found out, I had migraines for a week. I could hear buzzing in my ears and threw away my vibrator. I wrapped it in newspaper and thrust it into the trash bin behind the apartment.

I stand naked in front of the bedroom mirror. Clench butt. Lift legs. Smile. But I can't even get hard before the mirror. "Mushroom" they call me. A friend told me that there were three Chinese names for penis shapes: pagoda, column, and mushroom. A pagoda was larger at the base and smaller at its tip, the most common. A column was narrow and even. If the head of the penis was larger than its base, it was a mushroom. That was most desirable, but the least common. I grab some Vitamin E cream and begin to furiously lather my cock. It stays soft. I close my eyes until I can see Uncle Apostol bent down, his mouth on me. Over and over again I'm shoving my cock through his membranes, flesh, and bones, against the green tiles. Blood flows, turning the water at my feet red. *Jesus—as sticky as the blood of Christ—*I think as I shoot into his mouth. He falls to the floor, suddenly old and crumpled. With the carved wooden *Bulul* I had carried with me to America, I pummel his face and body until there's nothing but his skin as transparent as a woman's nylons. A few strands of dyed hair stick on the tile. Two eyeballs, as dark as loquat seeds, roll toward me, staring. With my heels, I press down until they recede into the tiles. The dark face of my Ifugao rice god is shiny with blood and sweat; the face of an ex-lover who'd given it to me would probably recoil at the sight. Tomorrow is Tuesday. If I come through, they will send me to the Long Beach Club on Fridays. That's the big show, with two dancers. They pay the same, but the tips are twice as much because there are more guys. I can't decide. So I shower, throw on my sweats, and slip my key ring around my fingers.

I intend to stop on Western Avenue for a bite at Bangluck Cafe, my usual joint, for green papaya salad. But something else drives me on. Past well-tended pastel stucco houses in the foothills of East Hollywood, onto Los Feliz Boulevard with its windswept junipers, then straight into Griffith Park. "Open to Vehicles at Dawn, Close at Dusk, The Los Angeles City Park and Recreation Department," the sign says. The Gene Autry Museum—all Spanish stucco and red tiles. I slow at the display of antique railroad cars and make my way up "heartbreak hill," where joggers and runners run a mile straight to the topmost point. From there you can see the Hollywood sign, the Observatory, and sometimes the ocean.

I get halfway up the hill. No joggers this hazy weekday afternoon. Plenty of empty vans and cars are parked alongside the roadway, though, near the familiar row of overgrown oleanders. I fumble in the dash compartment for my stash, drop an "X" into my mouth, and wash it down with the bottle of Evian I always have in the car. I put another capsule in my T-shirt pocket for later, get out of the car, and make my way slowly off the road, into the bushes. I listen and smell for signs of life—the acrid scent of cigarette smoke, the crackling of dried eucalyptus underfoot. My Nikes brush against used condoms scattered like torn white petals. It is a netherworld only yards from the bright open road. Ahead of me, behind some trees, a man is tied to the post, his hands bound to the trunk. His torn Levis are down to his knees, and another man is crouched at his belly. I put my hand on the crotch of my sweatpants as I make my way toward them. They are about thirty feet away. As I move closer I see that I am not alone. Other men, moving steathily as animals, flicker then disappear between trees and shadows.

The scrunch of leaves underfoot seems louder than usual. A quick step behind me. A hand on my thigh. Eager fingers frisk the seat of my sweats. In no time I'm butt-naked. But I don't even turn around. I just put one arm against the tree trunk nearest me, lean my body against it, and lift my cheeks to give him a better angle. Leaves and branches camouflage our faces, bodies, and identities. He inches forward, around to the throbbing below my belly. I glance down. A dark-haired head bobs up and down. It's Chino. So my cover's blown. I take a capsule from my pocket and finger his lips until I can slip it down his throat. My thirst drives me to do crazy things.

Eclipse

LETA HUNTER is a transgendered, pre-op Afro-Asian American, mid-twenties. Olive-skinned, with expressive eyes and hands. A dancer's body.

DANTE WOO is a muscular Chinese male, shaved head, with a combination of rough good looks and street smarts. Artist/occasional hustler.

PROFESSOR RICHARD "DICK" KUSAI is a New York University professor of anthropology, Japanese American. Closeted, in his mid-forties. Is doing a study on sexual self-representation among Asian Americans, a comparison between straight, gay, and transgendered individuals. "Kusai" means "stinky" in Japanese—a pun.

WAITRESS

PATRONS

10:30 p.m. The Cafe Mou-Mou, a popular vegetarian cafe in the East Village, 2000. The cafe is usually slow until after midnight. A few patrons talk, read books, write on their notepads.

PROFESSOR: Another ginseng tea, iced.
WAITRESS: It'll keep you concentrating on those notes!
PROFESSOR: Ah, yes. It's for a research project. Thanks. How about some of your wildflower honey?
WAITRESS: Certainly.

Through the wooden door, DANTE WOO *steps in. He is wearing a black T-shirt and baggy gray wool slacks. A small gold Buddha hangs around his neck on a red silk cord. He smiles at the waitress and she points to a table, two tables away from the professor.* DICK *cannot help staring at the young man.* DANTE *smiles back; the* PROFESSOR *averts his head, nervously.*

DANTE (*to* WAITRESS): I'll have the same thing—is it iced ginseng or loquat tea?

WAITRESS: Ginseng. You've tried the loquat. Ginseng is drier, with a bitter undertone, almost.

DANTE: Okay. And a plate of tortilla chips.

As DANTE *wolfs down the chips, the* PROFESSOR *studies the young man's face and body, noticing a tattoo on his forearm. It is the Chinese character "nan" meaning "man." The* PROFESSOR *is tempted to walk over, but instead tears a sheet of notebook paper in half, then in half again. With his Montblanc pen, he writes: "Hi! I'm Professor Richard Kusai, NYU, Anthropology. I'm doing a survey on Asian Americans. May we talk?"*

DANTE *and the* PROFESSOR *glance at each other. Placing the paper on a small plate, the* PROFESSOR *looks directly at* DANTE, *who returns his look and reaches for the white dish that is thrust toward him. After unfolding the note,* DANTE *motions the* PROFESSOR *over.*

PROFESSOR: It's brazen of me. But I couldn't help noticing you as you walked in the door.

DANTE: And why me?

PROFESSOR: Because you must be an artist, or a dancer. The way you walk and dress yourself.

DANTE: You could say I'm in the arts. I work in a framestore part time. I just frame the art, that's all. Lift heavy paintings. (*He pulls up a sleeve to show off a bicep.*)

PROFESSOR: I may be able to offer you a small job.

DANTE (*laughs*): Whadda you think I am! I'm not lookin' for a one-night stand, man. I came in to freshen my lips.

PROFESSOR: No, you've got it wrong. I'm a professor at NYU. I am doing a study on Asian Americans—on sexuality and self-representation.

DANTE: Representing what?

PROFESSOR: Oh, it's just how people view themselves. How they express their sexuality through speech, body language, dress . . .

DANTE: And you're doing a study on it?

PROFESSOR: Yes, so far I've interviewed about twenty people. I'm actually going over some notes now. Here's how it goes. An interview, maybe in my office—or even here—for about an hour. I ask a few questions, you get fifty dollars. You want to answer, okay. If you don't like the questions, you remain silent!

DANTE: Sounds easy enough. Am I what you're looking for? I am sexual. And I love men. And I love women. Whoever.

PROFESSOR: Perfect. Tomorrow afternoon?

DANTE: How about meeting here? It's not busy around two o'clock.

PROFESSOR: A deal.

DANTE: How about if I bring a friend? A girlfriend.

PROFESSOR: Fine.

DANTE: Fifty for her, too?

PROFESSOR: I haven't met her.

DANTE: You'll love her. She's transgendered. Asian. Not the usual hangups. Beautiful.

PROFESSOR: I'll take your word for it. I'm a good sport. Now tell me about yourself, what you're doing here.

DANTE: It's personal. Tomorrow you can ask me anything, within the hour! Besides having good taste in men, and a job at NYU, what are you here for?

PROFESSOR: I get tired of seeing all the nannies from India wheeling the White babies of those professors in Washington Square. Their liberal ideology stops at the cradle. I come here to escape them.

DANTE: Yeah, the world is full of contradictions. For instance: what's a nice-looking man like you doing with your head buried in these notes and books?

PROFESSOR: Oh, just trying to escape myself, as academics are wont to do. When I look at you and think of my lost youth. Don't lose your . . .

DANTE: Nothing is lost, unless you let it go, man. See my Buddha—he's always reminding me that I could be reborn—better or worse. You can keep it or you can lose it, but ya gotta use it.

PROFESSOR: What do you mean?

DANTE: Tomorrow, all the answers, okay? Ciao.

The next day

DANTE: Dante Woo. So we meet again. This is Leta.

LETA: Leta Hunter. And you must be Professor Richard . . .

PROFESSOR: Dick Kusai, NYU. Thanks for coming. Uh, do you mind if I use this microcassette recorder? You understand that everything is confidential. And at the end of this session, I do have checks for you. A small token for your time. Let me reiterate: you are part of my universe of informants. But I look at each one of you as an individual with a unique voice.

LETA: No problem. But just call me Leta and ditto for Dante here, my boy toy.

PROFESSOR: Hmmn, that's an interesting term.

LETA: He's pretty, don't you think? That pout. Those long long lashes. Those pecs. Much too pretty. That's why he's my boy toy.

DANTE: What do you think it all means?

PROFESSOR: That you two are going together, perhaps?

LETA *(laughs)*: What does it look like to you, Professor!

PROFESSOR: But as I understand it, you're transgendered, right? And . . .

LETA: And have I cut it off? No. I haven't cut it off. Yet. I just swallow it between my legs, like everything else.

DANTE: She is my spore whore—my partner in crime.

LETA: That means wherever I lay myself, my body, something sprouts up.

PROFESSOR: What do you mean?

LETA: Whatever. Love or hate. Ecstasy or whatever. But no man can leave me without feeling something primal in his guts.

DANTE: Yeah. They can't get her out of their nostrils for two days.

LETA: Two weeks. At least.

WAITRESS: We have a special Wednesday veggie plate. Braised eggplant, turnips, and baked brown rice. It comes with two kinds of salted pickles.

DANTE: For me, the Yokohama veggie burger and iced ginseng tea.

PROFESSOR: Give me my usual California roll, thanks. And a diet Coke.

LETA: I'll try the special. With a mango shake. Can you add bee pollen and wheat germ?

WAITRESS: Certainly.

PROFESSOR: Tell me something about yourself, your background, Leta. What led you to want to become a female?

LETA: You can't generalize, Professor, though I know NYU is a good school. My background? First, I'm not the color you think is black.

DANTE: She considers herself the twenty-third descendant of Nefertiti.

LETA: Shush. You see, I was born in Okinawa. To a Black soldier and an Okinawan woman. My father and my mother. Oliver Norbett Hunter the third. He was handsome, with smooth black skin. Miyumi Kiya. She was beautiful, as pale as he was black, with wavy dark hair. But I wasn't raised by them. After Father died, when I was five, my mother sent me back to Oakland, and I was raised Afro-American by his sister. I haven't seen my mother since.

PROFESSOR: Do you miss her?

LETA: Sometimes I dream of her. Other times I curse her. But in real life, no. I don't have time to miss the past. I don't even know if she's alive. Do you want to see a picture of us?

PROFESSOR: Yes.

From her purse, she withdraws a small photograph of a Black soldier and an Asian woman, and a boy clutching his mother's hand. There is part of a wall and a sago palm in the background.

LETA: This is the only photo I have.

DANTE: They were hot, babe. You inherited their looks. And intelligence. Fusion, man.

LETA: Fusion may be good for music. But it hasn't always been good for me. If it weren't for my aunt I'd be dead. She taught me to love who I was, no matter what.

PROFESSOR: Hmm.

LETA: She told me, "God has his reasons for mixing and meddling, child. Now don't you go on messin' things up!" My skin may be smooth. No pores. No acne. But in some circles I'm too dark. In other circles I'm too light. I got Black lips and those tight Asian eyes.

DANTE: And cheekbones. And a Black ass. Men die for that. Shit, I'd trade my ass anyday for that.

LETA: But baby, I have traded my ass. And look how much trouble I've gotten myself into!

PROFESSOR: Getting back to . . . what did your aunt think of your desire to be . . .

LETA: Female? Oh, yes. My femininity, as it were. Why are you interested in the subject, Professor? I'm just as curious as you are.

PROFESSOR: You're the subject, Leta. And Dante. I am just the transmitter. I listen. I record. I interpret.

DANTE: Are you gay, Professor?

PROFESSOR: That's not relevant. But let's just say, for the sake of our little discussion, that I'm open. I'm exploring bisexuality. It's part of my work. Trying to define race, gender, and sexuality in terms of Freudian repression and desire. My Ford Foundation grant.

DANTE: I see. You won't cop to getting a hard-on when you first saw me in the restaurant. Leta here and I could teach you a few tricks, Dick.

PROFESSOR: I'm sure you could. But getting back to . . .

LETA: Oh! I'm not what you might assume. I used to lift weights. See these muscles? (*She flexes her well-toned biceps.*) And I'm very well hung. But one day I just decided that women's clothing and makeup were more natural for me. Even my features seemed to glow more as a woman. Sexuality is like an eclipse. Shadow over light. Moon over the sun. Interconnected electrons.

DANTE: Sexual poetry. She's an X-rated poet.

PROFESSOR: But what is a woman to you, Leta? Only a matter of clothes, makeup, drag, performance?

LETA: Too much theory, professor! Pay attention! My aunt, for instance. She said: "Man or woman. Either or neither. That's God's will. Who am I to interfere?"

PROFESSOR: So it didn't faze her . . .

LETA: Listen. I went to Oakland High, West Coast. The prom. I had no date. No female, that is. That's when me and Hansel (he's Black) decided to go as a couple. My first time in drag. No one knew. No one guessed. I dressed discreetly, elegantly. High neck, but very low backed. A long string of pearls. My hair was pulled back and tied with a matching silk scarf, forties style. My aunt sewed it up. We looked like a couple right out of the Harlem Renaissance.

DANTE: The essence of essence.

LETA: Then we drove to Lake Merritt, under the moon.

PROFESSOR: And after that time?

LETA: I just grew into womanhood. When I used to look in the mirror, I felt raw, naked, vulnerable as a man. Especially being of mixed blood. But as a woman, I could blossom, come into myself. Despite my blood. Being a woman, I learned to touch things. My thighs. Forehead. Hair. Ears. They felt different, as a woman. With another hand almost. I knew how my aunt or ma felt.

DANTE: Girl, even Kwan-yin, I heard, was a man in India. By the time she got to China and Japan, she put on those jewels and robes and shaved off her little mustachio. My ma prays to her every day.

LETA: So I started experimenting with makeup, hair conditioners, clothes. Clothes are like feathers are to a bird. They protect, warm, warn. They're delicate and dangerous. Me.

PROFESSOR: And emotionally, did you have satisfying relationships with other men? Did they know you were a man?

LETA: Some did and some didn't. Most didn't care. Front door or back door. They came and they went.

PROFESSOR: Oh, I see. But were you satisfied?

LETA: You sound like a Catholic priest—and I'm confessing!

DANTE: I bet those priests get all hot and bothered under those thick robes. They probably aren't even wearing underwear. The better to get themselves off.

LETA: Who ever is completely satisfied? I take them as they come. But I don't fake it. I am Leta. She is me. My dick—bad word choice!—is not the dividing line between male and female. Neither are my breasts or hips or my ass. Though for most folks, that's the line between heaven and earth.

DANTE: Yeah. Sometimes she is a he acting like a she.

LETA: Or a he acting like a she acting like a he.

DANTE: Did you see *Heaven and Earth,* Dick?

PROFESSOR (*flustered*): I'm confused. No I'm not. Yes, yes, I did see it. Oliver Stone, wasn't it? Now Dante, you're definitely a he acting like a he. Whew! How long have you known each other?

DANTE: Me? Why, about seven years, since she was fifteen.

LETA: Fourteen and a half.

DANTE: Okay. Whatever you say, babe.

PROFESSOR: And what is your relationship?

DANTE: Then? Now? We messed around when we first met. Leta hadn't come out as a woman yet. Yep. Just two guys suckin' and fuckin'. But I lost track of her for a couple a years.

PROFESSOR: And now?

DANTE: She is my sister. My main woman. I protect her. And she protects me. I am her shaman. She is my Miss Shasha Man.

LETA: I like that, Dante.

PROFESSOR: Tell me a little about yourself.

DANTE: Not much to tell. Second generation. Born in the projects. San Francisco. Ping Yuen. Peaceful Garden housing projects. Guys used to beat the shit out of each other. I could fight men. I could whip their asses. But then I decided that loving them was better. For me. I can't speak for others.

PROFESSOR: And how did you first come out?

DANTE: I didn't come out. It just came out.

PROFESSOR: What do you mean?

DANTE: The ME out of the me, man. Fluids and juices and semen and tears and sweat exchanging and changing and charging up my world.

PROFESSOR: Can you be more prosaic? A little less poetic? More specific.

DANTE: You're a sociologist.

PROFESSOR: Anthropologist.

DANTE: Forgot! Lemme see. Hmm. I didn't respect the other yellows who were hanging onto the arms of old White guys. Or even the young White guys, for that matter. I had more self-respect than that. So I started hanging around in Oakland. A Black jazz club. Thunder Alley. I grew a beard so I could get in the door. My first lover was Black. He played bass. Man, he could seduce a sunset.

LETA: And you have loved that blackness ever since!

DANTE: Could say that I found the blackness in me. Under my yellow skin, under these oblique lids here, was a darker man waiting to be born. A dark man desiring a darker man. That is, until you came along.

LETA: And I did come, honey.

DANTE: Friend and companion. The most beautiful being my tight eyes had ever seen. I had to put on my shades otherwise I would be blinded. I offered my body to her. Every muscle of my 150 pounds. Like burning black incense and offering black foods to Rahu, the four-armed dragon.

PROFESSOR: What's that?

DANTE: It's a Hindu god, I think. Maybe Thai. Who burns in a chariot of fire. Who tries to eat the sun and the moon. Like during an eclipse.

PROFESSOR: I see.

DANTE: Me and Leta have this word chanting we do. I'm Rahu. She's Kwan-yin. Wanna hear it?

LETA: That'll be twenty bucks extra.

PROFESSOR: I see.

Before the PROFESSOR *can make up his mind,* DANTE *and* LETA *push two empty tables together. Other patrons turn and stop talking as the two scramble onto the tabletop.* DANTE *strips off his T-shirt to reveal a solid physique. They begin chanting;* DANTE *taps his booted foot on the table. The* WAITRESS *rushes over but stops as the two appear to mesmerize the audience with their bodies and voices.* LETA *bends her arms in a slow, sinuous movement; in contrast,* DANTE *continues tapping the table and slowly running his hands over his throat, chest, and stomach. The two, trancelike, begin to recite, in alternating lines.*

LETA: From the thigh of Tehran, the moon's shadow unfurls.

DANTE: Racing to reach the belly of Calcutta, to touch the forehead of Bangkok.

LETA: To clasp the ears of Phnom Penh. Seventy-seven seconds to the millennium.

DANTE: This is the color you think is black. But I am not it.

LETA: Sky darkens at dawn.

DANTE: Already, sparrows wing back to their nests.

LETA: Sun suffers. Soothe it, soothe it.

DANTE: Walk full circle. Start a fire in the hearth. Light flames in the temple.

LETA: Toss roots, herbs, nuts, rice sugar, dried almonds, apricots, peaches, and millet into the flames!

DANTE *jumps off the table, bends at the waist, looks directly into the eyes of the* PROFESSOR, *who is sweating with excitement.*

DANTE: If you are pregnant, remain indoors.

LETA: Burn black incense and offer black foods.

DANTE: Appease Rahu, the four-armed dragon.

LETA: Who burns in a chariot of fire.

DANTE: Who tries to eat the sun and the moon.

LETA: If you believe that the moon can hide the sun, then bathe and chant holy hymns.

DANTE: Blow conch shells and ring brass bells. Fire your pistol at the sky.

LETA: Wear your shades, boys and girls.

DANTE: Race your bikes to the beach. Look up.

LETA: This is me. Dark as you are light.

DANTE: The one you think is black.

Patrons and PROFESSOR *applaud.* WAITRESS *rushes over and admonishes them.* DANTE *and* LETA *smile and rearrange the tables.*

DANTE: So that is how Leta and I became friends. She started as a he. I lost track of him for a couple of years, but I found Leta—as a woman—later. But as I said, she and he are the same to me. The same in my eyes. I look for structure. If I had gone to school I would have been an architect, I think.

LETA: He brings out the structure in me. I feel like I am whole. A man and a woman fused when we are together.

DANTE: Simple. Like a temple. Or a house. A house is not a home.

LETA: Not a home unless you have a bed.

DANTE: And a window. A wall. A step. A toilet. A yard. You can't separate them. Otherwise you don't have a house.

LETA: We share a one-bedroom closet. Brooklyn.

PROFESSOR: Hmmm. Let's backtrack a bit. Now, you and Leta are just platonic friends. But Dante, tell me a bit about your relationships with other men—as lovers, friends.

DANTE: We're telling this priest here a whole lot for fifty bucks. Even if he is so damn sincere and searching so hard for enlightenment. Shit, even those Times Square booths don't give that much detail, honey. I don't think we can talk much more, can we, babe . . .

LETA: Unless we get a little more. Rent's due tomorrow.

PROFESSOR: Well, that's the standard fee I'm paying for informants on the project. That's what was budgeted in the grant.

DANTE: So, how much are you getting paid?

PROFESSOR: As an academic, nothing. Of course, I have two research assistants to process and transcribe the interviews, a travel budget, miscellaneous expenses, a computer, conference money, that kind of thing. All standard. I'm not hiding a thing!

LETA: Where are you going?

PROFESSOR: This is a four-city study, maybe I didn't explain. I am interviewing people in San Francisco, Los Angeles, Chicago, and New York.

DANTE: Professor Dickhead—understand we are not standard. We are boy toy and a spore whore. Or, call us Kwan-yin and Rahu Woo. We know our names. We are a team. We are talent. And we will talk no more to you before we talk to our agent.

PROFESSOR: I am sorry. You misunderstood. I can't pay informants differently, that might bias my sample.

DANTE: Cut this crap. We're not gonna sign any release form.

LETA: Forget it, Dante.

PROFESSOR: You know, I do have good intentions. My study, if published in a reputable referreed journal, will help gays, lesbians, and transgendered individuals. Like yourselves.

DANTE: It will help you. I don't know how it'll help us. Will it help us get laid? Will it make money for us? Will it help our parents so they can quit their fuckin' shit-pay jobs?

PROFESSOR: The academic world is really a terrain of ideas. Not a metropole of desire and desperation. It's hardly the street. Now, I've spent a good two hours with you. Most of my informant interviews are an hour and a half—at most. I have been very patient with you two. Trying to translate your—lingo . . .

DANTE: Lingo! Take your flat ass home, boy. Now. Fifty for me and fifty for her.

LETA: Plus twenty for our little ditty!

PROFESSOR: I'm afraid I need your Social Security number, address, and phone. Just fill out this release form.

> DANTE *takes the microcassette recorder and throws it to the painted concrete floor where it shatters in gleaming, black plastic shards.*

DANTE: Fuck you. Come on, Leta, let's split.

> *The two flee into the dark night air. The* PROFESSOR *morosely begins to pick up the pieces of his tape recorder from the floor.*

Samsara

"CHECK IN YOUR BODY!" Khai said. "We got to warm up before we go through what we're gonna do." I nodded. Good to warm up, check in my body—but for a new one, I noted to myself. Khai was a New Ager ready for the millennium. He looked like a teen-ager.

"How was your day?" Khai asked me, sitting cross-legged in the studio.

My body felt dull from writing on the computer all day. But I had agreed to collaborate with Khai on the performance for Highways, an alternative art space in Santa Monica.

"My day was okay, Khai. Now you be the visible body, and I'll just be the invisible voice. Can I trade in this old model for a new one?"

"No. Collaboration means two bodies and both of our voices."

"Your turn to check in. How did the day go?"

"Morning rehearsals with students at L.A. City College. Latino, Black, and Asian. And I am beat."

"You're young."

"Cut it out! Got to get over the age thing if we're gonna work together."

I looked at Khai, in his snug sweats and tank top, and felt awkward in my baggy T-shirt and shorts.

"We are going to play the mirror game. Every movement I make, with my body, you must follow. Every move you make, I follow. But we should move together. Slowly. Simultaneously."

"What?"

"Like this." Khai lifted his arms. I followed.

"Pretty soon we'll be moving right into sync."

"Sounds New Age."

"No, this is what I learned from the forest." Slowly, he brought his arms down, then crouched as he extended his left leg. I did the same. Sweat shone on his unlined face, on the fine arch of his eyebrows, above soft, wide-set eyes. There was no visible scar of the three years he had spent as a Vietnamese foot soldier in the Cambodian jungles. But he had lost so many friends, as he'd told me once, that he was forced to let go of his grief, or to let go of himself. Here in America, he just danced for joy and forged his own expression of freedom. Nothing else in the world mattered, he said.

"You tricked fate, Khai."

"Buddha kept me alive, Alec."

Each squadron was independent and responsible for its own survival—gathering food, keeping rations, taking care of its wounded, and setting and clearing camp each night. Ho Chi Minh's teachings were drilled into them during their training, but after six months in the jungle principles gave way to grueling practicality. They would learn to tread the rotting undergrowth with care. "The white eye of fire is waiting to catch your feet," they were warned. One summer he and his best friend, a soldier from the same village, were cutting down ficus trees to make tent poles for the night. As he'd almost cut through his own tree trunk, Khai offered to trade places with his slower friend. They traded spots. Khai began sawing. When his friend's trunk fell to the rainforest floor, it set off a hidden land mine. Khai was thrown to the ground; his friend died in his arms.

Khai continued to move, from Cambodia back to Vietnam, and finally to the U.S. via the Philippines. He finally brought both arms to a circle, his fingertips almost touching mine. Khai captured movement from the forest, from soldiers, and from Nayo. For the last three years, until he became ill, Nayo had trained Khai. The two had once been more than friends. Every wall of Khai's studio had large, blown-up photographs of the two dancing. Before, Nayo had also been close to me.

The collaboration that Khai and I had worked out was a piece on French colonialism and indigenous Asian peoples: oppression and resistance; power and sublimation; victor and loser; age and youth. We would re-enact that classic struggle once again, with a twist, five days from now. Khai had asked me to join the Queer Asian Pacific Men's Performance team. At first I said no. Performance was too public. Then I relented. He was curious about me, as curious as I was about him. We recognized that the two of us were linked through Nayo. We formed a strange trinity, three generations apart. Khai was twenty-six, Nayo, thirty-four, and I, Alec, forty-five.

Bare feet slid across the blonde wood. Northern light flooded the tall studio windows. Portland. Sudden rain on the glass panes raced against my pulse. Nayo was directing three dancers in his latest piece, set to lines from a poem I had sent him.

He was not positive or negative then, neither yin nor yang. Day by day his dark mercurial body alighted upon a new voice or a fresh gesture. He made dances about his childhood in Saipan, about poetry he found everywhere, at the corner laundromat, in the street walk and corner talk of refugee Cambodian, Hmong, or Vietnamese women who could be his sister, mother, or his cousin. From them he stole earthiness and elegance and modeled his dances on their cadences of survival. One time he told me that all energy was feminine. He was never ashamed of that in himself.

Nayo wrapped himself in a blue shawl and sat cross-legged on the wooden kitchen chair. I sat across from him. I rose to get the teapot on the counter and brought back two cups. With my hand I brushed against his shoulder. He brought my fingers down to his chest and the shawl slid to the floor. With both arms I lifted him off the chair onto the cloth. The red wig he was wearing caught on my fingers, revealing wisps of black hair beneath. With my teeth I snapped the length of fake pearl beads that dangled from his chest. He kicked off his spiked heels. He would have to put everything on again before we went to the Halloween party later. His face blurred from bleeding mascara, lipstick, and powder. But his arms and legs were hard as any boy's against the blue cloth. As I entered him he bit the back of my hand, then licked the blood off with his tongue.

All that was before he left me, for the others. That's when I burnt the picture he had given me. In a photograph, the exposure of silver particles to light results in a blueprint deposit of residue. That's what is left, resistance to further development. He was five years old. Dressed in a child's white sailor suit, next to a papaya tree. His handsome father smiled on one side, his delicate mother on the other. The same thick eyebrows, the same luminous eyes. Beauty was his inheritance. Sometime later, I told my friend about him. She just shrugged her shoulders and continued to pluck her eyebrows with a steel tweezer. "Serves you right," she said, and spat out the salted plum seed into the ashtray. So I was caught off guard between their eyebrows and lashes, condoms and nylons.

Still, through the papers I could follow him wherever he danced—Boston, Chicago, Minneapolis, Atlanta, Santa Fe. We sent postcards back and forth, conversing through time and space.

—I found a black rock for you in the Mojave desert, he said.
—Come back to me.
—The rock has a blue vein, like the one on your cock, he said.
—Where are you now?
—I am on the 54th floor and the wind is swaying the tower, he said.
—Don't jump.

He called me, he was in L.A. Would I see him? Come for dinner, I told him. Before he came, I cleaned house, vacuumed the carpet, dusted the shutters on the windows. Then I cut vegetables into bits and tofu into cubes. I was meticulous in my cleaning and circumspect in my fear. On the phone, I asked him whether there were certain things he couldn't eat now, what foods were his favorites, what he needed to avoid. No spicy foods, he said. He used to eat spicy—Thai or Korean. I dropped my knife. The kitchen floor was shining. I used a rag to polish the triangular spot on which I was standing.

The doorbell chimed. I walked to the door. He was wearing a brown knit cap, a scarf of scarlet and green, and a heavy Navy peacoat over a wool turtleneck sweater. He did not take his cap or coat off, though it was ninety-two degrees in the middle of August. I was wearing shorts and a T-shirt. We hugged. I could not feel his body under the thick layers of clothing. He sat on the kitchen chair. I began to cook. He asked for a glass of water and I brought one to him. With a grimace, he took a brown plastic vial of pills from his pocket and opened the white cap. He had lost weight. I went back to stir-frying the vegetables. When he smiled, his teeth were too big for his narrow jaw. We talked about his diet, his doctors, and his mother and father. A year before, I saw him dance outdoors at the Salk Institute, in La Jolla. In repose, he sat on the concrete floor, arms at his sides and legs loosely folded into a lotus posture. He extended his arms and lifted his legs, his fingers and toes pointed toward the sun setting in the sea. To his left, two women dancers did the same, embracing the empty Pacific.

Nayo did not eat much tonight. It was difficult for him to swallow. Half-chewed food stuck in his bowl. Without a word, he began to touch my wrist.

I recoiled. He laid his fingers on my arm again. Then I whispered his name. "Nayo."

He coughed.

"You must trust people," he said.

On my left arm, he began to slide his fingers up and down. But shouldn't I be the one to touch him? He was positive, I was negative. I did not speak. He spoke.

"Take a good look at me. I have already been to the other side. So I'll tell you this. Never shut yourself off from love," he said.

He pressed upon my arm insistently, with surprising strength. My dancer was half-way to the other side. His fingers began to strum upon my wrist, in a movement I had not foreseen. I looked into his eyes. He was smiling. He was releasing his breath to bring me back to him tonight.

This would be our last rehearsal before tonight's performance. I was sweating in a priest's black cassock, though I was naked beneath. Khai had nothing on but the rope I had draped around his neck. Slowly I began to tighten the noose. The other end of the rope was bound around my forehead, my veins pulsed against the taut twisted fibers. With his left hand he pulled at the rope, with his other hand he encircled my chest, his fingers tugging at the folds of dark cloth. If Nayo was the name of my brother, then Khai was the name of my son. I recoiled at his touch, for as we pulled harder, we discovered the ropes that bound us. I did not know how would we escape samsara, the cycle of desire, and rebirth without end.

3 Paradise

The Western Paradise of Eddie Bin

IT WAS DURING their sponsorship of the Miss Chinatown beauty pageant that he realized the difference between people like May and himself. Wherever he went he carried the loneliness of his displacement within him, like a smooth dark seed. That seed was always floating on the sea or skimming barren ground, never sending down roots. May, on the other hand, was rooted in America—carefree, immune to war, revolution, and civil unrest. She carried her emotions outside, for all the world to see, like the large red bag she was fond of swinging over her shoulders. It was this difference that irritated him and finally caused their rift. She spoke exactly what was on her mind, while, from the time he first left China, he did not speak freely, forming and reforming his identities from place to place, no matter how hard he tried to assimilate through local activities like the pageant.

Maybe it was a mistake for his agency to sponsor the attractive young woman in the first place. As a sponsor, you had to come up with one hundred dollars for a satin Chinese dress, a hefty fee to the Chinese Chamber of Commerce, and incidental expenses that added up. "Sunny" Loo was a five-foot-six brunette who was studying to be a physical therapist. Born in Chinatown, she was also skilled at the Chinese ribbon dance, at twirling the blue and red silk ribbons around and behind her body, without catching her legs or arms in the undulating pattern. What Mr. Bin had not taken into account was that half of the sixteen girls entering the pageant also specialized in the ribbon dance; that they all loved their mothers (and they would respond in the same way to the Chinese-language question section); and that most of them walked ungracefully in their high heels. Sunny was the epitome of the typical contestant for the last dozen years; she did not have a better chance than anyone else. Nonetheless, on the day of the pageant, Mr. Bin invited Sunny's mother, a hairdresser whose salon had taken out an advertisement, to sit with them in the Masonic Temple Auditorium on top of Nob

Hill. On that evening it seemed that half of the small-business people in Chinatown were at the pageant. Women in short fur wraps, permed hair, and Chinese-style dresses filled the lobby; their husbands, prim in their pinstripe suits, clasped familiar associates and clients. Some were obviously sponsors of the beauty contestants, and they were pointing out their candidates' pictures in the gaudy red-and-gold printed program that was for sale for two dollars. May was dressed up in a high-collared dress from China. Eddie was in his best suit, expecting that their candidate, Sunny, would take one of the two queen titles at least—Miss Chinatown USA, or Miss Chinatown San Francisco. If worse came to worse, Sunny could take first, second, or third princess, or Miss Chinese Chamber of Commerce, or Miss Congeniality. She was not unlovely, only nervous, he thought. She'd place and bring publicity, business, and good luck to her sponsor, the advertising agency.

The gray-haired judge asked Sunny in Cantonese: "Miss Loo, how would you help to improve this world?"

Sunny wasn't prepared, as she'd only memorized an answer about her mother. So, giggling and shrugging her shoulders, she said, in accented Chinese, "I can't remember the vocabulary about the world, but only about my mother. But isn't that enough?"

The crowd, made up predominantly of Chinese Americans like herself whose Chinese was also limited, laughed with her. The judge crinkled his nose. "Then what do you have to say about your mother?"

"My mother is the best person in the world, and the universe would be much less bright without her," Sunny said. No one could argue against motherhood and the universe, so she redeemed herself on that question. However, the girl from Hong Kong and the one from Singapore spoke flawless Cantonese and Mandarin, and chattered on and on about saving humanity through medicine and law and public service. They would score higher points with the judges, Mr. Bin thought sadly. Their sponsors, both Asian airline companies, had the money to find and train not only the tallest but the best-educated girls for the pageant, unlike what his small company could afford.

Maybe it was the swimsuit competition that did Sunny in. There were a few contestants from Taipei and Hong Kong equally skinny in their suits and heels, but they carried themselves arrogantly. Sunny, on the other hand, paced nervously, her hand going to her right breast because one falsie was slipping, thus affecting her posture and her walk. As for Sunny's ribbon dance, it wasn't distinguishable from the others.

May poked him in the ribs after the judges had announced all the princesses. There were only two titles more, Miss Chinatown San Francisco, which entitled the winner to local appearances, and Miss Chinatown USA, which provided a college scholarship. Sunny, needless to say, took none of the titles. Mr. Bin cursed under his breath, not at her, but at the other girls who had won: Neither the queen nor her San Francisco consort had been born in America. The local girls didn't have much of a chance, May said. Even though she told Sunny's mother that the judges were blind and had no taste whatsoever, May kept silent on the way home.

They reached the apartment door. "This little escapade cost us 613 dollars—three months' rent for the office. I don't see how we can last, Eddie," she said. They didn't talk about the pageant ever again, but certainly it was a factor in May's leaving him and the business six months later.

He checked the bedroom. The coverlet was neatly made, the closet emptied of her clothes. Her dresses hadn't taken as much room as he had imagined. Her jewelry cases were gone. He fidgeted with the television knob but the morning programs irritated him. He opened the refrigerator, took out the foil-wrapped ham sandwich from yesterday, and began to slowly savor the meat, mayonnaise, and mustard on the toasted wheat bread.

He ran his fingers through his thinning hair. May had finally left him. There was no one in the apartment. She was probably staying with her best friend in Palo Alto, down the coast. He didn't bother to call her, but went to his office down the street, to clear it out. Eddie Bin surveyed the bare walls. The calendars, spread sheets, and memoranda that had been tacked there a week ago were gone. On the makeshift Formica shelf in front of his desk chair were three Sanford Library Paste glass containers—"Utopian Jars"—filled with dimes and nickels, paper clips, and colored stamps of various denominations. He tossed the clips in the wastebasket, sorted out the stamps and slipped them into a plastic sleeve in his wallet, and stuffed the coins into his jacket pocket. These were the last tasks left for the owner of a defunct Chinatown advertising agency. Despite his ex-wife's excellent bookkeeping, he had declared insolvency. He had lost most of his accounts to the new overseas papers from Hong Kong and Taiwan in recent years. They did not consider him one of them. Mr. Bin, with his low-key appearance and direct Cantonese mannerisms, was the typical *lo wah que*, the old-timer Chinatown

Chinese, who had been born here or came at an early age. What no one realized was that Mr. Bin had painstakingly created his own Chinese American identity as soon as he jumped ship in San Francisco on October 1, 1948, one year before the People's Republic of China was born.

In a Hong Kong bar, Eddie Ming Bin had befriended a naturalized Chinese American seaman and paid him $500 to smuggle him aboard his ship, the *SS Buchanan,* en route to Honolulu and San Francisco. It was an American Liberty ship, retrofitted for cargo after the war. Eddie had left his Pearl River village, the war, and the Japanese occupation behind him, and made his way to Hong Kong. Now he just wanted to see the world, unencumbered by family or circumstances not of his making, so he told the seaman. The seaman, having worked his way up to third mate from steward and cook—the only kind of jobs Asians could get on U.S. ships in those days—had a soft spot for Eddie, whose round face, persistence, and articulate charm reminded him of his own brother. Following closely on the third mate's heels the night before the *Buchanan* lifted anchor, Eddie slipped into the mate's portside cabin. It was furnished sparsely with a single bunk, a desk and mirror, sink and toilet. Whenever the third mate was gone on one of his two watches, at four-hour intervals, Eddie would stretch out his body and sleep. Days and nights were uneventful. Throughout the small porthole, he glimpsed the Pacific. Eddie lived entirely within the cabin, subsisting on extras of beef, chicken, biscuits, spaghetti, and beans, whatever the third mate could sneak in. When the cabin boy came to straighten the room, Eddie would lock himself in the metal locker, suppressing his urge to cough in the stale air. Eddie and the third mate had little time to talk. A few days before they reached Honolulu, the mate told him that their ship had almost collided with another on the starboard bow, because the lookout had been drinking. Sprawled out on the front deck, he hadn't noticed the two lights coming up on his right. The two ships, both pushing a steady eight knots, barely missed each other.

Between the port and starboard cabins, in the open middle space and stairwell that housed the engine below, Eddie would hear voices and footsteps, usually at breaks between watches. He recognized, "Hey, Second, or "Hey, First." He didn't know what time of day it was, and depended upon the intensity of light through the porthole, or upon the changes in temperature and humidity he felt as they reached the Hawaiian Islands to unload cargo. They were halfway to San Francisco. Eddie counted the days when he would first see the mainland.

His first glimpse of the city on hills, the western paradise of his mind, was through the luminous fog at dawn. Foghorns sighed in his ears. Everyone aboard the ship, from engineers to mates to seamen, had to sign off on the routine quarantine before the local pilot could tug the ship into harbor. Eddie remembered staying in the closet for a long time. At the mate's pre-arranged signal, he simply walked off the ship, dressed neatly in a seaman's uniform.

It was the end of one life and the start of another. He named himself "Eddie," in honor of the stocky, taciturn mate. They had a meal in Chinatown together, before the third mate shipped out for Panama and Perth and promised to keep in touch. The first three months, Eddie waited on tables and lost most of his money on horses. He owed rent, stopped betting, and began to change his life. He worked his way through two years of City College, perfecting his English and observing how the Chinese born in America worked and thought among themselves. He got a job as an advertising assistant for the *Gum Shan Journal*. The paper needed someone who could speak English and Chinese to sell advertising space. That is where he met his May—maiden name of Lau. She strode into the editorial offices one windy March afternoon. Barely twenty, petite, with bangs flying across her forehead, she demanded to speak to someone who knew English. Eddie Bin volunteered. She blurted out that she was a Chinese American City College graduate with straight A's in English and business. She wanted to work for a local paper. But the "old fogey" editors were prejudiced against Chinese Americans like her, she said.

"Why?" he asked. "I'm not."

She laughed. "But you're not the editor. You only sell advertising. Plus, they're probably afraid that we'll take away their jobs someday!"

He liked her directness. But Editor Chew, told him, in Chinese, that one English-speaking person was enough for the three-page English supplement. By the time he finished explaining the paper's position, she was fuming. Several weeks later he ran into May in a coffee shop. She teased him.

"War refugees—like you—are taking jobs away from us local folks right and left!"

He defended himself. "If I stayed in China—I would have become skinny and scabby under the Japs!"

"You're a remnant of the old world, Eddie," she said.

"A new patch on old clothing," he retorted.

Because they enjoyed sparring and joking about their differences, they took a liking to each other. They saw each other for two years. She found a secretarial job for an import/export firm. She learned everything there was to know about running a business, even refreshing her accounting skills at a City College night class. For their engagement, Eddie took her to a small Italian restaurant around the corner from his office and confessed his undocumented status to her. She didn't seem to mind. He applied to stay as a war refugee, and May got a lawyer to handle his case.

After they married at City Hall in April of 1952, they found a two-room apartment overlooking the Stockton Street tunnel. Because May was good with figures and tracking delinquent invoices, they soon had healthy accounts. Year after year, they thought of having kids. But after her first miscarriage during the fourth month, May grew morose. The second time she got pregnant, she suddenly stopped eating for a week. He would stew beef tendons or stir-fry flank steak to tempt her appetite, to no avail. Fasting on pineapple juice and water, she miscarried again.

They bickered. She demanded that Eddie have a check-up. But Eddie stalled for time, regularly missing his doctor's appointments for months. He told her she was crazy in the head. Nothing was wrong with her, she insisted. Her own mother had borne her at twenty-nine. So the possibility of having children remained mired in their daily working and quarreling.

They argued again on the eve of her thirty-sixth birthday. It was also the day after he had lost a big account—Datong Shipping—to a rival agency. From their cramped apartment, they walked through Chinatown to Sorrento's in Little Italy.

Below plastic ivy and empty Chianti bottles entrapped on the ceiling, they ordered antipasto and veal. She wasn't paying attention to the food. He ate mechanically, thinking of the lost account. Staring at the dregs of a silent meal, she blurted out: "You want me to die early, don't you?"

"Why do say that?"

"No noodles on my birthday, not even a side of spaghetti!"

"Look, May, this is where I proposed to you. It's been a lot of good years—so, happy birthday!" Eddie lifted his wineglass.

She continued. "You of all people should know that Chinese have to eat noodles—for long life!"

"Is that all? Let's get a side order now." He motioned to the waitress at the bar. "Waitress, one side of spaghetti, no meatballs."

"Is that all!" she repeated, glowering. "Too late for noodles. Too late for children."

He winced because he agreed with her, but not for the same reasons. He had sensed the change in her after the doctor had told them that the miscarriages were not unusual, indicating that May's inability to conceive again might well lie in his glands. A child would complete their family, she would chide him. Yet, because children had always shied away from her, and she couldn't tolerate them for more than ten minutes, Mr. Bin never took her sentiments earnestly to heart. For him, children were a memory of hunger and sadness. He'd seen too many during and after the Japanese Occupation. The sooner you could escape childhood, the better.

But Mr. Bin decided that she would not understand this because she was born in America. From that point on, coolness had crept into their marriage, like a draft from their apartment's hallway window. They still worked together on accounts during the day, but they slept under separate blankets at night. May would take to their bed, thumbing through *Life* and *Look* until she fell asleep. Eddie slept on the living room sofa. Each night he would drape the wool blanket he'd lifted from the *SS Buchanan* over the sofa, without even removing the stiff plastic tarp that, for over fifteen years, had preserved the dark green pattern beneath. Then, stretching his body on top of the blanket, he would pull the sheets over his head, imagining a younger man smuggling himself into a new country.

During their first mutually agreed-upon separation, watching Vietnam on television exhumed his memory. That surprised him. He thought he had gotten rid of all traces of war and Asia when he left. On the trail of a flickering news report on the capture of a squad of Vietnamese soldiers, he fell asleep on the sofa. When he awoke, his pants were damp around the crotch. "A wet dream," he laughed, before he felt, under his thigh, an empty beer bottle.

From the corner of his eye, he spied her squinting at him—in derision. But he was mistaken. He had already filled ten plastic trash bags with the contents of his files, the carbons of every bill, advertisement, and note he had written for fifteen years. For the janitor, he would leave stacks of newspapers: the *Gum Shan Journal, Oriental Digest,* the *China Daily,* the *U.S.-China Association Newsletter.* His fingertips were smudged black with ink and he had gotten a few paper cuts. He liked the smell of paper—newsprint or typing stock—even if it was being thrown away. It was comforting to feel the sheets in his hands, as he methodically tore some and scrunched others into a ball in his palm, depending on the contents. He'd always been faithful to May, but now and then he'd use his office late at night to surreptitiously read the pornographic magazines he enjoyed. The apartment was too small to hide or read the magazines he'd been buying for over a decade. At least, he rationalized to himself, he didn't bring the White prostitutes that prowled the side streets off Grant Avenue to his office. Not that he hadn't ever thought about doing it. He could see them laughing at the small space they'd have to work, squeezed between bookcases, a Royal typewriter, and stacks of papers and bound magazines. They'd literally have to make love standing up. Mr. Bin had the key to the office building that occupied the entire corner of Pacific and Montgomery Streets. Built in 1913, it had marble floors and offices that had been divided up into small wood-paneled cubicles, with high ceilings. Late at night, after ten p.m. sometimes, he would tell May he had some matters to catch up on in the office. He'd walk the eight blocks downhill, unlock the entrance door, and climb the two floors to his office, where he'd scurry to the locked filing cabinet behind a stack of newspapers and pull out the magazines. He would sit alone in his revolving chair, flipping through the images of big-breasted women with their legs spread, wearing different colored panties and g-strings, and then begin to loosen his belt. In half an hour, he'd pull up his zipper, wash his hands in the old-fashioned marble men's room, and be on his way home. It was a clean act— sex in solitude. As their marriage fell apart, he had relied more and more on his office, which was now no more.

He hurried to Cathay Fidelity Savings and Loan to close his account. He picked up his suit from the cleaners and had his shoes shined at the Italian shoestand. The dark smell of wax and spit soothed him. He would appear at the Long Hop Association that afternoon.

In the third-floor meeting room other Chinese who had emigrated from the same district greeted him. Mr. Bin wrote out a check for next year's dues. He inquired as to his grave-site plots. "My wife," he muttered, "does not want to be buried next to me. Can I get a refund on the double plot?"

"No," the treasurer snapped.

Mr. Bin was silent. Then he thought that a double plot would actually be advantageous when he died. Knowing that he would have more leg room than others made him smile. He ate more than he should have of the buffet—chow mein, pork buns, roast duck, and pastries. He poured himself a shot of Seagram's and toasted the continuing prosperity of those around him.

He had stuffed the debris of his life into the black plastic trash bags. By now, a truck had probably carted it all away to a dumping site outside of the city limits. Maybe his bad luck would be recycled and come out better for someone else. Mr. Bin joked with the other small-businessmen. He told them that frankly he was bankrupt—even he, even in America. They offered to lend him money from their informal rotating credit club, as he was a fellow from the same district. He declined, yet he felt grateful and flushed with the right degree of camaraderie and liquor by the time he left the association.

For the next hour, before dusk, Mr. Bin half-heartedly canvassed the Tenderloin for single rooms. To save money, he had decided to give up the apartment. He rang the manager's doorbell at the Wawona Apartments. To his relief, no one came to open the barred glass doors. On the next block, he peered into the lobby of the Evergreen Arms. Old men in plaid shirts stared into the darkness.

As he strode into the lobby, he collided with a swarthy, slight man in a vest. "Sorry sir, but we have no vacancies available," the man said.

Mr. Bin said nothing. The Patels, from India by way of expulsion from Uganda, seemed to manage all these run-down hotels.

He strode on in the early evening darkness as if he had somewhere to go, but in fact other than to find a room, he had nothing to do and no one to see. Mr. Bin passed the Cambodian grocery store and the pawn shop. They were probably ethnic Chinese, he thought, like him, just tugging on his heels. Soon, they'd surpass him, own their house, and send their children to college, while he'd still be struggling to make ends meet. In front of Roscoe's 24 Hour Nudie Palace, he hesitated, glancing quickly at the passersby closest to him. They paid him no heed. He withdrew three dollars from his wallet— not noticing the driver's license that slipped out of the worn plastic sleeve— and paid the cashier. As he walked into the theater the familiar smell of vinyl, grime, Lysol, and the sweat of men assailed his nostrils. It was as familiar as old newspapers and magazines, and the odors were oddly comforting to a man who'd lost everything else.

He settled in the center row, anticipating the mild arousal he had experienced here in previous times. He had begun coming here after their first arguments. The first few times, he could not get used to the furtive hands, the overcoats and briefcases on top of the laps of businessmen. Then, as he started to understand the secrets and the shame of men, he himself began to remember to always wear a long jacket or bring an overcoat when he came to the theater. He would just ignore the tiny noises of cloth against hands, of zippers unzipping, of the thud of an occasional briefcase sliding to the floor. He even ignored the one time when he felt a hand, from out of nowhere, touch his thigh. That day his eyes hadn't adjusted fully to the darkness, so he could not know that the seat he had chosen was next to another man's. Thereafter, he made sure to blink his eyes several times before he looked for an empty seat in a solitary row.

The screen threw its usual array of flesh at him—red lips, pink breasts, pale shoulders, and smooth legs. As his eyes adjusted to the darkness, he saw other profiles. He was not alone. He put the palm of his hand in front of his eyes to break the screen's fevered rhythms. But the images flew right through his fingers, lodging themselves in his brain. He shivered, as he felt dampness rising from his feet to his calves and thighs. He felt it spreading to his fingertips and toenails, and his body stiffening, like a mouse the second it realized it was caught in a trap. His wife. They had lain side by side for years, then lay apart in separate rooms.

"You must have left your heart on the ship you jumped, expecting to find another one here. But I can't give you back the one you lost," she said.

He protested. "I thought I understood you."

"But you never will," she said.

He rose from his seat, waded through the littered aisle, and left the theater. As he walked in the darkness, he remembered leaving his village on foot, trekking through muddy fields, soon after the Japanese surrendered. He had said good-bye to his parents and said he would make his way to Hong Kong, that he would get to America, by hook or by crook, even if he had to stow aboard ship. For years thereafter, he had sent money to them until they died. He had gone back only once to Sun Ha Village, in 1981. He, with a gaggle of distant uncles, nephews, and nieces dressed in blues and grays, chopped his way up the hillside. The smell of leaf, wood, and wet earth filled his nostrils, its rawness making him dizzy. He was surprised at how small and insignificant the gray stone markers looked in the noon light. He sprinkled what was left of a bottle of Scotch on the hillside grave sites and placed oranges, bananas, and a freshly killed white chicken in front of the markers. There would be no one, he thought, to tend to his gravestone in America.

He turned into Ellis Street. A wig store with a "Sale on All European-Styled Hairpieces" sign caught his eye. He imagined thick female hair, shorn or shaped into sleek bangs, twisted into French chignons or oriental braids. For all he knew, they might have been hardened filaments of chemical waste.

He walked into the shop. An attractive middle-aged woman greeted him—in Japanese, in Korean, then finally in broken English. "You want to see nice hairpiece? Women like. You look younger."

"No, I'm just looking. Maybe a surprise for my wife."

She just smiled and shrugged, making one last attempt: "We have all sizes and all prices. Real hair costs more."

Disconcerted, he pulled the dark wig closest to him over his head and smiled. Reflected in the mirror was an unfamiliar face, its pudgy cast made feminine by the longer wavy hairpiece. For an instant, he had seen himself as she had seen him: as a scavenger, a picker. He tore the wig off, threw it on the counter top, and fled into the darkness.

On the street, he pondered the fate of a friend in Los Angeles whom he had once met at the association. This friend, acquaintance really, consigned "seconds"—plastic watches and transistors from Taiwan—and sold them at weekend swap meets at drive-in movie theaters. Mexicans and Blacks bought a lot, his friend said. The start-up capital was small. Mr. Bin wondered whether his friend would split the cost of a stall for a few months.

With nothing more to lose, he found himself a week later with two valises in hand, waiting in the open-air Greyhound terminal. The night express would leave San Francisco at midnight and arrive in L.A. at dawn. He paced between the snack machines and the knot of waiting passengers that grew thicker as the bus eased into Gate 26. He let the elderly and families board first and found a seat toward the middle. His shoe caught on a sticky candy wrapper. He almost cried aloud.

Phoenix Eyes

AT THE SAME Buddhist temple downtown where my friend P. and I used to go whenever he visited L.A., I prepared to don the gray robes of a layman. There was no chance of my becoming a monk, but I wanted to hear the five precepts for myself.

A dozen people would take the vows today. The monk would state the same precepts to each of us. Some simply nodded their heads in affirmation; others answered with a soft "aye." I was the last to step before the altar. Now the monk was repeating to me: "Do not kill sentient beings. Do not steal. Do not lie. Do not drink alcohol. Do not have improper sexual relations." At the fifth precept, I balked. The monk looked me directly in the face. I cast my eyes downwards. My days of pleasure and sensation it seemed, would cease. I was past forty. Yet sweat was flowing down my back. I squinted in the haze of the burning punk sticks and yellow candles.

Twenty years ago, I graduated from Washington State University with a double major in theater arts and business communications. Ba and Ma had high hopes for me, of a wife and children soon, and a stucco duplex where they could live with us in their old age. When I told them I would never marry, they threatened to disown me. From then on, I did not show my face at family banquets, at baby parties, or even at funerals. It was as if I, the offending branch, had been pruned from the family tree. I was hurt, then angry. But I also felt free to pursue my life as I saw fit. As always, older sister supported me after I explained to her why I wanted to live in Asia.

"If I'm going to make it as a theater designer in America," I said, "my training in Asia ought to open a few doors. Look at Black artists in Paris. They make it there first, before they come back here." I promised to keep in touch. I promised to send money for the folks if I had any to spare.

But besides my artistic ambitions, and unbeknownst to my family, I was leaving the U.S. because I had fallen for an airline steward based in Taipei. We had met the summer before on a Tokyo-Taipei flight—I had been spending July studying Mandarin. He would be my first Chinese lover; at the time in the States, Asian men going together was considered "incestuous." Even if we were attracted to men of our own race, we didn't move on it, fearing we'd be ridiculed.

Every other month, I drove my beat-up blue Mazda from Pullman to Seattle, where I would spend a weekend with the steward. When I finally graduated I worked the summer to save for a ticket and then in the autumn moved to Taipei to join him. His tenth-floor condominium was on Chunghua Road, near the hotel district. The teakwood furnishings were a far cry from the wooden crates that had surrounded me growing up in back of a grocery store by the tracks in Seattle's International District.

Besides sex, he wanted me to serve him—draw the bath water, polish his shoes, massage his brow with green eucalyptus oil, teach his friends dirty jokes in English. Even with my help, he took half an hour to tie a silk ascot around his neck; I took one minute to throw on a T-shirt and Levis. He drank at odd hours and chewed candied ginger and Wrigley's gum to cover his breath. Where was love, I asked myself. It was hell. After six months, it all ended one night after I was eyeballing the singer at the Hilton Skylounge. The steward and I got into a brawl in the parking lot. He kicked me out the next day.

That year—1972—Nixon, Kissinger, and Winston Lord broke twenty years of Cold War policy toward China. I was stranded on a hot, dusty street in Taipei, with a hundred dollars U.S. in my pocket, a duffel full of clothes, and an art-and-business degree to my name. I sat at a fruit stand, drinking a concoction of condensed sweet milk, crushed ice, and mango, trying to decide what to do with my life. Taiwan was a small island near the equator shored up by coral reefs, U.S. dollars, and cheap labor. In all fairness, the Portuguese were right when they named it Formosa, beautiful island. Between the hills and the sea, though, shanties hugged the dirt, poor relations to the mountains of condos and mansions above them. Certainly I did not want to be overwhelmed by lack of money, by lack of love, or by too many English students, which is what usually happened to foreigners forced to earn their keep.

I found a cheap room in a prewar Japanese-style boarding house. A notice posted on the inside of my door read, in Chinese, "Do not use over 30 watts, no loud music, clean the toilet after you're done." The absentee landlord, a widow, would rifle through our rooms while we were at work, unscrewing bulbs with too high a wattage and unplugging radios and television sets. But the boarders, mainly office workers, tolerated the "widow's house" because of its convenience to bus lines and the low rent. Jerry-built townhouses edged up to either side of the wooden structure. It had been beautiful in its day, but it was now only a matter of time before this colonial relic would be demolished.

Before I ran completely out of money and out of luck, I ran into P. at the National Palace Museum. I was taking notes and sketching Tang dynasty terra cotta burial figurines. I noticed how the wide sleeves and low bodices—fashions influenced by the foreign traders who plied the Silk Route—accentuated the body. These styles seemed to reveal rather than hide the body's robustness. Absorbed in my observations, I was startled when a man standing next to me suddenly began speaking in perfect, high-pitched English: "You're an ABC on a summer visit?"

"Me? Yeah, like you said, I'm an American-born. Here to learn what I can. How did you know I spoke English?"

He looked me up and down, smiling and pointing to a stocky, half-naked clay figure tethering a yellow-glazed horse.

"Persian or Turkish, not Chinese," I said.

"Imported labor," he said. "Exotic, like you. You'd have been a good model for a stable boy."

I blushed, realizing that no local boy would have dared enter the museum dressed as barely as I was—in cutoffs, tank top, and plastic sandals. I retorted: "And you are a Tang prince waiting to mount the horse?"

It was P. who brought me out—to the *hung kung hsien,* the international call line. The circuit was made up of high-priced young men and women who made themselves available in Taipei, Hong Hong, Manila, Bangkok. As the tiger economies began to flourish in the seventies, so did the demands of Western businessmen for after-work entertainment. Most of our clients were German or American, with a few English, Dutch, or Spanish—and even a few Asian businessmen thrown in. On our part, we could be of any nationality—Taiwanese, Thai, Chinese, Vietnamese; and of any gender—man, woman, or pre- or post-op transsexual.

We hung out in the same cafes and shopped the same boutiques. After our clients spent over $100 on food or clothing, we'd get a 5 percent kickback—

and a New Year's bonus in an embossed red envelope. As I saw it, food is food to the belly, and cloth is cloth to the back. Most of us ordered vegetarian dishes for ourselves, but for clients we selected the richer braised meats and fancier seafoods they preferred.

The boutiques were staffed by the same slender, clear-skinned young men or women. The clothes, as everyone knew, might have been labeled "Bluette Mode-Paris," but they were knit in a local factory that made "imports." No matter, the salesperson would try the clothes on for the buyer in the private dressing room. My well-built buddy, Wan, would wear nothing under his trousers. A certain Ivy League professor known for his translations of Sung poetry loved to stop at the boutique whenever he was in Taipei and have Wan undress and dress for him.

As P. taught me, the main thing was not what you did in bed, or even how good you looked; the key to referrals and comebacks was skill and charm in "talking, walking, welcoming, and leaving." You had to make your client feel intimately involved, you had to make him long for your presence after he'd left. After all, P. said, if they could afford you, they could afford someone even younger or better-looking. But not necessarily smarter or more personable. A street hustler or bar girl didn't need education or social graces, but an escort or companion did.

That meant you had to know at least two languages and the common cordialities in Japanese, Chinese, and English. Read the newspaper every day. Know your food. Hold your liquor. Don't order the most expensive entrée or wine, but something appropriate to the season, to the country you were in. "Take a lesson from me," P. said facetiously. "In Kyoto, don't order Hunan pork. Admire the view from between the shoji, and accidentally brush your hand on your client's thigh without looking directly at him." Bringing his hand to my face, P. suddenly traced my lips with his fingers. "Save this part for me."

Last, but not least: keep it simple, but as good as you could afford. No white shoes or polyester shirts. Not too much jewelry or luggage. When business was slow, P. said I might consort with horny American sinologists from prestigious Ivy League schools who had come to Taipei to hone their classical Chinese. They were suitable for conversation and culture, as they loved to pontificate about their studies, but not for their allure or their dollars. They were the orientalist tightwads of the Orient, he joked; they didn't know much about fashion, food, or how to spend money. But, as P. said, you could always learn a bit more about Sung *tzu*, from them. "That might come in handy with your next client. Watching the moon from the hotel balcony, you could recite a stanza or two."

P. didn't need the money like we did, but he did what we did anyway, for pocket change and for fun, he said. Sometimes, after double-dating with clients, or having drunk too much of our favorite cognac, P. and I would fall asleep on the same bed, feeling safer in each other's arms.

One morning, after we had woken up together, he had a sudden desire to visit the lotuses that would now be at the peak of their bloom. I asked him why today, because I knew that he had a valued client flying in.

"Then I'll just cancel him. He can wait until tomorrow." He dressed, tossed me a diet Coke and a banana, left a message for his client, and rang for a taxi. We were on our way to the Lin Family Gardens, just south of the city, a classic eighteenth-century Fukienese family compound. We passed through endless corridors, dank rooms, and carved door lintels to the lotus pond in the back. There seemed to be no tourists anywhere. From the depths of mud and dark water, hundreds of white lotuses had pushed themselves up to reach the sun. Upon seeing these, he began to tremble. I put my arm around his shoulder. His grandmother, who had raised him, had always looked forward to the beginning of summer and the blooming of lotuses in the small rock pool in back of their family house. As the third wife of her husband, and a woman from the countryside, she had the lowest status in the large household. Her room was the smallest, her clothes the most meager, because she could not produce a male heir. Yet she had raised P. as her own son, picking his hair for lice, bandaging his scrapes when he would fall. Each year, during the two or three weeks that lotuses were in full bloom, she would, just before dusk, pour clean water onto the bulb of each pale flower. At dawn, she would, with a tiny spoon, transfer what remained on the flowers into a jar. This precious liquid, mixed with morning dew, would make the purest water for tea, enough to brew a single cup, which she would sip with him.

The red taxi whisked me to the peaks of Yangminshan estates, to where the sour smog of the city basin gave way to the scent of pine and jasmine. The doorman smiled and opened the black-lacquered double doors, flanked by two sago palms.

Making my way to the outdoor bar, I spied Tan Thien, the thin, effeminate scion of the Tan Tan ice cream family, which had branches all over the island and was establishing plants in Singapore. Then there was Jerry, a muscular Taiwanese, kept by a restaurant owner in Osaka. And Marie, a French-Algerian student who had found it more exciting not to study Chinese—we'd had a brief affair. One night when we were making love I went on and on about the Jun vases I had seen that afternoon at the Palace Museum. She told me that I opened my mouth at all the wrong times instead of putting my lips where they belonged—quietly between her legs. She swore at me in French, and I at her in Cantonese, and we parted. After me, she drifted to pretty-boy types who usually borrowed money from her and never paid her back. About then, I think, she started going out with older businessmen, again through P.'s referrals.

I kissed her lightly on the shoulder. "Marie, *ni chen mei li*. You look wonderful." And she did, in her simple black cotton dress and pearl earrings, her upswept chestnut hair.

"So do you, Terence. But you're as dark as a peasant. Your phoenix eyes give you away, though."

"Eh?"

"Longing and lust. That's what I see in them."

I kissed her again, and moved on.

I moved among Otto's usual crowd of slender Asians in their twenties, and important antiques—a gilt Burmese Buddha, oxblood porcelain vases filled with orchids, and Ming country furniture.

Otto was a Swiss cookware manufacturer and a regular at the Hilton Skylounge. Because of his bent for Asians, he kept villas in Jakarta, Chiang Mai, and Taipei, along with his family home in Geneva. He preferred, he said, the sensual aspect of darker Malays, but tempered with common sense, "at least one quarter of Chinese blood."

I pressed the gold pinky ring chiseled with my Chinese surname tightly against my palm. We were all accessories. Whether we were from the country or the city, whether pure-blooded Chinese or mixed with Japanese genes during the colonial occupation. Or Malay. It didn't matter. We were beads on a string. A rosary of flesh. We gave up our youth to those who desired youth. There was some room for variation, for beauty was in the eye of the beholder. I myself was called *feng yen* or "phoenix eyes" because of the way the outer folds of my eyes appeared to curve upward like the tail of the proverbial phoenix. Such eyes were considered seductive in a woman, but a deviation in a man. Thus, the male phoenix sings by itself, as it dances alone.

It was at one of Otto's get-togethers that I ran into Li-ming again. He was a well-known modern dancer who once asked me to design a stage set for him that would give him the illusion of height and weight—he was well under five-four. I ended up creating a series of painted silk banners that moved up and down on invisible nylon strings. During the last act, the banners slowly lowered behind him, effectively shutting out the rest of the troupe, so Li-ming appeared much taller. The editor of *London Dance Magazine*, who was making his annual Asian junket, saw the performance at the Sun Yat-Sen Memorial Hall and was impressed not only with the dancers and the stage set, but with the designer, me. We ended up at a Taiwanese restaurant eating garlicky sautéed squid, boiled peanuts, and noodles, downing it all with beer and getting thoroughly drunk. I was in no mood to talk design with the balding British editor because I had been smitten with the dark, long-haired waiter. I gave the editor my card and insisted my friends take him with them.

After slipping the manager a few bills, I asked my waiter to spend the night with me. Even though I'd moved out of the "widow's house" to my own fifth-floor studio, I'd never bring people home. P. was the only one who would visit and sometimes stay the night. So I drank coffee until the last customers and the manager left around three in the morning, and the steel door clanked down over the entrance. I helped sweep the floor and refill the condiment jars—pepper sauce, soy, and oil. In the airless basement dining area, the waiter set the air conditioner higher and put on a tape of Dionne Warwick. We pulled out the table from between two red vinyl banquettes, then pushed the upholstered seats together. We lay on the slick vinyl, sweating and breathing hard, undoing each other's shirts. In the darkness, I fumbled for the glass jar on the table that now blocked the aisle. Pouring the liquid onto the palm of my hand, I sniffed it: sesame oil. I began to massage his shoulders and the small of his back, steadily working the oil and sweat between his legs.

The barking of dogs on the streets awakened us. Bleary-eyed, he stumbled to the kitchen and fried eggs over leftover rice. We ate and drank last night's cold tea in silence. His damp hair fell in a mop over his forehead. I brushed it away from his eyes. We smelled of sesame, stale cologne, and sweat. He smiled and shrugged his bare shoulders. Could I introduce him to customers, he asked me, as he had to pay for his brother's tuition in a private English-language school. He wanted to know if I had any American "friends" studying in the colleges who needed companionship. I pulled out a fifty-dollar bill from my pocket. "My pleasure."

"No," he said. "Brother, you are Chinese. We look the same. Swear the same. Fuck the same. *I ch'uang t'ung meng*—though we sleep in different beds, we have the same dreams!" I hugged him, and promised to bring American friends to his cafe in the future.

That's where my dual career began: in Taipei, then on to Hong Kong and Osaka. Twice a year, P. and I flew to Hong Kong to set up private parties and modeling shows for jaded wives of rich businessmen. A family limo would meet us at Kai Tak airport. When their husbands were on trips to the U.S. or Japan to meet their mistresses, we would set up parties for these tai-tais, who paid well for good-looking men. Struggling (but handsome) students, and out-of-season soccer players were my specialty. Women, we found, went for the strong thighs and tanned calves of the players, which performed more diligently than the listless limbs of their pale husbands.

One thing led to another. Shopping for fabrics one day in the Landmark Mall with a Mrs. Chi, we were introduced to her Tuesday-night mah-jong partner, a gallery dealer from Shanghai. His gallery, Contempo, showed modernist Chinese artists from the twenties and thirties, now very collectible. He would take the time to educate younger collectors, including me, about painting styles that derived from Qi Baishi's minimalist renderings of fruits, flowers, and vegetables.

The following day he drove the four of us to the Chinese University of Hong Kong to see paintings by the eight eccentric Qing masters of the Yangzhou region. They were, he explained, the eighteenth-century precursors to the art of the New China. Yangzhou was near the tributaries of the Yangzi river and the East China sea, a cosmopolitan metropolis based on the salt and fish industries. I was impressed by his erudition. At the same time that he could appreciate esoteric old masters, however, his sensual tastes ran to young, unschooled hairdressers and bartenders with thick hair and bright eyes. Through him, my appreciation of Chinese modernist painting—and of men—improved.

Men were no problem, but I couldn't spend money on this caliber of paintings. Twice a year, I sent some money home to Ba and Ma, care of my sister. Besides, my own studio in Taipei was as sparse as a stage, with books, a bed and desk, and track lighting. I needed spaces to exercise, to create, and to escape. Out of odd pieces of stone and lava rock I had assembled a rock garden on the balcony and potted some bamboo to hide the high-rise apartment across the way.

I was three years on the Taipei–Hong Kong–Osaka circuit before I got to do anything bigger in London, Canada, or New York. P. and I used to match our clientele in the same Asian cities so that we could rendezvous later and compare notes. In the meantime, I was the only Chinese American male on the *hung kung hsien*. Despite my eyes, I never considered myself exotic or different. But I used my English and art background to advantage with my clients: mainly men, but an occasional female. I always sent flowers to the women after I left them, usually a spray of pink orchids, or a subtle-patterned tie to the men. In Bangkok, on a trip with a Chiu Chau business-man, I had picked up three dozen silk ties at discount. My callbacks and re-ferrals were no worse, and probably as good, as those of men who were much better-looking. I had strong features and never hid the irregularity of my slightly rough skin with makeup, like the others who tried to smooth their imperfections. I smiled or complimented a person, however, only when I really meant it. I guess even my jaded clients could appreciate that.

Evenings, I would drink with middle-aged Chinese or Japanese businessmen: average length of marriage, eight years; one wife, maybe a mistress, two chil-dren. The Japanese were fastidious about their skin and bodily cleanliness, bathing before and after sex, so I preferred them. Then again, Chinese from Hong Kong or Singapore enjoyed talking, and eating, before and after the act.

After dinner I would go to the Club Fuling, a bar for Japanese and other foreign businessmen near the Majestic Hotel, in the Shilin district. Unlike other clubs, the Fuling had no neon sign, just an engraved bronze plate with the club's address. Membership was by referral. New members—and that in-cluded locals and foreigners—could join only through an introduction. No street trade. Even we—companions, escorts, or entertainers—had to pay a nominal fee.

Entering the inner courtyard, I would pass through a Japanese garden with its plantings of red-leafed nandina—heavenly bamboo—and wisteria. The club had two entrances. The left door, sheathed in verdigris copper, led to a western-style bar with leather and chrome chairs and glass tables. The right entrance, sheathed in rosewood, led to Japanese tatami rooms and was considerably more expensive due to the imported foods served. I usually worked the western-style side. No food, just local salted peanuts and dried cuttlefish.

The club's waiters were at least five feet eight inches tall. Some were of aboriginal origin from the Hualin mountain area; others were ethnic Chinese from Seoul or mestizos from Manila. The club catered to Japanese and other Asian men over forty years of age. Being a shorter generation due to the war, the patrons were fascinated with younger and taller men. The waiters turned heads and opened wallets. They were dressed elegantly, in white linen shirts, black slacks, and black patent-leather shoes. They slicked their short hair back behind their ears. They would never go home with clients, otherwise they would be fired. Each had been selected and trained by the Fuling's rich owner, a local trader who had made his first fortune exporting refrigerators to Southeast Asia.

Daytimes, I would read, go to museums to research, or go shopping. I recall that one day, as soon as I entered the neighborhood around Lung Shan Market Street, my shoes started kicking up dust. Lung Shan was in the older, western side of the city near the river, for locals, not fixed up for tourists. The air was raucous with the voices of straw-hatted peddlers selling everything from watches to perfumes to human-shaped ginseng roots laid out on blankets on the street.

The leveling of some pre–World War II housing blocks had turned the sky yellowish-gray with dust. Shoeshine boys prodded me until I gave in. One examined the leather of my shoes and said the hide must be expensive. "We do not have this here." I turned to him and nodded my head, mumbling that a friend had sent them from Hong Kong. I tipped him a dollar for polishing them.

In the middle of the sidewalk, people with shopping bags were pressing around something or someone I could not yet see. I walked toward the crowd. Edging my way to the side I saw a man with a short haircut sitting on the ground. His eyes did not look up. He was a young man no older than I, pale skinned, with the leanness of a soldier. His straight shoulders ended abruptly at the armpits. It was warm, and he wore no shirt. His gray pants were rolled up to his knees.

He was painting. I looked at the crayfish emerging as his toes deftly controlled the bamboo brush. A bowl of water, a wooden box full of various tipped brushes and tin pots of paint were at his knee. Passersby tossed coins into a tin cup.

I squatted down so as to be the same height. A voice in the crowd shouted: "How much?"

"Seventy-five dollars."

"Too much," the voice said.

He calmly answered: "I don't lower my price, but neither do I raise my price for anyone." With his feet he pushed two pebbles to each corner of the painting to hold it down. Squatting, he repositioned himself to prepare another sheet of white. This time he bent over, inserting the brush into his mouth, between his teeth. As he bent down, I could see the inverted triangle of his shoulders and back tapering to his bare waist. Someone kicked the stone on the corner of the unsold crayfish painting. He lifted his eyes for a second and looked at me without expression. I lowered my gaze. The green carapace of a grasshopper emerged. Coins continued to drop into the can. The crowd thinned out, and then thickened again with the newly curious. His tongue flickered pink for a second, to moisten his lips. He had gleaming white teeth, except that one was badly chipped. His forehead and chest were lightly glazed with sweat and a line formed on his brow as he continued to paint in the humid afternoon.

Had he been maimed? Or had he been born without arms? His eyes were the gray of an agate. As I examined the crayfish painting, I wondered if he washed his face in a plastic basin at home. Or if his sister or wife or mother did that for him. How did he bathe or cook or make love? Despite his lack of arms, he seemed to have a part that I lacked.

The pock-pock-pock of a monsoon shower took us by surprise. Quickly, he used his feet to roll up his paintings before the rain could spoil them. From the crowd, a younger man, perhaps a friend, helped him scoop up the rest of his materials. He rose from his haunches. He was taller than I expected. The shower was now a torrent, and the painter and his friend turned into a muddy alley off the main street. Without thinking, I hurried after them, sloshing my way through uneven, pot-holed streets. The rain pummeled down; I sought shelter under a doorway. When the rain stopped, as quickly as it had begun, they were nowhere to be seen. Soaked, lost, and breathless, I flagged a cab to take me home.

That evening, I went back to the Club Fuling, where the head waiter introduced me to a number of visiting Japanese businessman. We had a few drinks before I settled on Tanabe-san. He had a wife and children, he said. Every year he would go back to Osaka to impregnate her, to "keep her busy." I laughed, only because I had heard the same line several times before. He said that I reminded him of a well-known Kyogen actor—with the same square face, ruddy complexion, and red lips. We spoke in halting English, with a bit of Chinese and Japanese slang thrown in. I would write down the characters in *kanji* for him on a paper napkin. As I did so, he gripped my wrist in his hand.

His blunt fingers were strong. He asked if I had ever been bound. I said no, that I didn't do that. He laughed. He put my hand over his wrist and told me to squeeze as hard as I could. I did. He said, "Too weak. You've never lifted a shovel or a hoe! We must use other things." I asked what things, and he pressed his glass of bourbon to my lips. He had his ways. I looked toward the bar. The bartender squinted at me, out of the corner of one eye. It was the "Okay—he's clean and solvent" signal.

We taxied back to his hotel. He turned on the bath water. I turned on the television, ordered two Remys from room service, and stripped down to my jockeys. I had emptied both glasses before he emerged from the dressing room in a blue and white cotton robe. Flustered, I began to run my hands over the covering that concealed his body.

With a click, he opened his leather valise. It was full of thick white cotton cords, organized by length. He had me tie his wrists and arms back, pinioned to the sides of his body. Between the bands of white, his blue and red tattoos glowed: dragons and serpents attempting to escape from their prison of bound flesh. I placed my lips on the head of the red serpent that encircled his chest. Then I drew back until I could bend my knees and place the soles of my feet on his belly.

I worked my toes downwards, foraging in a triangle of dark hair until I managed to insert his cock between my feet. With my soles, I kneaded until it became engorged, the bluish veins pulsing beneath the skin. I did not touch him with my arms or hands. Flexing my calves and thighs, I pressed my feet together until finally he could not contain himself. At that moment, in my mind, I could see the painter I had lost in the rain.

I remembered reading Thomas Mann's *Death in Venice* at fifteen. I saw that perfect beauty could kill, as the pursuit of it had killed Aschenbach and quite a few of my friends. Death, like beauty, could arise slowly, through frustration, liquor, or disease, or strike quickly, through anger, accidents, or suicide. I decided I could live better with imperfection, as long as I could live with myself.

In time, as my theater and design work materialized and I began to earn more from those efforts than I did from "other" work, I told myself that I would leave Asia for good. I was happy that I had been able to put a hefty down payment on a stucco duplex for my parents, who were, at last, able to tolerate me, in their way. From L.A., where I had settled, I flew to Seattle for my father's seventieth-birthday banquet. I had not been seen at a public family banquet for twenty years, though I had visited Ba, Ma, and Sis briefly, on and off.

That afternoon, Ba put on his Brooks Brothers navy suit, bought in San Francisco; Ma donned her best jade rings and pendants. Sister was in charge: she had arranged the menu and tables at the Hong Kong Low, bought the 24-karat "long life" gold peaches from the jewelers, made sure that a play area for infants and children adjoined the main room. During the dinner, members of the Hop Sing Association praised Ba's contributions to building a high school in the Pearl River district that he was from in Guangdong; the International Settlement Civic Association of Seattle gave him a plaque; and Sister, on behalf of the two of us, talked about his virtues as a father to his daughter, the pediatrician, and to his son, the designer. I had no words to say, but led the toasts after the speeches.

Accompanying my parents from table to table, I felt the heat and sweat seep from my body. I could see questions in people's smiling faces: Where are his wife and children? Why isn't he married yet? Does he make money? What exactly does he do for a living? I was imagining things, I told myself— these kith and kin of Cantonese farmers and small businessmen didn't really care that much about me to begin with. If I had stayed in Seattle and lived their lives, I would be asking the same questions. I was glad when we reached the last table to toast. We lifted our shots of brandy, like I had at my own farewell meal at the Club Fuling, before I left. There, the members of my adopted family—P., Marie, Wan, Tan Thien, Otto, Li-ming, and the others whom my blood family would never meet—used me as an excuse to toast each other, the future, and the next man they would meet. I suddenly felt orphaned with my memories. At the same time I felt moved to see Ba and Ma in public, flushed and beaming, until the last guest had shaken their hands.

Sis and I drove them back to their apartment where I picked up my bags.

"Bye-bye, Ba, Ma," I said. "Have a good trip. Sis and I have already reserved the hotel in Vancouver and boat tour."

Without ceremony, Ba suddenly thrust a large package wrapped in recycled green Christmas paper and twine, into my arms. Ma told me to open it. It was a red Pendleton blanket, a Pacific Northwest specialty. He grunted. "For you—king size—big enough for two, eh?" Ma said: "See the label here—all virgin wool. Not a cheap one. We get it close-out." I could only nod my head. My eyes were wet. I had not realized how much I had missed them all. Sis touched the material but didn't say anything. It was late, so I bowed to the three of them. And I left for my hotel.

P. moved also moved to the West Coast—San Francisco—after I had moved to Los Angeles. Wherever he moved, his family would buy him apartment houses to manage.

The last time I saw P., five months ago, I noted that his features had aged well. In his late forties, he could still pass for thirty-five. He attributed his glossy black hair, pale smooth skin, and flexibility to his Southern Yunnan ancestry. I always thought that it was due to his vegetarian diet and yoga. He had no outward symptoms of the disease. At the time, he was drinking bitter melon *fugua* juice daily, a native drink favored by Beijing researchers studying immune-building drugs at the Johns Hopkins Medical School.

A card I had got from him, postmarked San Francisco, read, in Chinese: "Dear Terence/When my feet leave this earth the calendar will turn a new leaf, with a new birthday in a new month./Light incense for me, wherever you are./P."

I had called immediately but his line was already disconnected.

Three days later, I read about his death in the Chinese paper, but the family and the police did not disclose details. The family whisked the body back to Taipei. No funeral services were held in the States. His family had apparently not been willing to admit at all that the myth of Asian invulnerability is simply a myth. But they were not alone in their desire not to see or hear about AIDS. In Asian families, you would just disappear. Your family, if you have one, rents a small room for you. They feed you lunch and dinner. They leave the white Chinese deli boxes pushed up—discreetly or not—against the door. Asian families do not want to have anything to do with what the American welfare system can offer the afflicted: Supplemental Security Income, food stamps, Medicare, hospice care, etc. They simply could not call AIDS by its proper name: any other name would do—cancer, tuberculosis, leukemia. Better handle it yourself, keep it within the family. Out of earshot.

Perhaps our lives are marked, as our bodies are destined to be beautiful or maimed, before we are ever born. But neither prayer nor desire worked to bring back anyone whom I loved. Only now I can say his name, because now it doesn't matter. Peter Hsieh, the beloved grandson of the general, Hsieh Hung, who so valiantly fought the enemy during the Sino-Japanese Resistance of the thirties. Now there's nothing more to fight against, or resist.

Even though I'd tested negative for the virus, I'm afraid of simple moves: Today I won't open the door and walk across the street, not even for a six-pack of beer or aspirin. I don't trust cars, pedestrians, clerks, janitors, nurses, bank tellers, not even children anymore. Nothing to do with the L.A. riots, car jackings, or fear of being robbed in this city. It's something else entirely.

I thought that I was prepared to accept the news of his death. But I wasn't. Rereading his card, I began to tremble from the fear and beauty of his words, "a new birthday in a new month." Being nominally Buddhist, he believed in rebirth, and in good or bad karma begetting similar karma.

Enveloped by spiraling smoke, the monk had been waiting for me to answer. His clean-shaven pate and face were beaded with sweat, but his black eyes were steady and cool. I had repeated "aye" three times to each of the precepts, including not lying, not stealing, not drinking, and not killing. And, finally, "aye" to the last, not having improper sexual relations. If taking these vows would change things, or if it was too late to change my life now, I did not know. *Dok. Dok. Dok. Dok. Dok.* As he began to strike his mallet on the wooden fish-drum, others in the room picked up the chanting, *Nam mo ah ye da fo . . .*

I could sense his presence nearby. He was not the one whom my eyes had sought and loved, or the one who had already lived and died. He was another—the one still waiting to be born.

No Bruce Lee

IN THE HEAT of a Los Angeles afternoon a Latino with a torn satchel and a Filipino nurse in a rumpled white uniform wait for the bus. Empty-handed, I stand a few feet behind them. Sundays mean those hours I reserve on the Day of Rest for those spare, routine actions that serve to tide me through the coming week.

Number 376, the downtown bus, stops. I get on, picking a side seat in the rear. The brown plastic seat facing me is impervious to knives, most scratches, and even to the L.A. aerosol-paint graffiti. It's made to last. The bus speeds through Santa Monica and West Los Angeles, stopping occasionally for passengers, mostly Salvadoran or Mexican or Black. The same mix. I note my own strong round kneecaps, not thin and pointed like a White man's, but sturdy, attached to muscle, to the punch and gravity of the bus, the street, the earth. Another time I might have felt like kicking my feet out, or dancing with them, but not today.

I am sweating. The cool, camphor smell of the Tiger Balm salve that I had dabbed on a fleabite under my ear before leaving my room vibrates in my nostrils. The Chinese medicine was an orange paste, but for me its smell was green.

I reflect on this anomaly. Color and smell can deceive me, can make my senses palpitate after things foreign and imaginary. Which is worse, I can not decide, warm color or cool odor.

The bus, I know, will carry me past the rich greenbelt of Beverly Hills, then southward to the Jewish section with its seedy rest homes and bakeries. Eventually it will reach the flat expanse of Olympic Boulevard lined with Korean signs and shops. The Korean alphabet is not sinuous and cursive like Chinese or Japanese, but stolid, rather no-nonsense, like Korean food— meat, fish, and hot pickles. The bus will speed on. Korean signs will transform themselves into svelte Spanish syllables for burrito and taco stands replacing the Korean cafes and bars. The giant 76 gas station sign on Figueroa Street will loom in my face, an orange and blue eye surveying all traffic to the inner city. Thus, a Sunday afternoon will be a third spent by the time I reach downtown.

In the aisle, a man camouflaged in green army fatigues weaves in and out between the standing passengers. His hair is the color of rust and he holds a red transistor radio in his hand. Muttering "crissakes" to no one in particular, his voice becomes louder at the lack of attention. His eyes appear gray and as opaque as smoke. He sports a plastic hospital wristband, probably from the county hospital. He looks at each passenger intently but they look through him. The man snorts, turning to the Latina woman next to him who presses her child closer to her body and uses her grocery bag as a shield. The man repeats himself. "If you don't understand English—go back to where you came from. Christ. To where you belong. Crissakes."

The bus driver turns his head once but does not say a word.

I am most honest with myself on Sundays, when I make the lone bus ride downtown, have a coffee and lemon creme pie at Lipton's, and then return on the same bus going the opposite direction. At one time, I could afford bar hopping, Sunday Chinese tea brunches, real woolen slacks, and two pairs of shoes per year. Under the dim lights of any bar, I would pass for an eternal thirty. But as the summers came and went, the sunlit days seemed longer. The happy hours that began at four or five o'clock in most places grew interminable. The brightness of L.A. summers began to hurt my eyes. I squinted more. Vanity did not permit me to wear either clear or tinted glasses. Finally, I had to curtail my bar hopping. I found myself bringing home bottles of gin purchased at the discount liquor store near my apartment. I began to get careless. Even the expensive cologne could not hide the liquor that slackened my skin and soured my breath. With each emptied bottle my countenance and authority had gone. The length of time I could hold on to any job became shorter and shorter.

The quake had been the last straw. I could not sleep, thinking of the brick apartment complexes on my block that had been condemned by the city building inspectors. Each day as I passed the red-tagged buildings I could see the bricks out of kilter and the dry wall of the rooms inside exposed by gaping cracks. The domed roof of an Armenian bakery was fully exposed to the sky. I felt as naked and vulnerable as the warped structures around me.

One evening in June I had ended up at the downtown Greyhound terminal. I had two hundred dollars in cash in my wallet and a small duffel bag with shirts, underwear, and socks. I fumbled with a fifty-dollar bill, the price of a round-trip fare, then folded it neatly into my imitation alligator billfold and stuffed it into my back trouser pocket. It caught on a seam so I pushed it further down. I would walk a few blocks in the cool evening air before making the long bus ride home. It was really a dirty street, I decided, after side-stepping a mound of damp slop. A drink might lift my spirits. I harbored the hope that the right mix of alcohol would realign the complex code of my brain and heart and ease the burden of my uneventful life.

Catty-corner, I spied a neon bar sign with a flaming green palm tree suspended over a blinking red island. I started to walk toward it. The Oasis was one of the last businesses not yet boarded up on a block slated for demolition by the city redevelopment agency. At the swinging double doors I almost collided with the two cops coming out. Once inside, I took a moment to adjust my eyes to the murkiness. Jukebox rap raced with the familiar pulsing of my heart. On the torn red vinyl stools sat mostly Black males, of varying ages, and a few Spanish-speaking men. The black and white tile floor was heavily worn, revealing an older orange floor beneath, the color of Tiger Balm ointment. A hand-lettered sign above the jukebox stated:

No men in costumes or cut-offs above the knees. No prostitution. No selling of drugs. We have the right to refuse service to anyone.
Signed: The Management.

Before surveying the bar I laid down my duffel on the counter and ordered a brandy and water. The Christian Brothers tasted sour and watery at the same time. I gulped it down quickly. I was the only Asian. The Blacks seemed to be enjoying themselves, bantering and laughing. Despite the sign, I noticed two men of indeterminate ethnicity with white powder covering their beardless skin, dressed in unisex green polyester hot pants and blouses. Their narrow hips and muscular calves gave their sex away. There were no women.

A young Black man to my left started to speak to me. He insisted that I reminded him of Bruce Lee, the martial arts star.

"Yes, he died at thirty-three and so did I," I told the Black. He chuckled and slowly sipped his rum and Coke, watching me intently from beneath his short-cropped curls. Perhaps he had some Indian blood in him, I thought, glancing at the oblique angle of his eyes. I thought better than to ask and instead ordered another rum and Coke for him.

"Bruce man, thanks for the drink. You don't look Korean or Jap to me. Your eyes are bigger. You're a Chinaman I bet."

"Close. I am Chinese."

"'Scuse me, my man. 'Chinaman' is like a honkie calling me a nigger, ain't it?"

"Depends. Forget it. Whatever name I am, I am for tonight."

"So watcha up to, Bruce?"

"I was planning to go to San Francisco to visit some relatives. But they can wait. The city will be there unless there's an earthquake tomorrow."

I had planned to go to San Francisco to visit my mother's sister, an aging spinster who lived in Chinatown. But I vacillated, better to save the money and buy a new pair of shoes. My aunt, whom I had not seen for ten years, had raised me while my parents worked. It was she who had fed me canned applesauce over hot rice, slapped me on the hands, forced my tiny fingers around the hard ceramic Chinese soup spoon. She turned angry if I spilled the contents of the spoon. At a later age, pressed into the Chinese Christian language school in Chinatown, I learned to handle a skinny bamboo brush quite decently. My aunt would lift the transparent writing paper and examine each character, stroke by stroke, and tell me what was right or wrong about it. Where she obtained the knowledge she never told me, but one time she read my palms and said that I was destined to become famous with my hands.

"A three-star chef or a major screenwriter?" I asked. She did not answer. That was the first and last time she had predicted the future for me. Wisely, she left the other lines on my hands unread.

I could imagine the chagrin on her face if I told her I could no longer hold down a job. I decided that she could wait.

Before I left my room this morning I had clipped down my fingernails with the nail clipper I had picked up at the drugstore. At a furious pace, I started on the pinky and worked my way to the thumb, left hand to right. My hands were small and pared down, almost to the bone. My rather flat and now fleshy face belied thin hands.

It had become a ritual, this paring of nails down to a point, so that the tender pink flesh was raw and flinched at handling salt or citrus fruit.

Satisfied with the minute bleeding and inflammation that sometimes occurred when my fingernails were too short, I swathed them in imaginary bandages. In a sense, it was an effort to punish myself for the good life that my hands had failed to create in forty-four years. Paring down my nails made the tips of my fingers all the more sensitive to changes in heat, cold, acidity, salinity, and texture. Seawater almost devastated my freshly cut fingertips.

To curb my passions—that was the intent—but not to the point of numbness. On the contrary, to the point of realization and pain. My fine-boned hands, which had served thousands of restaurant customers, had not paid off as handsomely as I'd planned. Two years ago I was fired as the head maitre d' at Flamingo West, the Chinese supper club on Sunset Strip. I had worked there for almost ten years. It was an expensive, dreary tourist trap, with Sichuan shrimp and sweet and sour spareribs that glared purplish under the ornate Chinese lamps. In its favor, however, the place possessed a sweeping view of the Hollywood Hills. The tips were good. My old coterie of friends and acquaintances, who loved sipping the Flamingo West's giant margaritas and nibbling greasy shrimp, scattered, moved to Florida, had strokes, or just became more miserly with their affections and their cash.

During my hours off I had learned to cater even more closely with my hands. I even put an ad in the gay papers: "Experienced Asian American masseur with western hands and eastern touch. Total sensuous body massage, versatile. In and out calls." But my amateur massages weren't all that good. My clients preferred a younger man for the sexual services that were usually demanded with a rubdown. In recent years they were harder to please with their peculiar demands. Their tips grew meager. Some wanted their asses slapped before they could get excited; others wanted me to wear a jockstrap or a leather cock ring while giving them a massage on specific parts of the body—usually the feet, butt, or nipples. One client who tipped me well lived in a mansion in Hancock Park, an elegant enclave for "old-monied" WASPS. The neighborhood streets were lined with pepper and oak trees fronting brick and stucco buildings. I usually entered the house through the "merchants'" side entrance and pressed the door chime. The door opened electronically. I'd make my way to the small elegant study on the first floor that faced the garden. He would have already drawn the linen shades and dimmed the lights. Under bound gilt volumes of Pushkin, Tolstoi, London, and Mark Twain, he'd be in his pajamas drinking a vodka tonic.

"Take off your leather jacket, dear, it's hot today," he'd always say, whether it was summer or winter, handing me the white envelope. Without speaking, I'd pocket my fee and do what he wanted. In my white tanktop and tight Levis, torn at the crotch, I would tease him until he grew excited. I would walk over to his chair, take the drink out of his hand and help him finish it, leaving his hands free to fondle my body. He'd lower his head. I'd stroke the strawberry blonde toupee below my belly, as he began to methodically unbutton my Levis with his teeth. Under my pants I wore a jock of black matte rubber with a chrome zipper that he'd bought me. With my free hand I would take the flat wooden paddle, almost like the one I used to scoop rice at home, and begin to slowly tap at his shoulders, until his pajama top fell to the carpet. Half-closing my eyes, I'd work my way down his body, until his skin was flushed and glistening with sweat. Another vodka would dull my senses, four was my limit. That's all I would do, standing over him, my legs straddling his shoulders and heavy pink flesh until, with a loud moan, he would come, using a black towel to wipe himself off. I had refused, however, to wear a silken kimono outfit and formal wig that he had supplied to celebrate his sixty-third birthday—along with a braided leather whip. "M. Butterfly" was not in my repertoire, though I did use the whip on him, gently, that night.

"Happy Birthday," I said, whacking him nicely on the back of his thighs and splashing the remains of my last drink over his body. Sometimes I wished that I was a blind masseur so that I could feel impartial toward all flesh.

"As I said, man, you sure do remind me of Bruce Lee. More and more. Let me get you a drink. Carlos, get this Chinese man another," he said, drawing out the last few words.

Carlos brought over another brandy and water.

"Thanks for the drink. My turn to ask your name."

"Brother Goode. Goode for tonight, and ba—ad tomorrow! And yours?" he asked, extending his hand.

"Hell, why not just call me Bruce. I'm beginning to like that name."

"Bruce, just look at yourself in that mirror over there."

I turned to the mirror and laughed. "My face is so red I probably look more like Mao. Goode, are you a native of L.A.?"

"Let's just say I've been here a long, long time. But my folks are originally from Louisiana. They call us Geechies down there."

"Geech . . . what?"

"In the ol' days, folks used to say that the Blacks and the Indians and the

Whites got down together and what all turned out was Geechies. I got some Indian blood in me. So my color is red, 'specially when I can catch some rays. But not as red as you." He grinned. "As I was saying, I'm Brother Goode. Ask anyone around here." He poked the guy on the bar stool next to him. "Ed, what do you say now? Am I, or am I not, Brother Goode?"

Peering at the two of us from under his white baseball cap, Ed was non-committal. "Good as you can be. Which ain't saying much."

I laughed, and studied Brother Goode under the red bar light. His face was smooth and delicate, with high cheekbones and hair that had been processed to give it a fine copper sheen. Late twenties, at most, I thought. After something, I suspected, but attracted, I continued to listen.

"You see, Bruce, I was in the Orient, in Okinawa. Naha. Stationed there in ninety. I dig Orientals. I myself had the craziest, the best Oriental chick in the whole world. Haru was her name."

"So, you have girlfriends?"

"Yeah. Back then. But you know how fast things can change for a man. Changing every day. Anyway, some chicks are fine. Some are real bitches. Some men are fine. Some of them are bitches too." He shrugged. "Now take yourself for instance, you're cool. Nice skin, I bet."

"Yeah? Not as smooth as yours, Brother."

"Skin against skin. One picture's worth a thousand words, that's what you orientals say, don't you?" He smiled.

"It's getting late. I got to run. I enjoyed talking with you, Brother, but the last bus going back to Hollywood leaves at 1 a.m."

"Why leave now? It's only eleven o'clock. You scared of this joint? Of all of us niggers here? Of another earthquake and this damn building falling on you? Brother Goode will take care of you. Don't you worry yourself 'bout that now. You got any weed?"

"I don't smoke."

"Look, I got me a nice little room down the street. The Alonzo hotel. Chinaman owns it I think."

"I don't know it. As I said, I hardly ever come down here. First time in this bar. I'm going by bus to San Francisco."

"But now you're not. C'mon. What's a lone Chinaman gonna do this time of night anyway?"

"You win," I laughed. "Bartender, another one for this young man and one for me. Soda back. Goode, you make sense. But who's kidding who? I'm old enough to be your father. Bruce Lee's father for that matter. And I . . ."

"Every man for his self, Bruce."

"Let's just finish our drinks and call it a night."

We wound up having three more drinks for the road never taken. It was well past one o'clock. I rested my arm on Brother Goode's shoulder and let myself be dragged out of the bar before the cops kicked both of us out. Goode half-carried and half-pushed me down the street to the hotel, up the stairwell, and along the dingy hallway. We reached the room and stumbled in.

"Bruce, now watch yourself. Just take it easy here while I help you get those clothes off. Why are you looking at me so strange. You feelin' okay?"

"Very tired. But I'm not drunk. I'm very okay . . . No. I'm not okay. But I just ought to be getting home." I started to rise from the bed, then fell back.

"You're in no shape to do anything. Not even fuck, man. You just lay back while I run down the hall for a second." Yielding to common sense and weariness, I kicked off my shoes and closed my eyes. The door opened and shut again. I smelled the sweetish odor of marijuana. My eyes scanned the angles of his face and shoulders as he grinned and exhaled, blowing smoke at me. Inhaling, I felt my body relax. He began to stroke my chest and I stretched my fingers over the small of his back.

Morning light through the torn paper window shade turned the pinkish bed-spread into flame. I stirred, turned to my side, and saw a triangular expanse of copper shoulder beside me, topped by disheveled reddish curls. Then I re-membered that I was with Brother Goode. I saw that the man beside me was holding his dark flaccid cock in one hand. A small square of burnt tin foil and a match lay between us on the sheet. Maybe it wasn't what I remem-bered. Coke or Ecstasy or something else that I didn't know. I reached back toward my trouser pocket. Feeling nothing but my own flesh, I spied my pants folded neatly on the metal chair near the window.

I rose, tiptoed to the chair, and stuck my hands into the back pocket of the trousers. Anxious fingers yanked the wallet out. I quickly scanned the bills—two fifties, a couple of twenties and tens left after the drinks.

"You Koreans. All you think about is your money gettin' ripped off. I should have figured that out before I brought you . . ."

I spun around and the wallet dropped to the floor. Brother Goode wore a contemptuous smile, hand propping up his head.

"Uh, no, I was checking to see whether I had enough change for bus fare. I'm on unemployment, ya know."

"Don't jive me, yellow mother fuck. . . . Here I half-dragged your flat ass home. Didn't even mess with it and you think I took your money."

"No, no. It's just that I'm not a rich man."

"Who said anything about being a rich man? You're simple. SIMPLE."

"You got me wrong. I'm really thankful. Uh, how about going out to get some breakfast. On me. Really, I'm sorry. In this part of town you have to be a little careful."

"Who you sayin' sorry to? Not to me. But you should know one thing. You ain't no Bruce Lee. Not your face or your body."

"I never said I was, Brother. You said it."

"Brother? Bruce Lee? Shit, get outta here."

"Look—you want breakfast or not?"

Brother Goode turned his head, puffed up his pillow, and retorted. "I am stayin' right here. In my room. You get on home. But don't look too carefully in that mirror, Pops."

I threw on my shirt and pants, socks and shoes. I picked up my duffel and checked my wallet again, making sure it was lodged tightly in my back pocket. I made my way to the corridor. Downstairs, I nodded at the Asian manager who threw me a look of disdain.

The bus swerves to avoid hitting a pickup truck loaded with plantains and oranges, jolting me out of an intense sweat and camphor somnolence. I wipe my forehead with my perspiring right hand and push the thinning black bangs to one side. The bus reels and groans along its predestined course.

The man with the transistor and hospital wristband and the Latina with the child get off at the same stop. The child is dressed for church in a white lace dress and matching bib, reminding me that today is the Day of Rest.

Where Do People Live Who
Never Die?

ALL THINGS GOOD and bad in my life had something to do with feet. Two feet or one foot, or the lack of one or the other. The use or misuse of them. Walking or running. Whole or broken. Feet floating on a metal pedal; the body drawn forward by wheels. Generations of life beaten down, hobbled or raised up by feet.

Paw-Paw—Grandmother. My father's mother. Every night she washed her lisle stockings in a metal pan. The water darkened and blossomed with blood. She hobbled to the kitchen door and threw the water out. But she would never bare her feet to me. She unwound the bandages in her room. As a young girl her feet had been bound, but neither she, or anyone else, ever brought it up. One day I collided with her in the hallway, knocking her down. She pushed me away without a word even as I stopped to lift her by the elbow. She twisted her face at having to show me her pain. I walked her into the kitchen, then turned and closed the door, loudly. She would wash her feet in a metal pan in private. By now we understood her need for privacy and avoided that room during the half hour she was in there washing her hosiery. It was not because her feet were bound that they bled, for the broken bones and flesh had congealed decades ago. The bleeding was from the pressure of walking and standing on her feet, twenty years of cooking in the chop suey cafe my grandfather had owned. After a few years, the concrete stoop where she threw the water was darkish, brown with the indeterminate hue of blood and water.

Gung-Gung—Grandfather. The man she married. Daylight silhouetted him against the window. He wore a striped shirt and elastic cloth bands around the arms to keep his sleeves exactly the right length. After work, he wheeled back and forth in his wheelchair until he would limp to bed. He hardly spoke. Out of a hidden pocket he would withdraw a silver dollar to give to me. I would take it. His shiny black slippers peeked from under the brown blanket over his knees. So it was in his legs too, as much as in her feet. His legs could not walk correctly, his arches and calves and thighs could no longer stretch. He had had polio. One foot was slightly shorter than the other, causing him to limp. Every morning he would massage the arch of his afflicted right foot with ointment that smelled of camphor. These were the feet I remembered as a child. I ran in circles around them, knowing that they could never catch me. Maybe I was cruel without knowing it: we would play this game of encircling the silver dollar every other day.

One day, he told me a story about our ancestor, a notorious bandit born six hundred years before me. When he was caught by the provincial Canton authorities, one of his legs was cut off at the ankle so he would not flee anymore. In those days, a wooden stump made up for the leg. Wherever he walked someone would say, "There goes the man with a step and a stop. No good foot to speak of." Another would add: "He'd better use his third little brother to compensate!" Grandfather winked at me when he told the story, so I have no idea whether it was true or false.

All I know is that I am the offspring descended of a lineage of imperfect feet. I could see in my mind's eye the period of the wooden stump, the dots following one after another across the land. Trekking through mud and dust or cleaving the waters. Drifting through generations of families, or crossing oceans. This tale went as far back as I dared to believe. I vowed to cut the line there, at a story whose veracity was always in doubt.

But I cried when Paw-paw and Gung-Gung died. They were real. They were buried in the site they had chosen at the Chinese cemetery in Colma, just off the freeway. They had bought their plots long ago. We drove under the green-tiled Chinese archway, through groves of Monterey cypress softened by the San Francisco fog. We passed the leaning yellow stone markers that read *wu ming*—without a name. Those markers were unkempt, rank with weeds. We trudged farther up the hill. Black marble markers, or white ones, were set in neat rows. These had names. Fog whitened the hill. Even the grass was pale. Each year my sister and I returned to check on the condition of the gravestones. Grandma and Grandpa were okay. We remembered them because now we were alone.

As a child I played on the rooftop of the Chinatown apartment building. I could smell the sun on the clothing whipping in the wind. My nostrils sucked in the smell of clean sheets, underwear, socks, pants, shirts, blouses, bras, and skirts. I dodged between the pale moving walls of cloth. I peered down, four stories to the busy street below. I was barefoot. My feet could touch the gray pebbles that kept down the asphalt roof. I liked to look down. The smells and noise would rush over me. The sensation was the same, I found out a few years later, as squeezing model airplane glue into a small brown paper bag. I would sniff until I had had enough of my loneliness.

In high school I joined the cross-country team. We were the ones who ran the farthest. It was no glamour sport, unlike the 50- or 100-yard dash with the pretty girls cheering the ones who sprinted across the line. That was over in a minute. Cross-country meant we ran without spectators. Around the lake, crossing the Golden Gate park, under sun, rain, or fog. Running long distances formed a protective layer of skin on my feet. Sometimes I followed the feet in front of me, other times I did not, or lagged behind. My legs grew hard and muscular, especially my thighs and calves. My belly grew taut and my feelings grew lean. I did not want to feel anything besides the speed of the race and the sweat pouring down my back afterward. I was growing away from my sister into myself. My skin was browner, tougher, callused. I hoped that this new layer of skin would obliterate memory.

I haven't mentioned Ba and Ma, because they weren't here. I lived with my sister, Effie. She took care of me and our grandparents until they died, one right after the other, within the span of a week. My father, a U.S.-born teacher, had decided to stay in China after Liberation and help with the building of the New China. My mother, who was born and raised in Nanjing, stayed with him. By the mid-1950s, it was decided best for us to stop sending letters to them. It was the Cold War era. Any of us who supported the New China, or merely wanted to learn *hanyuromazi*, the new Latinized Chinese, could be arrested and detained by the FBI.

We lost track of our parents. Through friends of Father's in Hong Kong, we got a few letters about them in the sixties and seventies, addressed to Sister. One letter said they had been killed during the Cultural Revolution. An aerogramme said that Father, because of his overseas linkages, was toiling in the countryside, and that we should just forget them for the next few years. The cruelest missive was that Mother had committed suicide after the Red Guards had taken Father away. We could not prove anything one way or the other. Their images grew indistinct: after all, I had not seen them since I was two. They had sent me and my sister back from Nanjing, where we were born, to San Francisco to live. Effie was fifteen years older than I, so she was my guardian and best friend.

Around 1978 we got an official letter from the Overseas Chinese Commission, Guangzhou province, addressed to Mr. Andrew Tom and Miss Effie Tom. The letter said that our father and mother, Kaiser and Mei-ling Tom, had died, months earlier, in a train crash near Chengdu, in Sichuan province. They had to trace our addresses through Hong Kong, the letter explained, thus the long delay. That seemed official enough, with three red seals and a signature affixed to the letterhead paper. Effie dashed off a letter to the Chinese consulate and the commission. The consulate told her that they had no information. The commission, five months later, said that the person who had sent the notification was no longer at the Canton Branch, and had been posted elsewhere. Dead ends. I could hear Effie moan in her sleep for days afterwards. When I heard the news I did not cry, I shook with relief. Now I could cast away the residue that bound me to their history and to the country that was never mine. But the brain and heart play dirty tricks. I found myself writing them a letter that they would never read.

> Ma and Pa,
>
> Today I write you about my feet. All meridians of the nerves lead to my feet. I live from my feet upwards. All my life, as I have wandered, I have wondered why you abandoned me. I have a picture of you standing by the lake in Nanjing. It is 1953. You are leaning, Father, against a stone wall. Mother, your lips are parted with words in a language I will never hear.
>
> Love, Andrew

When I was younger, I vowed to live only for the future. But at the age of forty-nine, I had caught up with the future and vowed to let go of the past. That's when I signed up for a budget China trip—Chengdu, Chongqing, and the Yangzi boat trip to Nanjing in two weeks, via local transportation and hostels. I wanted to see some of the places my parents had been and to check for myself the railway records in Sichuan. But more than that, I wanted to see China, privatization, and post-Mao capitalism at its best or worst. You could say I was an inmate, returning to a country that had captured my parents, thereby also sentencing Sister and me to our peculiar exile.

The flight to Hong Kong over the Pacific, with a stopover in Seoul, was uneventful. From Kai Tak Airport in Kowloon I boarded a direct two-hour flight to Chengdu, the interior of Sichuan province. Through the mist I could see the city, divided by a river and by broad green boulevards that ran north and south. Once we reached the hostel I had a simple meal—fried bamboo shoots, soup, and rice. In my room, I lay down and fell into a deep sleep.

My dream began slowly. It was raining. Sheets of water turned into walls, into a small room, with iron bars on the window. There was a poster on the wall of a young soldier of the People's Liberation Army, rosy-cheeked, standing next to an equally healthy woman in simple village clothing. I heard marching music outside the window and a baby wailing. It was me. My mother was standing over me, a dark shawl wrapped around her Chinese dress, patched on the shoulders and sleeves. She was rocking me slowly and with one hand massaging my feet to keep them warm, until I stopped crying. She smiled.

Then I walked through a dim hallway into another room, quite different from the one I had been raised in as an infant. A large window was covered with white lacy curtains. A television was in the corner and a vase of silk flowers on top of the TV. The floor was carpeted, I recall that I could feel the thickness even through my shoes. On the table were stacked editions of the *Renminribao, The People's Daily.* My father was on the bed, with only his head visible above the blankets. He fluttered his eyes but did not talk. His mouth emitted a weak croak. On the chair next to the bed was a neatly folded blue Chinese-style suit, of good material. With the gold fountain pen I found in his suit pocket, I began to write Chinese characters on a sheet of white paper. I wrote the characters for "I" and "you," for "family," "father," "mother," "sister," and "son." I wrote the word for "health," "comfort," and "medicine." With the nib of the pen I pointed to each word sequentially to make different sentences from the verbs and nouns. He lifted one weakened hand for a second and pointed to the word *jia,* for family. I nodded. In the midst of our silent conversation Effie came into the room. She was dressed as a teen-ager, in a dark skirt and blouse. She did not say a word to me but began to rearrange his sheets. Suddenly, his thin ankles and feet emerged from under the blanket. I took them in my hands and stroked them for a second before covering them once again. Then I began to massage his feet to keep them warm. I sensed he did not have long to live. The light through the lace curtains became more intense until it flooded the room like fire, blinding me and obscuring my father and sister.

My bed sheets were clammy with sweat and humidity. No light came through the windows. Five a.m. on my watch. I dressed and left the small hostel. The night clerk's head was propped against a pillow in the lobby, she was sound asleep. Puddles of water muddied the streets. A man walking in front of me clicked two metal exercise balls in his hand. Women swept the streets with twig brooms; bicycle bells tinkled. At the bank of the Jinjiang River, a Muslim wearing a white turban stood out among the shadowy figures. He rapidly tapped his closed eyes and temples with his fingertips. In a nearby cafe, a man stoked coals and a woman poured tea for early risers. Three pedestrians converged, each carrying bamboo birdcages covered with cloth. Dawn broke and I passed a group of middle-aged ballroom dancers already waltzing to "The Blue Danube." The stocky bodies bundled in sweaters and jackets would have been about my parents' age. Roosters began to crow.

By the time I returned to the hostel, Chinese tourists from Beijing, Shanghai, and Guangzhou were chattering in the lobby. Their intonations—Northern, Central, and Southern—struck the ear as if they were played on different harmonic scales. My own blood was a mixture of Southern and Central—father and mother respectively—but English was my real language. In the dining room directly adjacent to the lobby, early risers were breakfasting on hot tofu milk and fried dumplings liberally dipped in hot sauce. Our guide got the stragglers onto the morning tour bus. Because I was Cantonese, I found myself placed on the bus with a group of retired government tax collectors from Guangzhou who were taking a retirement vacation together. Even the guide knew a few words of our dialect. She took us to state monuments, brightly lit auto and garment factories, and indoor shopping malls selling music, cosmetics, and clothes, most details of which I have forgotten.

Between stops the guide squeezed in bits of history that she'd memorized about the city, "built on the site of an ancient lake bed composed of boulders and pebbles." She went on at each stop, but we didn't pay her any attention. Instead we focused our eyes on the obvious sights, such as the white statue of Mao Zedong towering over the broad expanse of Renminlu, the People's Boulevard. Locals didn't go to exhibition halls or museums, only tourists like us. In the Sichuan Museum, workmen were carrying huge mirrors down from the second hall exhibition rooms. The museum, located in a dingy 1950s socialist-style gray building, was mostly closed because of the renovations on the second floor. On the first floor, as we exited, we passed workmen reinstalling a carved wooden boat, around twenty feet long. It had been owned by a nobleman from Baolunyuan Village, near the water, the marker said, and had carried food, bronze axes, and clay vessels. Though hemmed in by concrete walls, the shapely prow seemed ready to depart on a new journey.

Before I left Chengdu, I made an appointment with the records manager of the Sichuan National Bureau of Railways, located on North Renminlu Boulevard. Effie had arranged all that for me through the Overseas Chinese Bureau. She had written a letter in Chinese explaining who we were and why, as the only surviving daughter and son, we wanted to find out more about the train wreck.

The taxi pulled up to the 1940s red brick building that had been modernized with an ugly two-story concrete addition at its rear. The guard pointed down the hall to the office of records, where the bureau manager would meet me. Once I was inside, the clerk told me to sit and help myself to the thermos of tea on the table. "You're early. Mr. Hao is expecting you in ten minutes," she said.

As I was drinking my first cup of tea, Manager Hao appeared. He was tall and wore a dark blue sports jacket and tieless white shirt with an enameled pin of the railway on his lapel.

"Welcome to Sichuan. I understand you've come all the way from America to search for information about your father and mother," he said in Chinese.

"Thanks so much, Mr. Hao. You received the letter from my sister, Effie Tom?"

"Yes, and so we did have time to pull our records. Would you step into my office, at the back?"

I sat across from him, below a poster of a giant panda playing among bamboo, with a blue express train running through the mountainous province.

"Mr. Tom, a cigarette?"

"No, I'm afraid I don't smoke."

"I've heard of all the anti-smoking campaigns in the West, but it would never go over here," Mr. Hao laughed. "Now, back to the matter at hand. You must understand that in 1978 our railroad system was undergoing renovation and new tracks were already being laid for the German cars that we were going to import from Braunschweig. At that time, I believe your parents, along with other passengers, were riding even farther, to Qinghai and to Xinjiang in the Northwest."

"I don't know the details."

"According to our reports," and he shoved a printed report at me that I couldn't read very well because of the simplified Chinese characters, "apparently workmen had left one small section of the track unfinished, while they were taking a break for lunch. They had incorrectly estimated the time that the train would pass, as they had planned to finish before that. The train skipped over the section of old loosened track. A front car overturned, causing the entire train to derail into the gorge at 12:45 in the afternoon. Not all the passengers were killed, most were injured in fact. But it is possible that your parents were among the fifty or so who died."

"How did they die?"

"Some were thrown directly into the gorge, and others died later of their injuries."

"Were their names on the passenger list?"

"I'm afraid that we don't have passenger lists."

"Then why did my sister and I get a notice that our parents were on the train? Who could be sure of that?"

"Mr. Tom, I was not yet working at the records office at the time. I can only surmise that another person, perhaps, knew they had taken that train. They must have recovered identification documents on their bodies. Your father was working for the Chinese government, as your letter mentioned?"

"He may have been. But he was an American citizen."

"And your mother?"

"She was a Chinese citizen."

"Identities are always more complex than they appear, Mr. Tom. You might have to check these things in Beijing, or even with your own consulate, not here."

"You've been quite helpful."

"I am sorry that we couldn't be of further help. At least be assured that our trains are safe and running more smoothly than ever here. Enjoy the rest of your stay—this is a scenic province. Oh, and I've made a copy of the report for you and your sister."

I took the report, and thanked Mr. Hao. Then, because I'd almost forgotten, I took an envelope from my pocket with the two hundred-dollar American bills inside, as Effie had told me to do, and handed it to him.

"What is this, Mr. Tom?" he said, unflapping the envelope and smiling. "For the report . . ."

"This is unnecessary—the report is the least we could do for you!"

"Just cigarette money, Mr. Hao. If you do recall more about the incident, or about my father, please contact me. I'll be in Chengdu one more day."

As I turned to walk out, Mr. Hao suddenly stopped me. "Mr. Tom, step back into my office please."

I found the same chair, and he closed the glass partition leading to the front offices. From his pocket, he pulled out a white handkerchief and started to blow his nose. Then he began.

"Mr. Tom, the Chinese bureaucracy probably irks you as much as it does me. We have a well-deserved reputation. But it is not just red tape that impedes us. It is the burden of our history, upon our backs and upon our shoulders. Our ideas and ideologies, our fears and frustrations. On the other hand, our history keeps us—vigilant. But history and bureaucracy are very much a part of the West too, am I right?"

I nodded. "But what does all this have to do with my parents?"

"You have an honest face, Mr. Tom. So what little I'm about to tell you is basically rumor, hearsay. It may dismay you. Or enlighten you." He lit another cigarette.

"I will listen impartially, Mr. Hao."

"Good. I can't verify what I'm about to tell you, but I heard more about the accident during my orientation trip to Beijing, ten years ago. At that time I had checked official reports about the wreck, the survivors, and the dead. It was such an unusual occurrence, and appeared to be hushed up by everyone involved. The accident was confined to a small news brief on television."

"I've been impressed at the excellent quality of broadcasts here, Mr. Hao."

"Your father, Mr. Tan Kai-Se, or Kaiser Tom, had, as you know, stayed in China after Liberation. His wife—your mother—was a ranking member of the Communist Party."

I took a deep breath. "That I never knew, Mr. Hao."

"Actually, it was she who persuaded him to stay in China. He wanted to go back with you and your sister."

"I always thought that it was his choice to stay. But Mr. Hao, may I ask you, where did you hear this story and how do you know so much?"

"What you're really asking, Mr. Tom, is how I, a mere provincial bureaucrat, should know these things. Let me say because I am thorough, or because I wanted to know the history of this railway, as much as I could. Or that I am well connected. But for your sake, I am telling you because I also lost my parents at a young age. Not because of the *hungbao.*" He proceeded to hand me back the envelope with the money.

"I'm grateful. Please accept it as a token from my sister and me," I insisted.

"Very well, Mr. Tom. Let us continue. Your father finally gave up his American citizenship in order to work with his wife, and to serve the motherland. This is why he had difficulty communicating with you, probably."

"But what exactly were they involved in, Mr. Hao?"

"That I am not quite sure. But it had something to do with translating documents from English into Chinese. Your father then became a professor at Beida—Beijing university—for a period before the Cultural Revolution. They were sent to the countryside and rehabilitated. They came back to the capital and lived quietly for a number of years. They eventually ended up at the outer level of the politburo, as strategic city planners, so I'd heard."

"You are unusually well informed, Mr. Hao. Why are you telling me this?"

"Communists are not heartless, Mr. Tom, as we're so unfairly portrayed by the Western media. But I'm coming to the most distasteful part. Perhaps I should not tell you."

"Mr. Hao, at this point in my life, it won't make much difference, will it?"

"Your father wanted very much to return to America, to see both of you. After the Cultural Revolution, he had become increasingly disenchanted with living here. Our nascent Western capitalism held little appeal for him. But his wife insisted that he stay. In fact she threatened to have him placed under house arrest if he tried to leave the country."

"I loved my mother and father very much."

"It is said that he was planning to flee the country, not by sea, but through Sichuan, continuing westward by land. Rumors were that he was carrying strategic state documents to sell to the West or to the former Soviet Union."

"I can't believe that, or that he'd give up his citizenship!"

"Mr. Tom. Before you jump to conclusions, you must ask yourself how well you really did know your father."

"Then what about my mother?"

"His wife did not flee with him, she stayed in Beijing."

"Is she still alive?"

"I am not sure. The story about the railroad tracks was only an official version. The train was blown up by a bomb."

"A bomb?"

"Yes. But I do not know whether the bomb was deliberately set to kill your father."

"Was it the party—or the military that placed the bomb?"

"I cannot answer that."

"Did my mother have anything to do with it?"

"That I also do not know. This is all I know, Mr. Tom."

"Mr. Hao, you know far too much. Who are you?"

Mr. Hao snuffed out his cigarette. "Mr. Tom, enjoy the rest of your stay. You can believe me or not believe me. That is your choice." He stood up, shook my hand, and handed me the envelope again. I thrust it back into his hands and fled. I did not want to choose among the stories he offered me.

From Chengdu, it was a short plane ride to Chongqing, where, according to my sister, my parents had lived and worked for a spell. I slept until the plane descended. The recurring dream of my parents and Mr. Hao's tale of divided loyalties had shocked and exhausted me. I did not care about their loyalties to either country; I only cared about their singular relationship to me. Their presence did not dissipate during the days of my trip but insinuated itself into the atmosphere of each place before me. I saw my father sitting on a train reading or looking at the mountains when a sudden fiery explosion catapulted the train and him to his death. But his body was a blur among the twisted metal, wood, trees, and rushing water. I could hardly be sure it was him, or him alone without Mother.

Below, the Yangzi River and bridge that connected the two halves of the city were hazy under the smog. Chongqing, the most industrialized city in Southwest China, was a city built on hills. Blocks of old housing were being razed for new apartments, throwing dust into the air. As the tour bus moved through streets jammed with trucks and motorbikes, I wondered if Ba and Ma had ever lived in any of those skeletal apartments, their inner stained walls now exposed. As dust blew through my window, I flicked my wet tongue over my dry lips, tasting fine grit. We stopped at yet another tourist spot. I got off with the others, seeking my escape from hawkers selling tea eggs simmering in iron woks, bags of peanuts, candies, soft drinks, plastic pens, and Mao trinkets. Our mini-skirted guide said that we could go shopping in the stores that sold karaoke machines, clothes, and watches, and to meet her in two hours. As soon as hawkers and proprietors heard our Cantonese chattering, they grinned, trying to palm off their goods.

I managed to slip away, walking the opposite direction from the group, up a hill through the dusty blocks of a neighborhood about to be demolished. Around a small bend behind a grove of trees, I spied a brick building that appeared to be a small temple. The gate did not have the usual guard or ticket collector, so I walked in. The main hall was not a temple, but a storehouse or depository. The hall was illuminated by lightbulbs and lined with carved stone tablets, more than twenty of them, ranging from a foot tall to the height of a man. Most of the carvings were mythical creatures—anthropomorphic dragons, phoenixes, lions, and combinations of animal bodies and human heads. To my right, the fly-spotted sign read in Chinese:

Where are the forests made of stone?
What animals can speak?
Where do people live who never die?
And where do giants stay?

The lines were from a work called *Tian Wen*, by Qu Yuan, and the stone steles from the same period. As I examined the steles I became aware of the presence of another person. In one corner, under a bulb, was a man standing on a wooden stool. He was moving his arms in a circular motion, positioning the weight of his body on his thighs, bent knees, and feet, like a dancer. One hand held a small cushion, black with ink. He faced a rectangular tablet, around six feet high and four feet wide. A white sheet of rice paper was affixed to the stone. As he moved his hands clutching the black cushion of ink, an image emerged onto the paper. I stood, transfixed. It could have been my father's body, and the cushion in his hand, the compact weight of my infant's body. I had missed my father's touch, but I could never admit that to myself.

The man got off his stool and turned to face me. Bespectacled, darkish, with blunt features, he did not look like my memory of my father at all. He laughed, asking me if I liked the rubbing, a tiger grappling with coiled snakes. I nodded and asked if he wouldn't mind my watching him. He gave me a curious look, as he could discern my accent. But he didn't question me.

"I'm an art student. Whenever I have free time I do these rubbings for the provincial museum. With all this razing these steles might end up as cement for some apartment building!"

The building was actually a depository for artifacts that would have been destroyed or mutilated during the Cultural Revolution. Its contents were not of interest to anyone nowadays except for art students like himself and Japanese scholars, he said.

The Japanese, ironically, were also the best buyers of traditional stone rubbings, and a large one could fetch quite a good sum. He himself, he said, did not harbor hatred toward the Japanese people personally, just against the military. Without skipping a beat, he asked me if I was a Japanese tourist. "No," I replied, "I'm a Cantonese, that's why I have an accent. I came to visit the city that my parents had lived in during the 1960s," I said.

He adjusted the spectacles over his round, mole-speckled face, and began to prepare his tools for the stone rubbing. He took the black-inked cushion he had used and removed the cloth cover. Inside was what appeared to be a ball of white cotton strings, with wormlike filaments. He kneaded it tightly, then tore a piece of unused muslin and wrapped the ball, squeezing it with the palm of his hand. From a plastic bottle, he poured black ink onto one side of the cushion, and then flicked open a cigarette lighter to heat the muslin and rid it of excess ink.

He took his stool and a large sheet of rice paper he had moistened with a wet brush to an adjacent carving. It was, he explained, part of a tombstone stele about a husband and wife who became immortals due to their virtue on earth. He attached the paper by its corners to the top of the carving, then with a dry brush began to smooth the paper, with circular motions outwards, to eliminate air bubbles or wrinkles between the stone and the paper. On bent knees, he began to pat the stone with the inked muslin ball, from the center and top portions downwards to the corners. He danced on the stool. Energy flowed upwards from the soles of his feet through his ankles, thighs, and torso to his arms and hands. Speed was crucial, otherwise the paper would dry and the black ink would not stick to the surface. Through his mastery of breath and bodily dexterity, he forced the stone to yield its carvings to his hand.

On moist paper, the profiles of a man and a woman emerged as they had been engraved by an artisan two thousand years ago. But it was the wrong millennium, my parents had not yet been born. I did not recognize their faces on the chiseled stone. I did not even know if they had been buried, under stone markers in this province or another. Perhaps they were still alive and had been exiled to a distant region where they decided to stay. Catching his breath, the man turned to me. I asked him how long it usually took to complete a rubbing, for it to dry. He shrugged his shoulders.

"Depends on the weather," he said. "On the amount of humidity in the air." He told me that if I wanted to come back the next day, he would be doing others in the smaller back room.

"I will be cruising down the river tomorrow," I said.

"Then enjoy your journey," he said, "because it's not easy to come here again. The government is damming the river, so who knows what will happen to the land in the new century."

My group, the Cantonese tax collectors, joined other travel groups and boarded the dilapidated local riverboat, entitled *The Empress*. Local meant no Westerners, but mainly Chinese travelers and a few from Hong Kong. Noisy students from Shanghai intended to ride the ship all the way home. We were four to a second-class cabin. We took turns washing socks and underwear in the single sink so they'd be dry by morning. I took a lower bunk so as not to catch the wet garments flapping on clotheslines that crisscrossed the room. Most of my bunk mates, in their sixties, dealt cards and drank beer, waiting for our room number to be called for dinner. The dining galley served meals in three shifts.

We got to know one another better in the small cabin. One balding retiree told me about his mango and pomelo trees in front of the suburban townhouse to which he had retired, another bemoaned the divorce of his youngest daughter, while yet another recounted his trip to Hong Kong and Bangkok. Since I was from America, they were simply glad I could recall some Chinese. It wasn't recollection, I said, for I had studied the language for years in school. I told them the bare facts of my life—that I was born in China but had left at a very young age, that I was single and worked as an associate editor for a museum arts magazine. My sister, a retired executive secretary for a law firm, had once married but preferred the single life. They thought our lack of family was odd. Yet they accepted me as a fellow overseas Chinese, like their own nephews and nieces who had moved to the U.S. and to Australia.

As I shelled peanuts and listened to their stories, I was pouring the metal thermos of boiling water into my tea glass. The boat swerved. Hot water from the thermos splashed onto my legs. I felt a burning sting of pain and pleasure, almost as if Mother had slapped me across the face, or as if Father had struck a bamboo cane across my thighs. But this could never have happened. I dropped the glass, where it hit the floor and broke into shards. Immediately my top bunk mate withdrew a small brown bottle from his duffel.

"Lower your pants and underwear," he said.

I did what he said, unfastening them. Swiftly, with a cloth, he applied a viscous green medicine to the area between my legs, right up to my testicles. "My wife gave me this first-aid kit for me for emergencies like this."

"Do you have children?" another chimed in.

"Not yet," I said.

"Good thing we have the oil. Otherwise the burn might have affected your little brother!" my bunk mate said.

As *The Empress* went down the river she picked up locals who would sleep on the floors of the lower decks, bringing their chickens, bamboo hampers overflowing with produce, and rolled-up mats and blankets. Downstream, she sometimes passed the fancier versions with glassed-in decks, luxury cruise ships for European and American tourists. Though my bunk mates and I always ate together, I spent hours alone on the top deck, watching the sky and the mountains change form and color with the light. Blue and green precipices would soften into violet and purple valleys rising from the water, depending on the time of day. I would squint at the water, at the passengers on passing riverboats. The distant faces would laugh, shout, and wave hands, tossing banana and other fruit peels, empty bottles and peanut shells into the muddy river, oblivious to me.

By the third day we had reached Hubei province, where the river cuts its way through mountain ranges running in a transverse direction. Its channel now narrowed to some eighty yards, shut in by precipitous mountain walls on both sides. From the barge, we transferred onto motorized boats that held twenty people each, a mixture of people from our riverboat. The steep mountain walls, being closer to the boat, exuded the smell of cold river and warm earth. Our guide didn't need to point out what was visible to the eye—though she said that ancient iron coffins could be found in caves dug into the mountain walls. Because of her Sichuan accent, I could make out only about half of what she was saying. A man sitting in front of me thrust his arm out the window, trailing his metal cane through the green water. Perhaps he hoped that the water's energy, via the metal rod, would rejuvenate his limbs and restore mobility to his bum leg.

The water embraced our boat and all who rode within—the Cantonese tax collectors, the young woman guide, the man with the limp, and myself. My thoughts raced with the river. I no longer desired to follow the hidden tributaries and submerged streams of my parents' lives. What Mr. Hao told me might have been entirely true, or false. Another story lay behind the one I had heard. Even if I could have charted each day of their lives, it would add up to no more than a heap of river stones, a dry bed of facts.

The burn on my thigh was forming a scab, a dark flower of memory. Their blood, bearing the pain and hope of a woman and a man, coursed through my hands and feet. Despite Father and Mother leaving me, they had also left traces of their presence, elements of water, fire, wood, metal, and earth that had drawn me back to them.

Acknowledgments

To all those who taught me to see life as it happened, and to imagine other possibilities, I am deeply grateful. My father, the journalist Charles Lai Leong, my mother, Mollie, and my brother, Eric, encouraged my writing from the time I learned the alphabet.

Anne Wallach taught me to love words. From N. V. M. Gonzalez I learned about the controlling metaphor and the truth of fiction. Bienvenido Santos showed me the power of empathy for the subject. The writers of the Kearny Street Workshop in San Francisco, especially Janice Mirikitani and Al Robles, provided me inspiration during the past three decades. Frank Chin was always good for a bowl of noodles and a treatise on the art of war and literature.

The UCLA Asian American Studies Center has been supportive of my writing: Don Nakanishi, Glenn Omatsu, Mary Kao, Yuji Ichioka, Emma Gee, King-Kok Cheung and Gerard Maré, Jinqi Ling, David Wong Louie, Marjorie Lee, Eric Wat, Judy Soo-Hoo. Teshome Gabriel, Jessica Hagedorn, N. V. M. and Narita Gonzalez, Sauling Wong, Lisa Lowe, Edward Den Lau, Michael Lawrence, Joyce Nako, James and Dean Leong, Sesshu Foster, Minh Duc Nguyen, Josephine Foo, Sharon Hom, Alejandro Fu-Chang, Patrick Percy, Heinz Insu Fenkl, Armand Tran, Long Nguyen, Evelyn Hu-dehart, Hung Nguyen, Frank Jung, Tom Stanton, Arno Jahja, Walter Lew, and many others have helped me in ways big and small. Gratitude also to the staff and clients of the Asian Pacific AIDS Intervention Team in Los Angeles, where as a volunteer I held writing workshops.

Without the moral example of the Honorable Thich Minh Ton, of the Chua Phap Hoa Temple in Garden Grove, California, and the *sangha*, I would be even more attached to samsara.

To the spring of the millennium and to the memory of my soul brother, Ronald Preston Lewis (1949–1999), who shared his gentle and profound nature with me, I dedicate these stories.

Some of the stories in this collection were first published in earlier versions and under different titles in literary journals and anthologies from the 1970s through the 1990s, including *Charlie Chan Is Dead, Gay Fiction and the Millennium, DisOrient, Remapping the Occident, Emergences, Asian Pacific American Writers Workshop, Aiiieeeee! An Anthology of Asian American Writers, ZYZZYVA, New England Review, On a Bed of Rice: An Asian American Erotic Feast*. I thank editors Jessica Hagedorn, Howard Junker, Teshome Gabriel, David Maruyama, Bryan Malessa, Frank Chin, Shawn Wong, Lawson Inada, Jeffrey Chan, John Yau, Garrett Hongo, Terry Wolverton, Robert Drake, and Geraldine Kudaka, for their support.

Naomi Pascal of the University of Washington Press brought this project to fruition. Julidta Tarver and Lane Morgan provided helpful suggestions at the copyediting stage. Laura Iwasaki proofread with a discerning eye.